Charisse Tyson's got it all going on . . .
a quick wit, a gorgeous plus-size body, a hot
career, and an appetite for life's finest. So why
do all of her ex-lovers belong in the Losers
Hall of Fame? Does Rissy have a special talent
for attracting the totally wrong guy? And
when will her luck in love change?

Critics adore K. L. Brady and her heroine
Charisse Tyson—and find echoes of
Shakespeare's classic romantic entanglements
in two wonderful novels "in the outlandish,
comic, and charming tradition of the Bard
himself" (*Publishers Weekly*)!

GOT A RIGHT TO BE WRONG

"Book of the Year" in OOSA Book Club's First Annual
All Things Literary Award

"Brady draws readers in immediately from the prologue and propels them straight through the drama,
humor, and the various twists and turns. . . . [It] will
leave you satisfied."

—*Romantic Times* (4 stars)

"It's a *Comedy of Errors* for the hip-hop generation. . . .
Sassy, headstrong, successful realtor Charisse jumps
to one wrong conclusion after another—offering a
proclamation that gives this book its title. . . . Brady
updates an old theme for a new audience and finds a
thoroughly mode   lur-
ance of friendshi   —of
family."

ekly

K. L. BRADY

Voted **Female Author of the Year** by the African Americans on the Move Book Club for her sizzling, satisfying, and laugh-out-loud funny debut novel

THE BUM MAGNET

Winner of the 2010 Next Generation Indie Book Award for Multicultural Fiction and the Third Place Grand Prize winner overall for fiction books • A "Top Read" for book clubs, including RAWSistaz™ and OOSA • Featured in *10 Magazine* • Chosen as a Reviewer's Choice by *Midwest Book Review*

"Men can cause many problems in the lives of women, but swearing off them is quite the task. . . . *The Bum Magnet* is a highly recommended read."
> —*Midwest Book Review*

"It is a pleasure to recommend *The Bum Magnet*, as it focuses on Charisse Tyson, an African-American heroine . . . and size-14 sex symbol."
> —*10 Magazine*

"K. L. Brady has penned a clever, witty, insightful, and downright hilarious novel. . . . This debut author is one to watch."
> —*RAWSistaz*™

"Ladies, ladies, ladies . . . don't walk, RUN to get your copy of this book! *The Bum Magnet* happily blends surprise, humor, and wit into . . . pages of wonderful. . . . This book is FABULOUS."
> —Uptown Girl's Harlem Book Club

"The message of this book is something everyone can benefit from. . . . A well-crafted story."

—APOOO Book Club

"K. L. Brady gives you reality checks in laugh-out-loud scenarios. . . . Kudos!"

—SistahFriend Book Club

"A hilarious, tell-it-like-it-is story. . . . This novel screams perfection."

—AAMBC Book Reviews

"K. L. Brady's journey of one woman's dating woes and self-discovery was entertaining and real . . . funny and uplifting. Charisse's sarcasm is a perfect smoke screen for her inner struggles and insecurities."

—OOSA Online Book Club

"Highly enjoyable, entertaining . . . hilarious and insightful . . . K. L. Brady paints a vivid, heartfelt—and rather amusing—picture of the ups and downs of everyday romantic pursuits. . . . Witty, pointed, and real, *The Bum Magnet* keeps you rapt until the very end."

—*Apex Reviews*

"Entertaining, engaging, insightful, fast-paced, witty, and relatable. . . . K. L. Brady's imagination is through the roof. She is surely here to stay and I look forward to her next novel."

—Folake Taylor, M.D., author of
The Only Way Is Up

Also by K. L. Brady

The Bum Magnet

GOT A
Right TO BE
Wrong

K. L. BRADY

Pocket Books

New York   London   Toronto   Sydney   New Delhi

Pocket Books
A Division of Simon & Schuster, Inc.
1230 Avenue of the Americas
New York, NY 10020

This book is a work of fiction. Names, characters, places, and incidents either are products of the author's imagination or are used fictitiously. Any resemblance to actual events or locales or persons, living or dead, is entirely coincidental.

First Pocket Books paperback edition May 2013

POCKET and colophon are registered trademarks of Simon & Schuster, Inc.

For information about special discounts for bulk purchases, please contact Simon & Schuster Special Sales at 1-866-506-1949 or business@simonandschuster.com.

The Simon & Schuster Speakers Bureau can bring authors to your live event. For more information or to book an event, contact the Simon & Schuster Speakers Bureau at 1-866-248-3049 or visit our website at www.simonspeakers.com.

Manufactured in the United States of America

10 9 8 7 6 5 4 3 2 1

ISBN 978-1-4767-0475-3
ISBN 978-1-4516-1659-0 (ebook)

*To my Almighty Father for giving me another story to tell
and another day to share it with the world.*

*To my father, William Brady Jr.,
and in loving memory of Francine Brady.
Even though our lives were far from perfect, in my eyes,
your love for me always will be.*

Acknowledgments

To William Bullock Jr., my beautiful son and self-designated "Flyer Manager," who fills my days with joy and helps me in ways he'll never fully know. Mommy loves you more than anything in this world.

To my grandmother, Katherine Brown, whose excited anticipation for this sequel probably helped get this book written faster than it would have otherwise.

To my family, the Bradys and Browns, thanks to all of you who have supported me or spread the word about my book.

To my dearest friends, DaRell, Donna, Iris, and Lisa, thanks so much for your love, friendship, and support for the past twenty years. You are as close to me as sisters could be. A special thanks to Lisa for serving as my second set of eyes. With your busy schedule, I appreciate the time you take to help me.

To Brigitte Smith, Erica Feldon, Melissa Gramstad, Andrea DeWerd, the copy editor, cover designer, and anyone else at Gallery Books/Simon & Schuster who had a hand in helping me and/or bringing this book into existence. I cannot tell you how grateful I am for the opportunity to work with you all.

To my agent, Andrew Stuart, thank you so much for all of your feedback, help, and support.

To African Americans on the Move Book Club, OOSA, RAWSistaz, Uptown Girl's Harlem Book Club, APOOO, SistahFriend Book Club, RWA Book Club, Ladies First Book Club, and Reading Divas 12 for being among the first clubs to support me in my literary career. The value of your reviews and promotion cannot be measured but will always be appreciated. Thanks so much for doing what you do.

To my fellow author-friends (too many to name) on Facebook, ABNA, Twitter, and The Next Big Writer who have been supportive of me and my work over the past few years. You've been among my biggest cheerleaders and I cannot begin to tell you how much it means to have you on my side.

To every single reader who has ever supported my work, thank you, thank you, thank you. I cannot even describe the happiness I feel when you reach out to me and let me know how my stories have made you laugh or touched your heart. This is why I write.

To anyone I have inadvertently omitted, please forgive me and accept this as thanks for everything you did or will do.

Prologue

I had knocked Charisse's ass out. She was snoring like a security guard on the midnight shift. Unfortunately, sleep did not come as easily for me. I still felt anxious with the wedding only one week away. Couldn't shake the feeling something might go wrong and I wouldn't get my queen down the aisle, as crazy as she'd been acting—at least not without a shotgun and a case of Grey Goose. I could see the love in her eyes 99 percent of the time, but that 1 percent—her thinly veiled fear—might prove more than even I could overcome.

Hmph, maybe I should've told her.

Some of my anxiety might've emanated from my own guilt, as much as her fear. The one-night stand was nothing. Happened before Charisse and I even *thought* about getting together. She wouldn't care, would she? Not now. Not knowing how much I love her.

I tossed the remote control on the bed and scanned the nightstand for something to read. I'd left the latest issue of *Jet* magazine in the bathroom and feared my weak noodle legs might fail me. Puttin' Charisse out always drained me. So, I grabbed an issue of Zaina Humphrey's magazine—Charisse's second bible—and flipped through the pages.

I yawned repeatedly as I flipped through, wondering why women bought these stupid magazines. Clothes. Perfume ads. Shoes. More clothes. Who cares? Zaina needed to get a "Z" beauty, some phat centerfold bikini model. That's how you get men to read these things.

Nearly ready to give up and go get my first choice, I noticed an article that caught my eye, only because Charisse had drawn a letter *X* across the page from corner to corner. "Daddyless Girls: Women Who Grow Up Without Fathers and How They Cope." I read the article with microscopic intensity. Some words leapt off the page . . . "sense of abandonment . . . feels unworthy" . . . "low self-esteem . . . attracted to emotionally unavailable men (like the absentee dad)" . . . "trust issues, even in healthy relationships . . . fear of commitment."

I understood going into this relationship that Charisse was coming in with some emotional baggage. After all, she'd nearly been raped as a teenager. And the cousin she regarded as a brother stood by and let her get attacked. But until reading the article, I had no idea how her rocky, all-but-nonexistent relationship with her father had probably impacted her too. Whatever she said or didn't say about him, her father's absence still bothered her. Otherwise why would she even bother marking across this particular article?

Anytime I dared to mention the man's name,

especially as the wedding approached, her entire demeanor soured, her words turned to acid, but her eyes were filled with hurt. She'd been harboring some serious hate.

My father died from lung cancer, but I couldn't imagine growing up without him in my life. His presence had meant the difference between my growing up to become any old kind of man, and a good man, even though we often bumped heads. Since my father passed away, I'd have given my own life to have him back for a day, just one day, to tell him I loved him once again. Someday, Charisse would regret letting the rift between her and her father fester for so long. I wanted to help them heal their relationship. I was determined to find a way.

1

Charisse

How do men excel so well at exceeding your worst nightmares, yet still manage to delude you into hoping they'll someday live up to the dream? Mmm-hmm, you guessed it. My knight in shining armor, Kevin—the one who rescued me from being raped when I was thirteen years old, the FBI agent who arrested my ex-boyfriend for defrauding *my* clients and a hundred others in a real estate scheme, the one who'd dated me for over a year, the one I'd planned to marry—did not turn out to be the man I thought he'd be. No, he put me through some *straight* drama.

If I'm lying, I'm flying.

Oh, I'm not talking about the little, mundane, day-to-day "You didn't squeeze the toothpaste from the bottom of the tube" drama, you understand. I'm talking about the "If I catch you in a dark alley, I might beat you to a pulp" drama.

I can't even believe I once said, "Good men are like Santa Claus. Believing in them feels really good, and once you relax and stop watching for them, they appear when you least expect it." I'm permanently striking that remark from the record. Good men are more like the bogeyman—they lull you into a false sense of security, and when you least expect it, they jump out of nowhere and scare the shit out of you.

Only had myself to blame. I should've stood my ground and refused his proposal, but when I looked into Kevin's eyes, Lord have mercy, I couldn't tell my ass from a hole in the ground, you hear me? He had my head *twisted*. He could've asked me to fly to the moon and I'd have beat down an angel to get some wings.

That's why the night we got engaged had become a blur. Shoot, call me Usher because I was *allll* caught up. Moonlit, starry sky, slow-dancing to Luther Vandross, the resonant ebb and flow of the Caribbean Sea as we watched the sun fall beneath the horizon. One moment I was curling my toes in the soft, white, Bahamian sand as Kevin placed soft kisses along the nape of my neck, the next I had agreed to . . . to . . . *something*. I was so high on *loooove* I'm not even sure if I heard the question, steady cracking my mouth open to say yes.

We hadn't had much more to drink than a glass of wine or two, but we were completely intoxicated, lost in a brief window of time. I vaguely recalled the obligatory "I want to spend the rest of my life with you" speech he delivered, as if practiced from birth. And if eyes were windows to the soul, I could see forever in his. He loved *me*— the wholly imperfect, insane, way-too-analytical, but often insightful me. And he wouldn't have me any other way.

I can safely say that with my bum-magnet history and the resulting battle scars I'd donned in the wake of catching player after player with his zipper down, so to speak, I surely wasn't the *perfect* package, but he at least understood what he was getting. Good, bad, ugly, fugly, all my shit was on the table. His package, on the other hand, came with a few surprises—and not a single one pleasant.

Our problems started one week before the wedding. I was in the midst of nuptial planning hell when I overheard Kevin on the deck unburdening his soul to his boy Derek. First of all, why Derek was at our house at the butt crack of dawn on a Saturday morning was beyond me anyway. Then come to find out Kevin had his boxers in a twist because I pushed for a somewhat lavish (but small) ceremony. I mean, hell. I caved in and accepted his proposal because he pressed for marriage, the *least* he could do is let me plan a dream girlie wedding. An eye for an eye, tooth for a tooth, wedding for a marriage. Fair exchange is no robbery, right?

"Man, Charisse better be glad I know Jesus because I'm about ready to take her ass out. I realized she had gotten on my last nerve when I started googling things like *strychnine, cyanide,* and *arsenic.* If she ain't careful, her family might be planning for her funeral instead of our wedding."

"I hate to be the bearer of bad news but . . . aren't *you* the one who asked *her?*"

"I know man, I know. And more than anything in this world I want to marry her. She's my *baby*. I only wish we could skip the *wedding*, you know what I'm saying?" Kevin took a long gulp from his coffee and scanned the area to make sure I wasn't listening. "She came to me a couple of days ago with two pieces of fabric, while I was watching the Lakers game, and asked, 'Which one looks better—the blueberry or the sapphire?' I *wanted* to say, 'Listen, I do not *now*, nor will I *ever*, care about the difference between blueberry and sapphire. Hell, they're both blue, pick one!' But what I *said* was, 'I like them both. Can't you mix them together?' hoping she'd pose her question to someone else who gave a damn."

I growled.

Derek laughed. "Well, did your strategy work?"

"Yep! The answer was thoughtful enough to show I cared, but stupid enough to keep her from coming back with another question. Oh, oh, and the day before that she asked which looked better, high heels or kitten heels? I told her I didn't know cats wore shoes."

Mmm-hmm, as *stupid* as it sounded when he said that silly mess to me the first time. He must've thought I was a fool. Talk about fuming! I was boiling-grits mad. It's easy to sit around complaining when you aren't carrying your share of the load.

"The bridesmaids don't even need to *wear* shoes as far as I'm concerned. Here's all I want to know: Can they dress themselves? Can they put one foot in front of the other? They can walk down the aisle in flip-flops, and I wouldn't know the difference."

"Dude. Like I said. *You* asked *her* and you agreed to the wedding. What the hell did you expect? Weddings are for women, men are merely props. I should know; I've had three of them."

"Man, I ain't trying to become an *expert* like your ass. I'm just trying to get through this one. Sometimes I wonder if our wedding's gonna happen."

"Oh, it'll happen as long as you show up," Derek said.

"It ain't that serious, money. Of course I'm gonna show up. I just can't wait for the ceremony to be over."

I'd heard enough and stomped off. All Kevin did regarding the wedding was complain. Wah wah wah. He cried about the cost of the wedding even though I told him I'd pay for it. Said he wanted "us" to pay the expenses because it was "our" day. He complained about moving into "my" house even though I told him it was "our" house. Even agreed to put his name on the deed . . . and you know what kind of stupid-in-love shit I must've been on to agree to that. Still wasn't good enough for him. No, he wanted to get a place where neither of us had any past memories, a place where we could make new memories. I told him that I'd just paid more than a half million dollars for the house not three years ago, and because the real estate market had tanked, I . . . *we* would take a major loss if we sold before the market recovered. Besides, I loved the house, and all the memories I gave a damn about I'd be making with him. I got rid of the old bedroom furniture, mattress included—shouldn't my gesture have been enough?

I can't blame him for everything, I guess. Why did I have to fuck up a perfectly good relationship by agreeing to marry him? Hmph. He didn't want the *wedding*? Hell, I didn't want to get *married*! How about them apples! I repeatedly declared that marriage wasn't a necessity, but man of honor that he is, he *insisted* gettin' hitched was the proper thing to do with his old-school ass. Felt some innate need to make an honest woman out of me. For my part, sin and I had become bosom buddies over the years, so I had no problem living in it. I suspected his mother had more to do with his decision to press the marriage issue than he'd ever admit. A deeply traditional woman, she didn't believe in shacking up.

Shoot . . . I did!

And we're two grown-ass people who should be able to live the way we want. What would she do, ground us? Take away our car keys for a week?

Don't get me wrong, I wanted to spend every second of the rest of my life with Kevin; I just didn't think we needed to get married to accomplish that. Of course I couldn't tell him the whole truth because he'd think the worst—that I was harboring some deep-seated wish to marry Lamar. With his jealous self. How could a single black woman in this day and age possibly reject the idea of marriage?

I'll tell you how.

Marriage and the so-called dream of "forever" scared the buhgeebers out of me. It's not difficult to understand when you examine my personal history with the "institution." My parents split up before I was old enough to realize they'd ever *been* married. I had more philandering men and failed relationships than Elizabeth Taylor had ex-husbands—too many. My first (and only) marriage was to a twelve-year-old who couldn't keep his dick in his pants.

Oh, yeah, sign me up for some more of that!

Granted, Kevin was *beautiful*, for lack of a better word, a better man than any of those jackasses. But he was still a man. He was born with the "fuck-up" gene even if the trait lay dormant.

Of all the things I supposed I'd have to be alarmed about, I could say with some certainty that infidelity ranked among the lowest on the list—so did dishonesty. Kevin shared everything with me, and our lives were so integrated he wouldn't have the time, inkling, or energy to juggle another woman. And the beauty of Kevin, he wouldn't even if some miracle would let him indulge without my finding out. I'd never felt so incredibly loved in my life, and if I had to risk the ultimate commitment again with anybody, Kevin was the one. For him, I closed my eyes and jumped in the deep end.

So, there we were . . . sorta living together in a house I loved and he wanted to sell. I was scared shitless to get remarried and trust again; he was frustrated by my fear. He didn't want a wedding, no matter how small; I didn't need a marriage, shacking up would suffice. We were in wedding-planning hell, rushing to the altar before I changed my mind, and the time had come to finish up one of the last tedious nuptial chores—meeting the photographer. The day had already shaped up to be a pain in the ass, and we hadn't stepped out of the house.

"I hate to break up your little man-fest, Kevin, but don't forget our appointment this morning. You're still coming with me, right?" I asked. They fired looks at each other as if I'd thrown the monkey wrench all up in their plans. Derek rightly took the question as a hint to get the hell out and excused himself. Kevin was a little slow on the uptake.

"Do I need to go, baby? I'm supposed to play ball with the fellas."

Oh, no, he didn't! As sure as I was black, he was bringing his behind with me or he'd have hell to pay. Normally, I wouldn't mind going by myself, but El Cheapo Kevin refused to let me hire a wedding coordinator, who could've helped us with all the mundane crap. So, if I had to go, *he* had to go.

"I'm sorry. I must've misheard you, honey. Did you say you were going to play ball with the fellas?" I asked in my sexiest "you must be out of your damn mind" voice.

"No, baby, I said I'm really looking forward to meeting with the photographers," he lied.

"Oh, okay, that's what I *thought* you said." I smirked, walking toward the kitchen to get myself some orange juice. I had much attitude and wasn't at all happy with him, particularly in light of his little confession. Kevin said his good-byes to Derek and then ambled in trying to smooth my ruffled feathers.

"You know, I wouldn't let you boss me around if you weren't so cute. When you get old and wrinkled, you can fuhgedabouditt," he said in his *Sopranos*-worthy New York Italian accent. He walked toward me and wrapped his arms around my waist.

I softened a bit . . . only a bit. "That's okay. When you kick the bucket, I'll take your insurance money and buy me a *younger* man who can satisfy me *all night long*," I said, chuckling. I ran my hands up his firm biceps and clasped my fingers behind his neck. Yes, he'd pissed me off, but I adored him all the same.

"I fail to see the humor," he said, pecking my cheek. "Go ahead, mess around. I'll *haunt* both of y'all *all night long*. I'll be up in here like a cock-blockin' bogeyman. And I'm only gonna show up when you're ready to get busy."

"Ooooh, three-way!"

We fell out laughing and made up in the same breath, the entire nature of our relationship captured in one moment—laughter, lovers, friends.

2
Charisse

"Real quick, can we go over the 'things done' list before we head out?" I asked, pulling a small spiral notebook from my purse. "I can't believe we pulled this together in two months. Thank goodness the guest list is short. Only our nearest and dearest."

"Figured I'd better get you down the aisle before you had a chance to run," he said, smiling. Hadn't said anything but the truth.

"Let's see. Cake—check. Bridesmaid dresses and shoes—check. Ceremony slash reception hall—check. Umm, did you reserve the limos?"

"Ummm-hmmm, honey, took care of it yesterday," he responded.

"Honeymoon. Did you book the honeymoon?"

"Two all-inclusive, fun-filled weeks in Jamaica. I made sure the resort had a spa, just for you."

And no doubt a golf course just for him.

"Honeymoon—check. Rings—check. Flowers— check. Did your mom buy her dress?"

"The day I was born," he said. We both cracked up again. His mama's been dying for him to get married so he can finally crank out some grandbabies. "What about your dress? Did you find one yet?"

"No, and I'm starting to lose hope. I wish I could wear a black wedding dress. My butt looks too big in white."

"Your butt looks big in everything."

I cut my eyes at him and folded my arms. "Ex-*cuse* me!"

"I . . . I mean that's half the reason I'm marrying you, baby. You know I needs me some junk in my trunk. Come on now," he said, watching his mortality disappear before his eyes.

A smile slowly emerged and overtook my scowl. "So, what's the other half of the reason you're marrying me?"

"Your money." He laughed as he dodged a pillow I hurled from across the room. "I'm kidding, baby. You know I only love you for the sex. So, anyway, changing the subject . . . when are you gonna decide who's walking you down the aisle?"

The little smile he'd managed to get out of me vanished instantaneously with that question. I'd been avoiding that subject like a broke ex-boyfriend, but Kevin was determined to keep pressing the issue until I dealt with it, said I'd regret my decision if I didn't invite him. He didn't quite grasp he'd been fighting a battle he couldn't win.

"Yes, *James*. He's the *only* father I've known. *He'll* be the one who walks me down the aisle."

James, my mother's live-in boyfriend, is the only true daddy I'd ever known. He bandaged my knee when I fell off my bike, sat up with me until midnight when I had a fever of 103, chauffeured me to the prom in his pimped-out Cadillac because Mom refused to spring for a limo, greeted my first date at the door with a revolver (unloaded I hope), and did countless other things dads should do for their daughters. So, why in hell would I invite the *sperm donor* who'd pretty much abandoned me during my entire childhood to my wedding? More importantly, why was everyone—my best friend Nisey, Kevin, and even James—trying to make me feel guilty for *not* inviting him? I warned James I'd demote him to the cheap seats if he kept pushing me to invite Mr. Tyson, but he didn't care. He always said, "Right is right."

Well, I had a *right* to be *wrong*.

"Aren't you *at least* going to send your father an invitation?"

"Ummmm . . . no! Why should I? He hasn't so much as sent me a birthday card in four years. And I haven't seen him since my grandmother's funeral."

"Well, phones work both ways, don't they? Given your history, maybe he's afraid to call. Did you ever try calling *him*?"

"No. I didn't walk out on him; he walked out on me. Now, I don't want to talk about this anymore. End of discussion."

"But—"

"But nothing. That's the end of this discussion—okay, love of my life? Now I'm going to run upstairs and get my jacket, so we don't get divorced before we even get married. Is that all right with you?"

He shrugged and shook his head at my stubborn ass. *Hmph.* He could shrug all he wanted. He'd grown up with both parents in an old-school household. He couldn't relate to the hurt of being cast off by one of the people who helped put you on the earth, someone who was supposed to be genetically disposed to love you.

I ran upstairs and grabbed my jacket off the bed, and my cell phone started ringing. The caller ID read Nisey.

I wonder if she's gotten any news about the paternity test.

Among our many similarities, Nisey and I were both butt stupid enough to get involved with married men. Her faux pas, Richard, no doubt received his name because his mother foresaw he'd become the "Dick" who'd dupe Nisey into believing he was leaving his wife . . . knowing damn well he wouldn't. She took her mistake a step further than I, falling into bed and practicing unprotected sex with him and her perfectly single boy toy, David, whom she slept with during one of the Dick's "good husband" acts. She ended up pregnant and had no clue which was the baby's daddy. After she confessed this hard truth to the candidates, David stepped up to the plate and vowed to support Nisey and the baby no matter what—and Richard went back to the wife he never planned to leave in the first place.

For a prodigal husband who decided to return home and be a family man, Richard sure put Nisey and David through the ringer during her entire pregnancy . . .

with his sometimey ass. One minute he'd play daddy long enough to cause friction. As soon as he put a wedge between them, Nisey couldn't find him. She'd been on the emotional roller coaster from hell and, more than a year since Jamal was born, still hadn't found the exit. The way Richard had stomped all over her nerves, it was a wonder sweet Jamal wasn't a devil baby.

"Hey, Nisey girl! What's goin' on? And how's my angel?" I said, referring to my beautiful godchild.

"He's fine, girl. He said, 'Dada,' today and David was completely over the moon."

"Awww, I know he was. So . . . not to rain on your parade, but did the test results come back yet?"

"No, not yet. We're expecting them soon and I'm a hot mess. David fought me tooth and nail about getting the paternity test done. I kept telling him we'd stalled long enough. I can't stay in this limbo any longer. Meanwhile, Richard is threatening to take me to court for custody at every turn. He didn't want anything to do with the baby until he found out Jamal was a boy. Out of nowhere, the daddy genes kicked in and now he's just *got to* know. And now I'm scared David will leave if he finds out Jamal isn't his."

"But, Nisey, David already said he's gonna stay with you no matter what."

"Girl, please. That's like saying you'll split your lottery winnings before they call the numbers. Promises are real *easy* to make when you don't know the outcome. He's so hung up on being *the* father . . . I don't know if he can handle just being *a* father. And truth be told, I don't know if he loves me because he believes I've given him a child or if he loves me for me."

"Well, let me ask you this—do you love David?"

"Let me put it this way, I've let him see me with no *makeup* . . . and *no weave*."

"*Damn*, you really do love him, don't you?"

"I'm crazy about him, I can't lie. But I need to know if our life together is real or a fantasy he's living through me and Jamal."

"Hmph. Girl you can keep that drama. I don't envy you at all. But the bottom line is, you've got to know which one is Jamal's real father. You can't get around it."

"Yeah, you're right. I know you're right."

Kevin and I arrived at the photographer's, and Kevin almost went into cardiac arrest when the man told us the cost of the wedding photography/videography package—which came complete with still photos and a lovely customized video set to our favorite tunes. Kevin stood up and calmly walked to the back of the office.

"Charisse, can I speak to you over here for a second?"

"Sure, baby. What's up? Is something wrong?" I said, trotting behind him.

"'Is *something wrong*?' You expect me to pay almost three thousand dollars for some *pictures*? Are you kidding me? I can get my uncle Leroy to run my video camera for *two hundred* dollars."

"Oh, please, you're kidding me, right? Uncle Leroy is blind in one eye and can't see out the other one. Did you check out the pictures he took at the summer picnic? We got twenty lovely shots of Uncle Leroy's thumb, one of Mama's ankle, and one of Nisey's ass—which, by the way, was the only picture that he actually meant to take."

Every family had a pervert uncle, and Leroy wore the crown for the Douglass family. The only thing he spent more time doing than trying to look up women's skirts was actually trying to take them off. I swear he grabbed my ass one time during the Super Bowl party, but he said he was reaching for the tortilla chips—which were in the kitchen.

Kevin laughed. "Okay, baby, not Uncle Leroy. But let's please do some comparison shopping? We can find someone cheaper than this."

"Baby, I don't *have time* to comparison shop. Have you forgotten I work full-time like you and we're on a short deadline—only one week left? I wanted to get a wedding coordinator but you said no. We could've given the coordinator our budget and he would've done all the shopping for us . . . but you said no. I'll tell you what, though." I reached into my purse and grabbed the massive list of photographers that I'd prepared for such an occasion. "Here's the list that I researched. You're free to call as many as you want and tell me what you come up with. Is that fair?"

Kevin snatched the list from my hand and snarled, "Fine, I'll take care of it."

Oh, he has lost his ever-loving mind.

I snatched the paper, cranked my neck, and hissed, "Forget it! I might as well find one. I'm doing everything else with no help from you."

"What's *that* supposed to mean?"

"It means I'm up to here with your whining and crying," I said, motioning my hand over my head. "If you don't want this marriage, then end it!"

Who said that?

"Charisse, you take disagreements too far sometimes. I never said I didn't want the marriage. I just don't—" He paused.

"Don't what?" I snapped, looking down at my watch. I was supposed to meet Lamar, and our tiff couldn't have come at a worse time. "I need to get going."

"I'll find the photographer," Kevin said, holding his hand out for the list. I handed it to him and stomped off to grab my jacket. "Where are you going? I think we need to talk."

"I'm not ready to talk. And I promised to help Lamar pick out some new furniture." Kevin's face dropped. He didn't want Lamar within five feet of me, but he agreed to trust *me* and respect our friendship, even if he didn't always trust *him*. Lamar paid me no mind anyway. He was still celibate, although a few women at his church started sniffing around trying to hook up with him—feigning heifers. They viewed his celibacy as a challenge they needed to overcome to get him in bed, not a promise he'd made to himself and God to live a better life.

Unfortunately for them, Lamar had begun to view sex as a weakness, like an alcoholic who wouldn't take a sip or he'd plunge off the wagon. He'd focused his attention on being a father and keeping himself straight. Women were unnecessary complications.

"Instead of helping him find furniture, why don't you find him his own woman? You're taken . . . or did you forget?"

I cracked my mouth open to say something crazy, but caught myself and dialed down my original statement. "I'll tell you what. I'm gonna forget what you said and see you at home later," I said, gettin' my positive chi on.

When I got in the Beemer and glimpsed my narrowed, angry eyes in the rearview mirror, I wondered, *Are we doing the right thing?*

3
Kevin

I was glad to get home and chill after our meeting with the photographer. Told myself I'd actually call around to find a cheaper one, but knew I wouldn't. Just as I hadn't done anything else she'd asked. Not that I was purposely trying to be difficult . . . I guess I was just purposely trying to be difficult. Listen, I'd been down the big-ass wedding road before, a road that led straight to my cheating wife and a dead-end divorce. How had I evolved so much that I could guarantee my life with Charisse wouldn't meet the same fate? Shit scared me to death and I couldn't lie to myself about my fears even if I could deceive everybody else. The only thing more frightening than marrying Charisse was the thought that I might spend the rest of my life without her if I didn't . . . as good a reason as any to get married, I suppose. And with smooth-ass Lamar on the scene, up in her grill every chance he got, I couldn't be certain she wouldn't someday succumb to his charms.

On the way home, my boy hit me up on my cell. Derek was one of my best friends and a crime technician in the FBI lab. We'd worked together on a few cases and started hanging, playin' ball, catchin' a game, whatever. He'd been a positive brother and I hadn't met too many like him. He was a *three*-time divorcé, but not for lack of commitment or fidelity. He was unlucky in love, couldn't tell the difference between a chicken head and a queen. Derek had a better perspective than most hating brothers who didn't want their friends to find a decent woman if *they* couldn't find one. Derek hadn't been in a serious relationship in over a year, but he was a Christian-in-progress and helped keep me on the straight and narrow—most of the time.

"Whassup, man?" I said. "You didn't play ball with the fellas?"

"Hey, what's up? Naaah, man. I decided to try and get some work in. Your, uhhh, your ex-partner Kristen called me out of the blue and asked me to stop by her office on a case matter. Workin' on a Saturday." His voice sounded strange but I let the suspicion roll off my back.

"Oh, yeah? Some things don't change, I guess. I haven't spoken with her in a minute, not since we arrested Charisse's ex-boyfriend. How's she doing?"

"Well, man, she seems to be happy . . . doing okay. You know she had a baby a while back, right?"

A baby? She didn't tell me she was pregnant.

"Oh, for real?" I said, playing it off. "Well, she and her husband got back together. They got back on track fast! Did they have a boy or girl?" I tried to sound happy about the news, but my pulse quickened and the room started spinning like a mofo.

"A little boy. He's a cute kid. When I briefed her on a few things, I happened to notice a picture of him. Her husband, Greg, is actually one of my fraternity brothers. He and I are gonna hook up to play ball pretty soon. But, uhhh, you might want to give her a call, you know, to congratulate her?"

I knew damn well Derek wanted to say more. Sometimes brothers gossiped worse than women. I needed him to just come out, say what he was thinking, and stop beatin' around the bush. "Why do you sound like you're holding something back, man?"

"Well, I don't know. I just thought it was kind of strange. Both Kristen and her husband are very light-skinned. But their son is Cocoa Puffs brown, doesn't look like either one of 'em."

My stomach sank. In an instant, I knew. I didn't flinch though, continued on with the conversation not knowing whether I was trying to fool Derek or myself. Either choice was better than facing the truth. "Is that right? Well, you know how black folks are; we come in all colors. If there's some dark skin anywhere in your family line, you don't know what you're gonna enter the world looking like."

"True that."

"I'll give her a call, though. We need to catch up," I said. *Please, God don't let it be mine.*

"Well, let me holla at you later, man. Is your wifey gonna let you off your leash long enough to play some ball later? Or do you have to go buy some more cat shoes?"

"Whatever, man. I'm coming. Don't hate because you don't have a woman as good as mine."

"Yeah, right. Whatever."

I hung up the phone panic-stricken, held hostage by my own secrets, my own deception. I couldn't think straight. Kristen had a brown baby . . . a son. The child couldn't possibly be mine, could he? We'd only slept together once.

But once is enough.

Understand Kristen and I had spent a lot of time cramped up in a Bureau-issued vehicle while working the Dwayne Gibson case. Crazy hours. Late-night stakeouts. Sharing every intimate detail of our heartaches and heartbreaks. I'd left my wife, and Kristen had recently separated from her husband. Although I dreamed Charisse would someday be mine, I had no idea we'd end up together, engaged in just over a year. Yeah, I'd hoped for it, envisioned it, even said a quiet prayer or two asking God to make her mine, but my faith wavered just long enough for me to make the biggest mistake of my adult life, a mistake that might cost me everything.

The night of Charisse's fortieth birthday, Kristen and I were both subsumed in loneliness, craving the warmth of another . . . any other. We hooked up. I *thought* we used protection. Turned out to be the magic birth control pill. You know, the one that only worked when you actually swallowed it. I didn't carry any condoms because I didn't believe I'd need them. Nothing was planned. But a lack of planning was no excuse for stupidity. No excuse. Just thinking with the wrong head. The second we finished, we both called the hookup an accident . . . a mistake. Not an ounce of right in what we'd done. Made Kristen realize how much she wanted her marriage, no matter how broken it'd seemed at the time, and I became even more determined to win over Charisse.

We both went on with our separate lives.

After we locked up scamming Dwayne, one of the biggest cases of our collective careers, Kristen took a promotion with the White Collar Crime Unit at Headquarters, and I moved to the Organized Crime and Drugs squad at the Washington field office. Our paths rarely crossed and we never again spoke of what happened.

Now, that goddamned night had come out of nowhere to haunt me and threaten my future with the first woman I truly wanted to spend the rest of my life with. My first marriage was to a starter wife— Charisse was my forever.

I sat down on the edge of my bed and started doing the math, as if counting the months would make a damn bit of difference, as if tallying up the days would change what I'd already understood to be the truth.

Why now, Lord? Why now?

I shook my head.

Look at all the drama and heartbreak Charisse had suffered at the hands (and dicks) of the men in her life. I'd have to confess that I was one of them and break her heart yet again. I'd have to tell Charisse, one week before our wedding, that I'd impregnated the woman I claimed was only my partner, and now we had a little boy together.

Yeah, I tried to reason that I didn't *exactly* lie to Charisse. Rather, I'd omitted a key element of the truth. By the time our relationship had progressed, Kristen and I *were* partners—and nothing more. Charisse wouldn't believe the fling was a onetime thing, not the way Kristen transformed into a green-eyed demon anytime she was around. If I wanted Charisse in my life, what choice did I have . . . really?

Hell, the excuse didn't even fly with me and I was the one making it up.

My mind raced. I pictured Charisse slapping my face; the sting shook me to the core, reverberating through my entire being. She shrieked, "We're through!" Her words echoed over and over and over. I held my hands over my ears, but the sound wouldn't dissipate, only echoed louder and louder.

How could I live without her? What could I do to make her understand?

I resolved to get over the chickenshit whining and take the first step—call Kristen to find out the truth once and for all. The time had come to man up and accept responsibility for what I'd done, even though I thought—no, hoped—the baby might not be mine.

A small chance . . . a miracle.

I picked up the phone, hand shaking, and dialed her cell number. She answered.

"Hello?"

"Hey, Kristen, it's Kevin."

She paused. The heavy silence suffocated me. "I, uhhh, I thought you'd be calling. You spoke to Derek, huh?"

My hand shook and my inner bitch said one final prayer. *Please, God, say he's not mine.* "Yeah, I spoke with him. You got something you need to tell me?"

"Kevin—"

"Do you have *something* to tell me, Kristen?"

"I didn't want you to find out this way. I've wanted to tell you but didn't know how. Especially when I heard you and Charisse had gotten engaged. I kept saying I'd tell you tomorrow . . . tomorrow . . . and tomorrow never came."

Took her fifty words to say yes without saying yes.

"So, he's mine?" I asked resignedly.

"Yeah."

"How long have you known?"

"Since the first moment I looked in his face. He looks like you." Her voice started to crack.

"He looks like me?" I said, unable to hold back the tears—tears for what I'd gained and for what I was about to lose.

"Yeah."

"Well, what about your husband? Does he know? What did he say? How did he react?"

"Honestly, we hoped the baby would be ours. Not long after Dwayne's arrest, we reconciled. I laid my dirty laundry out and told him the truth about everything, including what happened between you and me. He forgave me for my mistakes and I forgave him for his. But he always understood a chance existed—"

"The baby wasn't his."

"Yes, he's a good man and he loves this baby as if we made him. He's such a good father, Kevin, to all of our kids. I didn't want to tell you, but I should've. You had a right to be told. I regret not saying something sooner." She sighed. "Listen, I'll understand if you don't want be a part of his life, if you want to go on and make your life with Charisse."

"What the hell are you talkin' about, Kristen? That's my son. He's my *child*, my *blood*. I can't pretend he doesn't exist. To know a part of me is alive in the world and not know him or see him . . . how could I do that? You know me well enough to know that's not how I roll."

"I know . . . I know. So what do we do?"

"I want to see him."

"Then what?"

"Then . . . I don't know, but I *need* to see him," I urged. "Let's meet at the park near Reagan National. I'm supposed to be playing ball with the fellas, but I'll skip the game and meet you there. I'll figure out what to do from there. I've gotta tell Charisse at some point."

"I'm sorry, Kevin. I'm truly sorry."

"You're sorry?" I said as a burst of anger welled up inside. I couldn't tell whether I was angrier at her or myself. "I just bet you are. You handled business with your husband and didn't give me the chance to do the same with Charisse—at least not before she accepted my proposal. Now, I'm not just losing my girlfriend. I may lose my *wife* and *the future* I had planned with her. So, thank you for your sorries, but you can keep them."

Kristen fired back, "I feel bad about this, Kevin, but you had the chance to tell Charisse the truth, and you chose not to tell her. How the hell can you blame me for your mistake?"

Her words struck my core. "I'll see you in a couple of hours," I snapped, and slammed the phone down.

Kevin

You had a chance to tell Charisse and you chose not to tell her.

Kristen's words ground in my head. She was right. I could've told Charisse and given her the chance to stay with me or leave. Frankly, I needed *her* too much to give her the option. She is the only woman I'd ever met who made me feel as if my love was enough, as if that was all she needed from me. She didn't care about my job. What I wore. She didn't need money. Not anything. Just me.

I called Derek, needed someone to confide in. I could usually count on him for decent advice. However, given the ridiculously bad advice I received (and accepted), I'd have had better luck calling Erykah Badu's Tyrone, whoever Tyrone is.

"Derek, it's Kevin." I stretched back on the couch, eyes closed. My temples pounded like a bass drum.

"Dude, I figured I'd be hearing from you tonight. I was about head over to your place to make sure you weren't home playing Russian roulette with six bullets in the revolver."

"If you knew, why didn't you say something?"

"What did you expect me to say? How would I look calling you and telling you that baby *might not* be yours but sure appeared as if you spit him out and named him Junior? You'd think I'm startin' shit. I didn't want any part of that."

"Whatever, man."

"So, what're you gonna do?"

"I don't know, man. This situation. Messed. My. World. *Up!* How could I be so stupid? I've jeopardized my wedding, my future—and for what?"

"Well, I can't tell you what to do, but if I were you, I'd wait until *after* the wedding and the honeymoon before I told Charisse anything. You don't want her canceling the wedding over some stupid shit like this. After the honeymoon, you sit her down, tell her the deal. What's she gonna do at that point, divorce you?" he asked, pausing for reaction. "Hell no! She loves you. Oh, she'll be mad as hell. She might even crack you upside your head. But she'll accept the baby and eventually get over it. If you tell her you lied to her about Kristen *now*, from everything you told me about her past, you can hang it up, dude. Your wedding ain't happenin'. And she probably won't speak to your black ass again. Plain and simple."

He hadn't said anything but the truth . . . but I was raised to do the right thing, to tell the truth even when it hurt. Of course, if I'd followed that advice I wouldn't be in this predicament. I'd accepted Charisse with all her faults, so she could do the same for me . . . couldn't she? "Man, I can't lie to her, not to *Charisse*. I'm gonna tell her the truth. Plus, she's like a damn human lie detector. I can't get shit past her."

Derek chuckled. "A'ight. You go ahead and tell her the truth, Mr. Forthright. I'll be watchin' your ass on the six o'clock news ready to plunge off the Woodrow Wilson Bridge. You better listen to me. Don't tell her until after you *get back* from the honeymoon or she's gone," Derek urged, before he added the final dig. "Need I also mention you've been concerned about that dude Lamar, right? She'll probably pass go and run straight into his arms. Is that what you want?"

Damn, he had a point. The *only* thing worse than Charisse's leaving me was the possibility that she'd end up with that bama Lamar. So, I reluctantly decided to take that fool's advice and wait to tell her after the honeymoon. In reality, I should've heeded my mother's advice. When I got into trouble as a kid, she always told me, "What's done in the dark will eventually find its way to the light. So, you might as well fess up. You might not save yourself an ass whooping, but at least you won't lose my trust."

My head fell back against the headrest, which vibrated as a 747 rumbled overhead. I had never been a fan of airplanes, but I'd have taken a ticket to anywhere. The Southwest Airlines commercial popped into my head, the one where they ask, "Need to get away?"

Hell yes! Take me wherever you want me to go, I thought.

I craved the comfort of Charisse's voice so I decided to give her a call. I had a feeling our lives would forever change after my meeting with Kristen and my son. I needed to speak to her before this meeting went down or I couldn't hold it together.

"Hey, baby," Charisse said. More than a year later and I still smiled at the sound of her voice. "I'm sorry about earlier, but you know I love you, right?"

"I know you do, baby." I stifled the tears as a tornado of emotions swelled inside me. "Y'all finished shopping?"

"You okay? I can hear something in your voice. What's wrong?"

"I'm fine, baby. Everything's cool."

"Okaaay"—she hesitated—"if you say so."

"I say so."

"Well, we're almost done here. My, uhh, my mother called and gave me some news, but I'll talk to you about it when we get home tonight."

"Why don't you tell me now?" I asked, watching Kristen's car pull into the parking lot.

"No, we can talk when we get home. I need to get my own mind wrapped around what she said first. This is definitely a conversation for Grey Goose. Anyway, what are you up to? Got a hot date?"

"Please. I only have eyes for you." Kristen stepped out of the car so I hurried the conversation along. "I'm getting ready to play ball with the fellas. Where're you on your way to?"

"We're gonna get some ice cream and hang out for a minute. After that, I'm going home. I'm wiped out. You gonna rub my feet for me?"

"You know I'll rub your hammertoes anytime."

"Forget you!" she said. "Alrighty then. Love you."

Glancing out the window, I caught sight of what appeared to be a father throwing a football with his son. The child couldn't have been more than three, cute as a button. He held his arms open wide as the wobbly Nerf ball sailed through the air. Once he caught it, the father raced over to him and swept him up in his arms as they did a celebration dance. The mother jumped and cheered and joined in. They were living my dream, the dream I'd planned with Charisse and the son *she'd* give me—not Kristen.

She tapped on my window and peered inside as a little brown boy hung on her hip. I opened my door and moved toward her, my body weighed down in angst. And then I set eyes on the baby's face.

Could I love him . . . really love him, this little boy who'd been thrust into my life by an unfortunate circumstance? The child whose presence likely meant the demise of a love that I held so close to my heart? Could I love him? Would I resent him? None of what happened was his fault, but it sure didn't feel that way.

I was jarred when the baby smiled at me. I'd never seen a smile like mine on another human face before. My heart thawed instantly.

"Hey, little man!" I said. He buried his face in his mother's neck. "What's your name?"

"Baby, tell him your name. It's okay. Tell him. Say, 'Javon,'" Kristen sang, trying to coax him. "He's a little shy around strangers. He'll be okay. You want to take a walk?"

"Javon? You gave him *my* middle name."

"Yeah," she said with a slight smile. "There's a bench over there. Perhaps we should go sit down for a bit."

"Can I carry him?"

"Sure . . . if he'll go to you." She leaned him toward my chest. Javon squirmed and whined for a brief moment, then rested comfortably in my arms. Holding him seemed like the most natural thing in the world.

"So, you're looking good," Kristen continued. "Still taking good care of yourself, I see."

"Well, Charisse takes good care of me." I looked off into the distance, as ripples from the Potomac River swept over the rocky riverbank. "She's the reason I've been so happy. I can't imagine my life without her."

"I'm glad to hear you two are doing so well," she said with a slight hint of insincerity. "Let's hope you'll never find out. So, when's the wedding?"

"Six days and seventeen hours."

"Listen to you! She's got you countin' the seconds. She must be putting something on your ass."

I chuckled and changed the subject. Hurt too much to think of how much I stood to lose. "You're looking good too. Marriage agrees with you."

"Nothing's ever agreed with me more. Nothing."

We sat on the bench and talked for almost an hour as she updated me on Javon—the day he was born, his first word. He'd started crawling and was on his way to learning to walk. By the end of our conversation, Javon had grown comfortable in my arms and whined and squirmed when I handed him back to his mother.

"I'll see you soon, little man, okay?" I gave him

a kiss on his forehead. "He's a handsome little man, Kristen. Handsome."

In an instant, I'd experienced the "wow" again. Love at first sight. From the moment I peered into Javon's little brown eyes, I'd been wrapped around the tiniest pinkie. Javon was my son, couldn't resemble me more if he tried. I was scared to death to tell Charisse, but I'd never turn my back on him. She'd need to learn to love us both . . . or neither of us.

Trust, I prayed like hell for the former.

As we headed back to the car, Kristen said, "Ummmm . . . Kevin. Is that Charisse headed this way? See her? Across the lot?" Kristen pointed at a black BMW. An angry-assed woman stormed toward us, trailed closely by a light-skinned brother yelling, "Wait, Charisse! Wait!"

"Oh, shit! Go! Get Javon to the car. I'll take care of this. Go!"

I mumbled to myself, "I'm so screwed!"

5
Charisse

Lamar and I met at Crate and Barrel—at his suggestion. Of course, I'd suggested IKEA. I asked him, "Why spend a million dollars when you can look like you did?"

He asked me, "Why look like you spent a million when you can afford to spend it?"

Let me find out he's ballin'.

We strolled through the aisles, chatting up a storm. We'd become the best of friends. Oh, how he made me laugh at the stupidest shit, and we had inside jokes out the wazoo. He and I talked to each other about anything, and he'd become my favorite listener, next to Nisey. In some ways, I liked him more than Nisey because he still had enough feelings for me not to slap me in the face with the truth when I didn't want to hear it. Nisey didn't give a damn. If the truth needed to be told, she put the hard, cold facts in your face and didn't mince a single word.

When Kevin and I fought about money (or anything for that matter), Lamar always lent his shoulder. He possessed an inner strength and wisdom that one could only obtain by making the world's worst mistakes and somehow surviving one's own stupidity. I recognized that strength in him because I bore the same mark on my own soul. We were two peas in a pod; both of us had the worst relationship histories, including the single point where our lives had briefly but passionately collided in college. We'd wallowed in the land of the love bottom dwellers, the place in life where we had no place to go but up . . . and we got up.

"So, you know my husband-to-be is still skeptical about our friendship, right? I've tried to tell him that you're harmless, but he doesn't believe me."

"He shouldn't. I'm not harmless."

I froze in the aisle. "What does that mean?"

"I mean, if I were him, I wouldn't trust me with you either. He understands what he's got. But in another time and another place you'd be mine."

"Excuse me? As I recall, I was yours and you didn't have a clue about what the hell to do with me."

"On the contrary. I knew what to do with you. Truthfully I wasn't ready at the time."

"Ready for what? A commitment?"

"No, marriage." He stopped dead in the middle of the aisle, right along with my heart. No, he didn't say the M-word. "Listen, Charisse, I'm about to school you on something women don't understand about men. See, men put women into several categories when we're considering a relationship."

I laughed. Lamar, the *original* player, was about to hip me to his knowledge of the female sex. The enlightening moment was like Colonel Sanders revealing his eleven herbs and spices. "Is that right? School me, Professor Think-You-Know-Women."

"Laugh if you want, this ain't nothin' but truth. Now, back to what I was saying. We recognize three kinds of women. There's the friend kind, the ones you can talk to you and hang out with but you're not sexually attracted to them. There's the booty-call kind, the ones you're *only* sexually attracted to . . . and you don't want to be friends with because you'll feel guilty about using them for sex. Last but not least, there's your kind."

"My 'kind'? What 'kind' would my kind be?" I said putting up air quotes.

"The marrying kind. You're the kind of woman a man takes home to meet his mother; the kind you know will have your back; the kind who becomes your world, a friend, a lover, and everything in between. The marrying kind."

"Oh, Lamar, I think you made my little heart go pitter-pat, such sweet words from an old player like yourself," I said, still scanning the furniture displays for the perfect couch.

"I'm serious, Charisse. Kevin's a lucky man."

"And you know this! Oooh, I like this sofa, right here. It'll be perfect for your living room. Really, the whole grouping works. You should tell them to wrap this so you can get it to go," I said, briefly distracted by the sea of home decor. "Anyway, change of subject. How are things going with you? Got any new prospects in your life? I think the time has come for you to consider getting back in the game. You've got too much to offer, and you don't want your nookies to go stale."

He laughed. "You're crazy. A man with everything to offer and no one to offer it."

"Lamar, please. You've got these Christian-lite women from church running around like poodles in heat trying you get with you. Give 'em a little Communion wine and you can take your pick."

He fixed his hazel twins on my eyes and said, "Uhhh, no—not *anyone.*"

Just then, my cell phone rang. My mother. Boy, talk about perfect timing. I planned to extend our conversation just long enough for Lamar to forget what he and I had been talking about.

"Hey, Mommy!"

"Hi, suga'," she said, her voice lacking its usual bounce.

"What's wrong? You don't sound like yourself."

"Oh, I'm not myself, baby. I'm not. James and I were fightin' all night." She sighed. My mother didn't sigh so I knew something was really wrong.

"You and James were fighting? Over what?" I asked, thinking, *What's she gone and done now?* "A few weeks ago, he was thanking God you survived your stroke last year. What happened?"

"Well, he asked me to marry him again and—"

"You didn't say no, did you, Mommy? Tell me you didn't say no."

"What else am I gonna say, Charisse?"

"Ummm, yes. The word *yes* springs to mind," I said, although I could totally relate to her dilemma.

Hell, if I could sacrifice for my man, she could do the same for hers, couldn't she? Or perhaps I'd contracted a case of misery loves company.

"I can't do it, baby. What I look like gettin' married? I'll tell you what I look like . . . a fool. Shoot, marriage at my age is like an old man's dick, don't work too good after the age of sixty without heavy medication." I rolled my eyes. Where did she come up with this stuff? "James said he don't wanna keep living together if we don't have a future. I said, 'A future? You sixty-five years old, you ain't got no future.' His future is dirt and daisies from the bottom side up and he's worryin' me about gettin' married. Why can't he just leave things be? We're happy just the way we are."

I wanted to holler "Amen!" but my holy praise would've been counterproductive to keeping her and James together. "Apparently not, Mom. Otherwise, we wouldn't be having this conversation right now. James is the best man we've ever known, what are you so afraid of?"

Let's face the facts. James had a long track record of doing right by Mommy. Sure, Kevin was undefeated—but it was way early in the season.

"I ain't afraid of nothing. Just don't see the point at our age. I ain't going nowhere. He ain't going anywhere. What do we need to get married for?"

"Do you love him?"

"Of course I love him. What's love got to do with anything?"

"Everything! James would walk through fire to make you happy. During the time you were in the hospital after you had the stroke, I had to force him to leave your side. He's supported you in every way. He's been a rock for me like no man until Kevin. All he's asking you to do is marry him. Maybe your decision shouldn't be about what you want this time. Maybe, if you love him, you'll consider what *he* wants."

"You talkin' crazy, baby. You talkin' crazy, and I don't wanna talk about this *no more*." I heard the proverbial *thunk* from Mommy's putting her foot down, so resistance was futile. "Anyway, I've got some more news you ain't gon' wanna hear, but I think you oughta know."

"Mmm-hmm. Trying to change the subject now, but go ahead. What's going on?"

"I spoke with your father . . . told him about the wedding."

"You did what!" I yelled. She intentionally went against my wishes. Talk about hot? She'd pissed me the hell off. He didn't have a right to be told . . . and he damn sure hadn't *earned* the right to attend, so what was the point? "I didn't even know you were in contact with him."

"We don't talk often, but I thought he should know his only daughter's gettin' married. I know you don't want to talk to him or invite him, but he told me something I think you need to know."

"What's that?"

"He's got cancer . . . prostate cancer."

"What!"

"Yes, baby. He was recently diagnosed. I'm not sure whether that means anything to you . . . or even if it should given that he hasn't been much of a father to you. But whatever happened between you two in the past, you only get one father. Only *one*. And when he's gone, he's gone. No takebacks, no do-overs."

I stood in stunned silence, my heart pounding. How had I conjured emotions for a man who practically abandoned me? I'd buried my hurt so far down for so long, I didn't realize caring existed where he was concerned. Couldn't decide whether to sit in numbed silence or cry. I needed time to process what she said.

"Okay, Mom . . . I, uhhh, I need to go now."

"Baby, I know this news is a lot to absorb. I'll give you a call in a couple of days."

I plopped down on the couch while Lamar stared at me in absolute confusion. Mom's news had floored me. I didn't associate with my father at all, didn't visit him. Neither of us went out of our way to speak unless we were attending a relative's funeral, so how had the mere thought of his dying of cancer left me paralyzed with fear?

"What is it? What's wrong, Charisse?" Lamar said through a dense fog of faint, distant memories filling my head.

"Nothing, Lamar. Nothing. Let's get back to shopping."

"No, we can do this another day. Something's wrong. What is it? Talk to me."

"It's my father, my biological father. He has prostate cancer."

"Oh, no." Lamar sat next to me. He put his arm around my shoulder and stroked my hair.

"Why is the news affecting me this way? I feel like I got the wind knocked out of me."

"Well, whatever he's done, he's still your father. You were bound to have some feelings for him."

"You're right. I can't fathom the thought of my parents dying, you know? Especially not from cancer."

"Don't put the man in his grave yet. Prostate cancer is very treatable. Survival rates are higher than ever, especially when it's detected early. Okay? Now, I can't stand this droopy face another second. How about we go spring us some Reese's Cup Blizzards from the Dairy Queen and sit in the park for a minute. So you can clear your head before you go home."

I somehow managed a smile and sighed. "Sounds perfect."

Lamar and I dawdled around Crate and Barrel for a while longer and paid for his purchases before we left for my ice cream sanctuary—the Dairy Queen. I suspected crack was the secret ingredient in those damn Blizzards because I was fully addicted, couldn't get enough. One of the most shameful moments of my life happened a year ago as I cut in front of a nine-year-old waiting to buy an ice cream cone when he turned around to find his mother. What can I say? I needed my fix. Oh, I bought him an ice cream cone . . . after I ordered, of course.

Anyway, we had grabbed our ice cream treats and headed for my favorite park, which was located adjacent to Reagan National Airport. Planes flew over as they approached the landing strip; they came in so low onlookers felt as if they could reach up and touch them. At night Arlington, Virginia, was visible on one side of the river and the DC city lights shone on the other. This little slice of serenity sat right off the Potomac River so the vibe was tranquil.

Kevin and I parked there whenever our nerves were on edge. Sometimes, we'd watch the planes fly overhead, and other times we'd make out in the backseat. Every couple should discover their own "spot," and the airport park was ours.

Speaking of Kevin, right after we left the Dairy Queen, he called to check on me. He was adamant about staying in touch during the day, but he was the first man with whom I didn't mind punching the clock. Understand, Kevin had never been one of those men who only called to check up on you because he wanted to ensure you'd be on the other side of town from where he'd be doing his dirt. You know how they do. Call you saying, "Hey, baby, where are you? I need to know where my boo is." Then hang up, slip on a condom, and get back to screwing the other woman. Some might've called Kevin controlling but I'd been with men who couldn't tell you from day to day whether I was alive or dead. They were so busy out running the streets or sliding up in some other chick's cookies, they didn't care whether I existed . . . at least until they wanted some ass. Mmm-hmm. Then they'd ring my phone off the damn hook, leaving indignant messages if I had the nerve not to answer. So, Kevin's concern for me had been refreshing and welcome. I trusted him implicitly.

As Lamar and I pulled into the park's driveway, my spirits lifted with every spoonful of ice cream and Reese's Peanut Butter Cup coursing through my veins. I gazed across the park and caught sight of a man and his son playing football. The poor child held his hands like twelve feet apart but somehow managed to catch it. His father ran over and grabbed him, and his mother joined the group hug, so touching. I leaned my head back on the headrest, peered up into the blue sky and imagined the three were Kevin, Junior, and me. I was engulfed by an inexplicable warmth. Kevin's presence in my life gave me the strength to dream and believe the dreams would come true. Once I got home and into my baby's arms, all would be right with the world and I'd figure out how to deal with the news about my father.

Then I turned my head right into my *nightmare*.

6
Charisse

I did a double take when I glimpsed *my* Kevin sitting on the bench with my least favorite heifer on the planet, Kristen (his ex-partner), and somebody's little boy. Hers, I guessed. I shook my head thinking, *Didn't Kevin—not two seconds ago—tell me he was playin' ball with the fellas?*

"Lamar, look over there." I pointed toward them. "Please tell me that's not Kevin. Do you see who I'm talking about? Over there, on the bench."

"That's not—hmmm. Yeah, he looks like Kevin . . . and isn't that his partner, uhhhh, what's her name?"

"Cruella!" I retorted.

"Uhhhh . . . Kristen, right? Didn't he just say he was going to play ball?" I couldn't tell if Lamar was being sincere or just trying to stir up some shit, but his question made my blood boil all the same. I zoned out like a veteran having Vietnam flashbacks. Black-and-white pictures of all the liars and cheaters I'd been with flickered through my head like a silent movie, and my emotions grew uncontrollable. I tried to tell myself, *Charisse, this is Kevin. Good Kevin. He's not a boneheaded cheater like the others, this is Kevin! Your knight in shining armor, your dream come true!* But Charisse was hearing no such bullshit. All she heard was *lying bastard!* and *No, this motherfucker isn't sitting here, in our spot, with* that *bitch!*

Before Kevin confessed he was the guy who saved me from being raped all those years ago, I'd always assumed he and Kristen had some kind of relationship. I believed they were married when I first met them and nicknamed her Cruella De Vil because she always copped a major attitude anytime Kevin glanced in my direction. She never spoke to me, at least not voluntarily. Women acted like green-eyed monster bitches when they were screwing somebody, not just coworkers riding in the same car. My every instinct told me they'd slept together, but I pushed the thought from my mind when Kevin told me he and Kristen were *just* partners. Never questioned his word another day because he'd been such a stand-up guy. But for him to be sitting on that bench with her and lying to me about where he was *supposed* to be, all doubts about the extent of their relationship dissipated. Something more had happened between them, and I'd become steadfastly determined to find out what that something was.

Before Lamar had even anticipated my next move, I'd already jumped out of the car and stormed toward my lying-ass fiancé. Lamar yelled, "Charisse, wait!" wasting his precious breath. I'd commenced my mission to *kill* Kevin and would not be deterred. Thought my days of catching men in midst of such bullshit extracurricular activities had ended the day I said yes to his proposal, but, to my dismay, I was still in the deep thick of it.

Kristen hiked her ass over to her car just as I swooped in. Kevin was well aware of the grave he'd dug for himself. He just needed a little help with the banana peel. I'd arrived just in time to slip it under his foot.

"Playing ball, huh?" I half yelled, sounding a touch breathless.

"Listen, I realize I lied but I can explain, Charisse." He reached out to grab my arm. I jerked back, out of his reach, and bumped into Lamar. I turned to Lamar and told him in an eerily calm voice, "Please give us a minute. I don't expect it'll take him too long to pull another implausible lie out of his ass."

"Alrighty then, waiting in the car," Lamar said as he headed toward the Beemer.

Kevin began to expel his verbal diarrhea after Lamar had walked out of earshot. "I'm sorry for lying to you, baby, but what you saw . . . it's not what you think." He paused. "Okay, maybe this is what you think, but I need you to let me explain."

I said nothing, only glared at him as tears began to form; his declaration of guilt was imminent. Ironically, the climactic scene from *A Few Good Men* flashed in my mind, the part when Tom Cruise yelled, "I want the truth!" and Jack Nicholson's character replied, "You can't handle the truth!" I didn't know if I could deal with what Kevin was about to tell me, so I tried playing his confession in my mind. The worst I thought he could tell me was that he and Kristen had slept together and were still involved, confirming I'd agreed to marry yet another cheating bastard. The urge to hurl overtook my body at the mere suggestion, but I braced myself and prepared to listen.

He continued, "Can we please go sit down?"

I shook my head no and remained silent. If I opened my mouth to say one word, the dam would break and tears would flow; I refused to cry.

"Okay. I, uhhhhh, I haven't been completely honest with you, Charisse." My heart pounded in my ears. "I told you that Kristen and I were partners and nothing else, but the truth is that we did hook up once. Only once. By the time I came to your house New Year's Eve, our relationship, if you want to call it a relationship, was over. She realized I wanted you and she reconciled with her husband."

I knew it! I always knew it. I was pissed as all get-out, but I could handle this. Oh, don't get me wrong, I planned to make him pay for that lie, but I didn't consider the revelation a deal breaker. After all, I'd had my suspicions all along.

"Is that all you can say?" I asked coolly.

"No, there's more."

More?

"I swear Kristen never told me. I just found out. The little boy you saw with us today . . . uhhhhh, he's my son."

Deal breaker! Oh. Hell. No!

"What?! Did you just say *she* had a baby and he's *yours*?! What the fuck, Kevin!" I shook my head as if I'd been swimming in lies and they'd saturated my ears. I couldn't shake the words out of my head. He *couldn't* be for real.

"She wasn't even going to tell me about him. Derek found out and told me. She and her husband—they're back together—were going to raise him by themselves, but he's my child, Charisse. I have to be part of his life. You know me. You know I can't have a child in the world and not be a part of his life. I can't do it."

"You can't—I don't even believe this shit! You lied to me! And you have a baby by . . . by her!" I shouted. Couldn't hold my tears back any longer, the dam broke, the floodwaters flowed, and my body trembled.

I took off, damn near running toward my car. Kevin scrambled behind me. I'm sure people were staring, but I felt like the only person in the world at that second. I'd never felt so alone and betrayed in my life.

"Wait, Charisse. Please! We can work through this."

"Leave me alone!" I yelled. "Leave me alone!"

I went to open the car door, but Kevin pushed himself in front of me and blocked it. Clueless Lamar jumped out of the car.

"What's wrong, Charisse?"

"I need to get out of here!" I yelled to Lamar, tears streaming down my face.

"Listen, Kevin. Maybe—"

"Lamar, man, stay the hell out of this," Kevin said, glaring at Lamar and giving him the hand.

Lamar remained cucumber cool and said, "I'm not sure what this is about, but let her calm down, man. Let her calm down. Emotions are obviously running high right now, and you both might say things you'll regret. I'll make sure she gets home okay and y'all can talk your problems out later. Give her some time."

Kevin nodded and released the door handle to let me get inside.

I fidgeted with the keys, couldn't get them in the ignition fast enough, fired up the engine, and took off so fast the tires screeched. Kevin faded out of my rearview mirror, and I wondered if he'd fade out of my life as fast.

Lamar asked, "What happened, Charisse? What happened?"

Through my sobs I said, "Kevin had sex with Kristen . . . and the little boy we saw—he's theirs. They've got a child together."

"Oh, damn! Listen, pull over and let me drive. You're not in any condition to drive. Pull over."

I eased onto the shoulder and put the car in Park. Lamar reached over to hug me, and my head fell onto his shoulder as streams of tears continued to fall. In minutes, my dreams had shattered. Our wedding was one week away. How could I go through with the ceremony now, a marriage I didn't even want, only to look like the queen fool? I'd had enough heartbreak to last me three lifetimes, and the burden on my heart weighed more than I could bear. After I calmed down some, we switched seats.

"Do you want me to take you home?" Lamar said, pulling back onto the parkway.

"Home? What home? I don't have a home anymore. Just a house with a lying bastard in it. Can we please go get a drink? This Blizzard just ain't gonna cut it right now."

• • •

When Lamar and I pulled into my driveway that evening, I was toasted. I ain't lyin'. My goose had been seriously greyed. I noticed a car sitting in my driveway, but didn't recognize it and didn't care because my bladder was screaming for the bathroom. Lamar opened the door for me, and as I stood up, I saw Kristen get out of her car, a second woman inside following close behind. I didn't know what the hell she was doing at my house, especially at that moment—or why she'd bring her little friend with her, but I was not in the mood to deal with them. I guessed she wanted a witness in case I commenced to whooping her ass.

"Kristen. What are you doing here?" I snapped, making it perfectly clear her presence was in no way, shape, or form welcome. The other woman didn't say anything, only folded her arms across her thick frame and smirked. She appeared fairly nondescript except for the blinging gold necklace around her neck with the initials STK.

"You and Kevin all right?"

"We're holding our own for the time being. Why are you here?"

"Well . . ." she said, unable to hold my glance. *Guilty bitch.*

"You're in love with him, aren't you?" I asked. Time to get the truth on the table so we all know where she stood. No need in faking ignorance anymore.

"Yes, I am. And he loves me too. His judgment is just clouded right now."

"He loves you? In case you didn't notice, he and I

are engaged to be married. I don't give a shit what you think. He bought *me* the ring. Count the carats," I said, waving my 2.5-carat ring in her face.

"Let me keep it real with you. If Kevin didn't have feelings for me, why wouldn't he tell you the truth about us?"

I stood silent. Didn't have an answer for that one. Perhaps when I finally spoke to Kevin, he would.

She continued, "I'll tell you how. Because he loves me. But he's so loyal he's not even willing to admit to himself. First of all, check yourself in the mirror. Do you honestly believe you can compete with *me*? Second, he and I are both FBI agents. We share a world you couldn't even begin to understand. *Now*, I've given him his first son. If you can delude yourself into thinking you can compete with *me*, do you think you can compete with *him*? You should give Lamar a chance. Anyone can see he's in love with you . . . and unlike Kevin, he's *not* in love with me."

Tears formed in my eyes. I might've been torn down by the Goose, but her words seemed true even if they weren't. I wanted so much to beat the shit out of her, hit her where I'd hurt her the most. So I walked over to her, glared in her eyes until the bile rose from my stomach to my throat, and threw up Grey Goose all over her new Louboutin stilettos.

As Lamar followed me into the house, he said to Kristen, "You might want to put some water on those. I heard Grey Goose stains."

7
Kevin

Charisse busted me . . . *cold*, and I couldn't do a damn thing about it. When I looked into her eyes, they rained hurt and distrust. In her mind, I'd become one of *them* . . . the same old tired brothas who slept around, lied, and couldn't do *right* by a woman if they had no *left*. I should've told her about the one-night stand, but, given her state of mind after everything that had gone down with Dwayne, I knew for certain we'd never have come this close to marriage. She'd have written me off at the speed of sound.

I paced back to the Range Rover, slipped in the front seat, and draped myself over the steering wheel. I hadn't cried since my father passed away, but guilty tears flowed. In an instant, I'd realized Charisse must become my wife because even the *thought* that she might never speak to me again crippled me. She'd become my heart's desire, and I'd be an incomplete man without the warmth of her laugh, the light in her eyes, or the curve of her hips.

I leaned back against the seat as my mind flashed back to our first year together. Shook my head and smiled, remembering our date. What an adventure. I realized from that day forward she was the woman with whom I had to spend the rest of my life. . . .

January 2011

"Does this make me look fat?" she asked as she tooted her butt in my direction. She wore a booty-hugging skirt that showed off her thick, shapely hips and legs. Almost made my mouth water. Yeah, the skirt did kinda make her look fat, but in my estimation, fat had never been a bad thing. Still I knew the question had a wrong answer. And with Charisse, the wrong answer might not be as obvious as it seemed.

"Is this a trick question?"

"Yep. Sure is."

"Didn't your mama ever tell you not to ask questions you don't want to know the answer to?" I asked, chuckling.

"Yeah. She also told me not to date a man stupid enough to call me fat to my face. So, now that you've had a few minutes to mull it over, what's your answer?"

"Yep. You look fat. Fatty fat fat fat fat fat fat. Fatty fat."

She walked over to the bar and grabbed a bottle of wine as if she were getting ready to swing a bat. "Excuse me? What did you say?"

"Not *f-a-t* fat. *P-h-a-t* phat. Come on, woman. My mother raised me with good sense. Now can we go? We've got reservations."

"Where are you taking me?"

"You'll see when we get there."

Almost immediately after I left Charisse's place on New Year's Eve—after spending the entire night eating ice cream sundaes and playing Monopoly—I started planning our first date. I wanted to show her that she could have a different life with me, a better life. That I could make her happy for a lifetime. Not all men were like lying, scheming Dwayne Gibson. I wanted to restore her faith in men, needed her to trust and believe in me. Okay, so I wouldn't accomplish everything during that evening. I'd give her a glimpse of how life with me could be.

As I pulled into the National Harbor, Charisse's eyes glimmered. I'd learned how much she loved to spend time near the water during one of our many New Year's Eve discussions. This time she'd have a much different experience from her usual restaurant hopping.

"Awww . . . you're taking me to McCormick and Schmick's?"

"No, some place much better."

"Better than McCormick's? Must be that new restaurant, what's the name again?"

"I don't know, but we're not going there either. Just be patient."

I pulled into the parking lot closest to the pier and boat launch where several large yachts were docked. Then I walked around to open her door and led her to my surprise.

"Isn't it a little cold for a boat ride?"

"Yes. We're not taking it out. I have a surprise waiting for you inside. A friend of mine is letting me borrow it for the evening."

"Wow. You sure know how to impress a girl, huh?"

"Well, you know . . . we do what we can," I said, smiling.

After boarding the luxury cruiser, I led Charisse inside the spacious cabin area, where a man in a chef's hat stood near a decked-out table, holding a bottle of wine.

"A chef and candlelight dinner? Oh my God. I can't believe this, Kevin," she said as she ran her fingers across my back; her touch gave me chills. "You did all this for me?"

"For you." I smiled and helped her off with her coat.

She took a long sniff. "What's for dinner?" she asked as I pulled out her seat and assured her comfort.

"That's a surprise."

Within five minutes, the chef returned wielding two plates containing our special meal. I'd hired a private chef for the evening and asked him to prepare a Brazilian shrimp dish. Several years before Charisse and I met, I traveled there with a tour group, and this dish was among my favorites, something I wanted to share with my sweet Charisse.

"Wow, that looks delicious," she said as the chef set the plate in front of her. "What is it?"

"Taste it. See if you like it," I said.

"Looks like shrimp with a cream sauce," she said as she filled her fork and took a bite. "Oh my goodness, this is delicious. Makes me wanna slap my mama it's so good."

"I thought you'd like it. It's Brazilian shrimp cooked in a coconut cashew sauce."

Her eyes grew big. "Cashews? You didn't say cashews, did you?"

"Yeeeah . . . something wrong?"

"Oh my God. I'm severely allergic to cashews."

"Allergic! I didn't know."

By the time I jumped up and reached into my pocket to get my cell phone, Charisse was holding her throat, struggling to breathe, and pointing to her purse. "Sh—ot, sh—ot," she tried to say, but her words had no sound. I could barely understand her. I grabbed her purse and rummaged through it until I spotted a syringe.

"This?" I asked as my panic kicked into high gear.

She nodded feverishly, hiked up her skirt, and pointed to her outer thigh.

When I saw her thick, chocolate goodness, I had an overwhelming urge to run my hand up her leg but shook it off and tried to stay focused. Her death would certainly spoil any romantic mood. "Here?" I asked, pointing the syringe into the thickest part of her thigh.

She nodded her head and closed her eyes as I jabbed the needle in her leg. Within minutes, her breathing improved, but I called 911 anyway. She was still pretty weak.

"Charisse, I'm so so so sorry. I had no idea," I said, pulling a chair beside hers and holding her in my arms until the ambulance arrived. "Note to self, you're a little allergic to nuts."

"Yeah, only tree nuts though. But you didn't know, so please don't feel bad," she said, rubbing my face to try to ease my angst. When that didn't work, she went for poorly timed humor. "Our first date and you're already trying to kill me. I hope this isn't a sign of things to come. Boy, you really owe me big-time."

I smiled weakly to acknowledge her effort to make me feel better. Decided to call the florist first the next morning to ask if they sold "Sorry I almost killed you" bouquets.

Getting involved with a woman who had emotional baggage with which I was intimately familiar had its positives and negatives. On the positive side, when she acted as if she'd lost her natural mind, I understood exactly what was at the root of her insanity. Knowing removed all the unnecessary mystery many men experienced in the beginning of relationships. On the negative side, I still had to deal with her insane behavior from time to time. Charisse could go from zero to crazy in about thirty seconds. Fortunately, when I set my heart on the target of my affection, I had the patience of Job . . . which turned out to be a necessity for loving Charisse.

About six months into our relationship, Charisse constantly tested my commitment and trustworthiness. She'd been through so many failed relationships she really wanted to determine—as soon as possible and by any means necessary—whether she needed to bother wasting her time with me or to run like hell for the nearest exit. Even with me, someone who had proven himself a good man more times *before* our relationship than all the other tired brothas put together had *during* her relationships with them, she *still* wouldn't cut me a moment of slack.

"I'll show you mine if you show me yours," Charisse said, holding her cell phone out to me as we cuddled on her favorite chaise. "I'm serious. Take a look at it. I don't have anything to hide. Do you?"

"No, I don't. But what's on my cell phone isn't any of your business. I'm a grown-ass man," I declared.

"I see," she said, the chill in her voice cold enough to freeze the Atlantic Ocean.

I had nothing to hide, but realized if I didn't relent, she'd hold the incident over my head and someday use it against me, maybe as an excuse to bolt from my life. I decided this battle wasn't worth fighting.

I reached into my pocket. "Here you go."

"You're only giving it to me because you think I won't look at it."

"No, I'm not," I said as I wrapped my arm around her. "Let's look at it together. If you have any questions, just ask."

She cut her eyes at me but sure didn't tell me to put the phone away.

"Hmmmm. Adrienne, Alice, Barbara, Charisse . . . Charlene?"

"Cousin, cousin, aunt, you, coworker."

"Kristen. Hmph. I know who that heifer is. Mary and Nancy?"

"Mary's an FBI agent. Nancy is my real estate agent . . . before I met you of course."

She smiled. "We can delete that one. Hmmm . . . Well, well, well . . . who is this Sophie D person? She's got an asterisk next to her name. Must be pretty special. Didn't even put an asterisk next to mine. Who the hell is *she*?"

"You don't need one," I said, turning toward her to see her expression when I responded to her question. "I guess you can say she was my favorite girl until you came into my life."

"Oh, really! Favorite girl, huh? What the hell's her number still doing in your phone? Are y'all still messin' around?"

"No! She and I *do not* mess around. And I'm with you twenty-four/seven. When would I have time?"

She snatched the phone from my hand. "Hmph. Men can *always* find time to cheat. I wonder what *she'd* have to say about your little relationship. I'm gonna call her."

I laughed. "I wouldn't do that if I were you."

"Why? She can't take me."

"I wouldn't be too sure about that."

"Whatever!" She hit the Send button. "It's ringing. You sure you don't want to make a confession before she answers?"

"Nope. No confessions. You go right on."

"Hello?" I heard the woman's voice, and saw Charisse's eyebrows furrow. She put a little attitude in her voice. "I'm Kevin's girl . . . friend. Who are you?"

Silence.

"Oh . . . I'm sorry, Mrs. Douglass. Kevin didn't tell me this was your number." Charisse punched me in the arm. "He's right here. Hold on."

She put the phone on mute and yelled, "Oh my God, Kevin. I can't believe you let me do that. She's gonna think I'm a nut!"

"Hey, I told you not to call, with your hardheaded ass. You got any more numbers you want to call?"

"Yeah, 911 for you!"

All I could do was laugh. I was time enough for Charisse. Always demonstrated I was a good man but didn't let her run the show . . . at least not every day.

A year later and I'd somehow managed to survive her insanity. She grew to trust me and I'd earned every ounce of it. Now, with one stupid mistake, one failure to tell the whole truth and nothing but the truth, all the effort I'd made to earn her trust had dissipated. As insane as she was, I loved her with every fiber of my being. I had no choice about being a father, but I wanted more than anything to become Charisse's husband. I prayed my dream was still possible.

8

Kevin

I straightened my back and resolved to save my relationship, whatever I needed to do. Problem was, I didn't have a single clue about how to deal with Charisse in the emotional state she'd likely be in—and she'd have to be handled with some finesse. She wouldn't be swayed with any BS bouquet of roses. She'd probably beat me with it if I had the nerve to even suggest the pain I'd caused could be fixed with flowers. Expensive jewelry might get the door open, but she'd probably snatch it and immediately slam the door shut. Take my hard-earned money and *still* leave me. I needed an idea, some perspective. Although I didn't want to talk to anyone, I went home and confessed the whole ordeal to Derek.

"Whaaat?"

"Yeah, man. I hadn't planned to tell her about the situation until after the wedding but she caught us. So what the hell am I gonna do now?"

"Well . . . how high is the limit on your credit card?" Derek said with a chuckle.

"Man, quit playing. This is serious."

"Who's playin'? If you don't want her to leave your

ass, you better give her everything she wants . . . and throw something extra on top."

"Dude, this is Charisse we're talking about, not some chicken head. I can't buy her off. No, you've got to come better than that."

"Oh, I see. I thought you were a player for real, but you're still wet behind the ears. Check this! Exhibit One—Kobe Bryant. Exhibit Two—Tiger Woods. Exhibit Three—Bill Clinton. Should I go on?"

"Please get to the point? I've got to figure out how to save my wedding."

"I'm telling you how to get your woman back, my brotha, but you ain't listenin'. The point is, no matter *who* the woman is, every single woman on this planet has a price. The only questions for you to consider are, what is Charisse's price and are you willing to pay it?"

Sitting on my bed, I buried my head in my hands and ran my fingers across my scalp in some futile attempt to relieve some frustration. When that failed, I jumped in the shower and let the hot water run over my body, trying to cleanse the shame away. I couldn't imagine what Charisse was thinking—or doing—but her activities likely involved Grey Goose, food, and plenty of tears. As much as I wanted to go straight to bed and pray that everything would be all right in the morning, I still had one last job to do before I could sleep in some semblance of peace. Couldn't let another moment pass before I shared the news with the other woman in my life—my mother.

My mother, Sophronia Douglass, affectionately

known as Mother Douglass around the way, wasn't nearly as off-the-chain as Mama Tyson, but she had her moments, and this news would certainly bring out her worst until she came to terms with it. I couldn't believe I had to call the most sanctified women on the planet and tell her that my baby's mama and the woman I was slated to marry in a week *were not* one and the same. Didn't matter that I was over forty, she didn't believe in "bringing no bastards" in the world. My stomach churned and burned when I picked up the telephone. As my fingers pressed the numbers, I thought, *Here goes nothing.* Braced myself, fearing her dainty hand might reach through the phone and yoke me by the neck the way she'd threatened on such occasions since I was a kid.

"Heeeey! How's my baby doing? And why you calling me at this time o' night? You know better! *Law and Order*'s coming on. That's my show!"

"I-I guess I'm okay," I said, tapping my foot nervously. I rested my forehead in my hand and shook my head. Felt like a twelve-year-old bringing home a D on my report card.

"Then why in heaven's name are you stuttering? You only stutter when you're about to lie or you're in trouble. So, which one is it?"

"I'm not stuttering, Ma."

"Yes, you are," she snapped. "Boy, don't you know how long I've been your mother?!"

Huh?

"Now, tell me what's going on," she ordered.

"Are you sitting down?"

"Kevin, don't make me reach through this phone!"

I chuckled. "Well, you remember the woman I worked with until about a year or so ago . . . Kristen?"

"Yeah, I remember her. Little high-yellow, scrawny thing you brought down here when you finished up your father's business. What about her?"

"Well, she had a baby some months ago."

"Is that right? Well, wonders never cease. How did some fool manage to make a baby with *that* ice queen?"

I shuddered, knowing I was the fool and would have to tell Ma that the son of the ice queen belonged to me too. "Ma, she's . . . uhhh . . . also your grandchild's mother . . . and I'm the father."

A long silence followed. Too long. As a matter of fact, Ma had *never* been that quiet, not that I could remember.

"Hold the hell up! Did you say my grannnnd-chiiiiild's mother?" she dragged, her Southern drawl even more pronounced than usual.

"Y-yes, ma'am."

"Kevin Javon Douglass, you gon' make me come through this phone and beat your forty-five-year-old ass!" She yelled all three of my names *and* cursed— always a bad sign. A series of indiscernible outbursts blared through the phone, as if she'd started speaking in tongues. "How you have a baby out of wedlock with that evil woman? I told you that little wench was trouble. What were you thinking, son? Hmph. Perhaps the better question is *what* were you thinking *with*?"

"Ma. I mean, I can sit here and give you excuses, but I can't do anything to change what's been done or right my wrong. He's here, I found out about him, and I've got to deal."

"He? It's a boy?"

"Yeah. She named him Javon, looks a little like me too," I said, praying talk of her first grandchild would calm her down.

"Javon?" she said, the pitch in her voice easing toward a happier tone. "Ain't that somethin'? You got pictures? He's probably cute as a spring bunny if he took after you."

I smiled as the grandma genes kicked in. "I just saw him for the first time today. I'll take some on my phone the next time I see him."

"My my my. I've got a grandbaby—" She paused. "Wait a minute. How did Charisse react when you told her? She's got to be beside herself. Y'all plannin' this weddin' too?"

"Well, she knows, but I didn't exactly get a chance to tell her. She caught me meeting Kristen and the baby at our favorite park."

"Lawd, Jesus! Boy, I raised you better! You shoulda told her the minute you found out," she said, letting out a frustrated exhale. "Well, she was aware y'all had some kind of a relationship, right?"

"No. No, ma'am. She didn't know," I said, instantaneously reverting back to a knuckleheaded teenage boy.

"Kevin Javon Douglass!" *There she goes again.* "Mhm-mhm-mhm. How many times have I told you what's done in the dark will come to the light? How many times? Sounds like you gon' have a tough lesson to learn. Hard heads make soft asses. Hmph." I could almost hear her shaking her head in disappointment. "Guess I'll be taking this KitchenAid mixer I bought for your weddin' gift back down to Dillard's. Ain't no way the Charisse *I know* is gonna go through with this weddin' and can't say I blame her."

What could I say? Ma had only spoken the truth. I should've told Charisse the truth long before, but sometimes the truth is as hard to *speak* as it is to *hear*.

After downing a couple of beers, I found balls sufficiently large enough to call her. Every day, Charisse's voice was the first I heard in the morning and the last I heard at night. She'd become my bedtime story, and I *needed* her even if she didn't *want* me.

"Hello?"

"Lamar?" I said, looking at the caller ID to make sure I had dialed her house phone. *No, this fool isn't answering her phone.* "What the hell are you doing there? It's almost two in the morning?"

"Heeeey, man, what's up? Listen, Charisse had a little too much to drink tonight and got sick. I didn't feel comfortable leaving her alone. She's knocked out in her room; I'm in the guest room."

"She okay?"

"I don't know. One minute she seemed fine and the next she was crying and yelling. Last thing she said is that she was calling off the wedding, but she probably just had too much to drink."

"I see!" I snapped, frustrated because his sneaky ass was with Charisse and not me. "Listen, dude, I'm trying to be understanding about your friendship with my fiancée but, just between you and me, don't let me find out you're starting shit now that we're having problems."

"Man, I know you didn't step to me like that. I'm here trying to help her. Listen, I've been in your shoes and had to confess the existence of new babies more times than I care to remember, but Charisse is a grown woman with her own mind. She'll make her own decision about you, and, and, sorry to say, her decision may not include you."

I chuckled. "Let's keep it real. This little nice-guy act you play doesn't fool me. *I'm* not Charisse. You think I'm not hip to your game? Trying to wait me out so you can slip in? Well, that's not gonna happen. And if you don't believe *that*, believe *this*—I'm licensed by the United States government to carry a gun, and I won't hesitate to pop a cap in your ass if you mess with me and mine. Are we understood?"

"Perfectly," Lamar said with a sinister smirk in his voice.

He must be tripping.

Lamar didn't know whom he was playing with but he better ask somebody. Yes, I'm a good man, but I'm not a stupid one—or a weak one. Figured there wasn't any sense in going over to Charisse's since she'd passed out, but I'd be there first thing in the morning. Talking with Lamar made me realize I needed to make things right—with the quickness.

Didn't get much sleep. Why I'd even tried was a mystery. Took another shower to wake myself up, threw on some jeans and a polo, and jetted out the door. When I pulled in Charisse's driveway, Lamar's Benz was *still* parked out front and her Beemer was gone. Lamar had to realize I'd show up at her house early and probably stayed to play with my head. As I put the key in to unlock the door, I felt it pull open from the other side.

Lamar yawned, acting nonchalant, and said, "Oh, *you're* here. I heard the car out front and thought Charisse had come back home."

"Where'd she go, man? And why are *you* still here?"

"I don't know where she went. I woke up to fix her something to eat because I knew she'd be hungover after last night, and she and her car had disappeared. I mean, I can't say for sure but I think we can both guess."

"Nisey's," we said in unison.

"Anyway, I don't know when she's coming back so I'm out. Help yourself to the coffee in the kitchen."

Listen to this cocky fool, offering me coffee in my woman's kitchen. He didn't even feign concern for my reaction. Lamar had made his position clear to me, if not Charisse. Lamar wanted more than friendship. He wanted lovership, wifeship, and mothership. Everything I almost had and nearly let slip through my fingers.

Lamar slipped into the powder room, ran the water, and came out with a damp face and his keys in his hands.

"I'm out, man. Holla," he said as he strode out the door.

"Peace." I walked over to lock the door and noticed Lamar had left a note for Charisse on the side table:

> Call me whenever you need me.
> I'm here for you.
>
>   Love,
>   Lamar

What kind of BS is he tryin' to pull? I thought, as I balled up the note and aimed my jump shot at the nearest trash can. I didn't have a single doubt Lamar's note was meant more for *me* than Charisse. He'd outright dissed me, wasn't even trying to cloak his intentions anymore. Trust me, I wasn't having any of that. No, the Lamar issue had reached a head and needed to be nipped in the bud sooner than later, but I'd need to handle the matter with care. If I even remotely appeared to be forcing Lamar from her life, Charisse and her hardheaded ass would do the exact opposite of what I wanted.

I walked into our office. Charisse had installed a second desk set so that I'd have my own personal space . . . and stay out of hers. I smiled as I pulled out the man chair she'd bought and assembled herself to surprise me. The hydraulic lift still didn't work, so the chair collapsed to toddler height whenever I took a seat in it.

Leaning back in my minichair, I thought about Charisse, thankful she'd gone to her girl's spot because Nisey had been my biggest fan. Now, she wouldn't let me off the hook, not on her *best* day, but she'd let Charisse choose her own course without any pressure. That's all I could ask.

With my nerves a bit more calm, I decided to check my e-mail and take care of some paperwork. Then the phone rang. The caller ID read ANDRE TYSON.

"Oh, snap!" I mumbled after taking a second to process the name. "This is Charisse's father."

9
Charisse

Feeling a little nauseous, I went into the kitchen to grab some saltine crackers to settle my stomach. I'd heard the saying "death warmed over" but never fully comprehended its truth until I woke up feeling like a twelve-pound sack of hot diarrhea the morning after finding about Kevin's love child.

More than anything else, I admired Kevin for his character. It's the only reason I trusted him enough to do the one thing I'd been scared shitless to do—get married again, commit my life to yet another untrustworthy creature. Like a newborn baby's ass, I'd been slapped with his deliberate deception. I didn't care that he and Kristen had sex before we got together. I cared that he didn't tell me the truth about what happened. I never believed he could hide something like that from me.

On top of that, I'd be lying if I said Kevin hadn't broken my heart because I wouldn't be the first to give him a child, a son. In an instant, he and Cruella had sucked all the joy from my reasons for marrying Kevin, and she confirmed, in no uncertain terms, she'd fallen in love with him, just as I'd always expected. Why were men so dense where women were concerned? Always insisting she had no romantic attachment to him when every fiber of her being screamed, *Kevin is my love muffin!*

Hmph.

I didn't give a damn about what she said or thought. I cared about Kevin's thoughts though. Wondered if he'd perhaps begun to think himself worthy of more than what I could offer. Kristen fit the standard of beauty with her fair complexion, Pantene hair, and Jessica Rabbit body. Me? I was the kind-of-cute chocolate girl with a big appetite, an even bigger ass, and a shitload of emotional baggage. Zero competition for the Kristens of the world in most circles. What if she was right? What if Kevin harbored some deep-rooted feelings he'd been unwilling to admit out of some sense of loyalty to me?

My emotions grew tangled in confusion. Part of me feared he'd leave me for Witchiepoo and her son. Another part of me—the part who'd fallen for one too many bums, who'd been cheated on and lied to with a frightening frequency—wanted to cut and run. The old cut-and-run had served me well through years, saved me from ever having to confront the *hard shit* in relationships—those in-your-face, can't-look-away problems that make you love and despise someone with equal fervor, that make walking away as heart-wrenching as staying. But the old cut-and-run had also prevented me from finding the long-term, in-it-to-win-it, for-better-or-worse kind of love I'd always craved.

The question I needed to answer was whether Kevin was the man I thought he'd be . . . or should I roll the hell out and safely avoid the hard shit once again? Who would blame me for leaving under these circumstances? So what if he had an ounce of good in him. He'd lied to me.

I had a right to be wrong.

Lamar was sleeping soundly in the guest bedroom closest to mine. He hadn't even bothered to take off his clothes . . . the thought of which sent a slight shiver through my back. I had to shake that shit off and get away from him. Didn't need any more problems than I'd already been dealing with—an estranged dying father and a fiancé who'd slipped and fallen into Cruella's cookies.

Kevin would be at my house at sunrise if he was still the man I thought he was. I couldn't face him yet. Didn't know what to say or do. So, I jumped in the shower, got dressed quickly, and hit the road. Hungover, I headed for the nearest Starbucks to find consolation in a hot, fattening drink. Then I headed to Nisey's place. I needed my girl. We'd always been ride or die for each other. And if I didn't ride over to her house, Kevin was gonna die the next time I laid eyes on him.

Latte in hand, I pulled into her subdivision not even thinking about how I hadn't called to let her know I was on my way. So consumed by my misery, I forgot she had a man. I decided to park in front of her house and text her to give her a heads-up that I was outside. Didn't want to disturb them if she was getting a little *morning glory.* However, my concerns were alleviated when I pulled up to her driveway . . .

And saw David's shit sailing out through an upstairs bedroom window.

Lawd, what's going on here this early in the morning?

I jumped out of the car and tried to quietly call to Nisey.

"Nisey! Nisey!" I whispered loudly. "What the hell are you doing?"

"I'll tell you what the hell I'm doing," she yelled about a hundred decibels above my volume, "gettin' David and his shit the hell out of my house, lying bastard!"

Sweet Jesus, I hoped David hadn't gotten caught cheating too. That would be more than I could handle in twenty-four hours.

"Listen, why don't you calm down and we'll talk about it. I'm on my way in. Oh, by the way, you *do* have neighbors. You really need to chill."

"Do I look like I give a damn about some neighbors?" She stuck her head out the window, arms flailing, and looked dead at the old lady who was eavesdropping from her porch across the street. "For all I care, they can bring their nosy asses over here and help him pack. Do something useful instead of worrying about what's going on in *my* house!"

I went to grab the doorknob to walk inside the house, but the door swinged open and David came storming out with a duffel bag flung over his shoulder and rolling suitcase behind him.

"David!" I yelled. "Jeez, you scared me to death! What's going on? Where are you going?"

His eyes were laden with sadness and pain. "I'm sorry . . . I can't. I can't."

"What can't you do?"

Finally, light dawned on Marblehead. The paternity test results had come back, and judging from the crazy scene, things hadn't turned out the way we'd all hoped.

Nisey came flying down the stairs not thirty seconds after my realization, dragging David's golf bag and clubs down the steps behind her. She pulled them out the front door and, like a spear-chucking Zulu, one by one launched them across the front lawn.

"Here! You forgot these!" she yelled, half out of breath from emotion and anger. "And don't bring your weak ass back!"

She stormed back inside, slammed the door so hard the house shook, and headed straight for the freezer. Before I uttered a single word, she pulled out the emergency Grey Goose stash I stored at her house, popped the top, and threw her head back as she gulped her breakfast of champions. She held the bottle out to me like a wino offering me a hit.

"Seven a.m., Nisey? I'm the alcoholic and even I can't drink this early."

"Hell, it's noon somewhere in the world." She let out a long burp and took a seat on the stool at her breakfast bar. The Goose gave the term *breakfast bar* a whole new meaning.

"So, I guess I don't need to ask what happened here. Test results came back, huh?"

"Ding. Ding. Ding. Tell her what she's won, Bob!"

She paused, turned her back toward me, and wiped her eyes, as if she had something to hide from *me*, of all people. "I told him Richard's the father and he said he needed some time. He's not sure if he can handle the situation, dealing with Richard's crazy ass and all."

"Oh, no!"

"Oh, yes. He asked me to give him a few weeks to sort things out." She took another gulp from the bottle. "So, I gave him *a few minutes* to get the hell out. Now he's got all the time he needs. Just like I told you, Rissey. He didn't love me or want me. He wanted the baby. No baby, no David."

"I dunno, Nisey. I mean, step in the man's shoes for a minute. Finding out a child you've loved isn't yours is a lot to deal with. I imagine his head's a little twisted right now."

She cut her eyes at me and shook her head. "Wait a minute. What the hell are you doing here this early in the morning anyway?"

Damn. I'd gotten so engrossed in her drama I almost forgot my own. I ain't gonna lie, dealing with her drama was far more entertaining.

"Hmmmm. Well, let's see. I've got bad news and worse news. Which do you want first?"

10
Charisse

Nisey walked over to the fridge and grabbed a bottle of cranberry juice, and I swear my mouth watered, but I needed to cure my hangover before I even thought about taking another drink. She mixed herself a cocktail and asked for the worst.

"Actually, I can't decide which one is worse. So, I'll start with this one. Kevin is a father. He and Cruella have a son together. This is a confirmed report. Caught them at the park yesterday."

She gasped and gulped down the entire drink.

"Oh. My. God! Please tell me they haven't been sleeping together all this time. Tell me now so I don't go over to your house right now and rip him a new asshole."

I laughed and regretted I hadn't thought of her idea first. "No, he says they only slept together once, and it was before New Year's Eve when he revealed who he was."

"Mhm. Mhm. Mhm. Ain't that some shit? You always said you thought something was up with them.

So, what're you gonna do, Rissey? Your wedding is less than one week away."

"I wish I had a clue. I mean, you know what I've been through, and I've had a hard time trusting again. I put so much of my faith in Kevin, and this is what I get for my trouble."

"Wow. I'm speechless, because Kevin's a good man. If *he* fucked up, we ain't got no more hope. I think I'm ready to become a lesbian. For real. I can't be butch though. I refuse to give up my stilettos."

I laughed. "Girl, you're crazy."

"Okay, we gotta come back to this story later. I gotta get my head wrapped around what happened. What's the other news?"

My expression grew somber; it never ceased to amaze me how the news had affected me. "It's my father . . . my real father . . . he has prostate cancer. Mom told me yesterday, right before I caught Kevin and Cruella at the park. I mean, this man gave me his name and showed me his ass as he walked out the door. And here I am afraid he's dying. What's wrong with me?"

"Nothing, Rissey. For better or worse, he's your father. It's only natural. I think all little girls are inherently daddy's girls. Even when daddy ain't there, we want them to be." She sat motionless for a few seconds, then said, "Shit, and I thought I was having a bad day."

"Please. You ought to know when drama's involved, I *will not* be outdone."

Nisey scanned her disheveled house, freshly abandoned by David, and let out a belly-deep sob. Her stomach muscles jerked. Reality had finally set in and she'd been overwhelmed with acceptance.

"I look around here and I can't imagine this house without David here. How could he leave me?"

I walked over and put my arms around her. I wanted to say, *One foot in front of the other, the way all cowards leave,* but instead I said, "Listen, why don't you pull some clothes together and come stay at my place for a few days. Let the baby stay at his nana's a little longer. The change of scenery will do you some good."

"Okay, we can be pitiful together," she said, smiling weakly. "What would I do without you, Rissey?"

While Nisey packed a few things, I reluctantly headed back to my house. Unlike Nisey, I hated to have witnesses to my drama, so whatever Kevin and I had to do to resolve this situation, we'd have to figure it out before she arrived.

I pulled in my driveway. Kevin's truck was parked but Lamar's Benz was gone.

Oh, hell.

If Kevin and Lamar had crossed paths, I didn't even want to think about the confrontation. While I probably shouldn't have given a rat's ass about Kevin's opinion, I didn't want him to be suspicious without cause . . . in case some miracle happened and we went through with the wedding.

I walked in the house and threw my keys on the side table. "Kevin? You here?"

He poked his head out of the office and half smiled, still hesitant because he didn't know where my head was. "Hey, baby. I'm so happy you're home."

"Oh, don't be happy yet. You haven't listened to what I'm about to say." I gravitated toward my favorite chaise and plunked down. He trailed closely behind. "Let's just dispense with the crap, Kevin. I'm hungover, emotionally exhausted, and I'm not sure what to say to you right now."

He sat next to me and held my hand. Part of me wanted to yank it back, but part of me needed his hand as much as he needed mine.

"Listen, baby, I understand I wasn't totally honest with you, but nothing's changed. I'm still the man you agreed to marry. I just made a mistake in judgment."

"A mistake in judgment? Is that a new term for *lying your ass off*? This isn't like a one-night stand you can sweep under the rug. You guys have a baby together—a living and breathing reminder to me that you deliberately hid something I would've wanted to know. You told me there was nothing between you and Kristen, and you'd slept with her. What am I supposed to think? If you can lie to me about this, what else will you lie about or hide? I bet you weren't even gonna tell me, were you?"

"Well . . ."

"No, you weren't. You would've let me marry you knowing you were keeping this secret. What does your way of handling the situation say about you, Kevin? What does it say?"

"I understand what you're saying, Charisse, and you're right . . ."

Mmm-hmm . . . funny how women are always right when men are cold busted.

"But I need you to tell me we can get past this. I need you to say that you forgive me and we're still getting married next week."

"I'm not sure if I can do that."

"What part?"

"Any of it." I pulled my hand away and turned my back toward him.

"Don't say that," he pleaded. "Look at me. You and I both know this isn't only about me and Kristen. You're afraid. Afraid of marriage. Afraid of loving and trusting. We're on the edge of our dream, so close we can reach out and touch it. Don't let this get in the way."

"Where I come from, finding out your fiancé has a child with an evil heifer you can't stand one week before your wedding ain't got shit to do with *dreaming*. That's a nightmare. I think you need to go back to your condo for a few days so I can take some time to think things through."

"Oh, so this isn't my place now?"

I rolled my eyes and shrugged.

"Well, I'd like to respect your wishes, but I'm afraid I'll need to be here for a few days longer. We have company coming to stay here with us, and I think you'll need me around."

"Yeah, I know. Nisey's coming to stay for a few days. I don't need you here for her."

"No, I'm not talking about Nisey. I didn't know she'd be here. I'm talking about someone else."

"Who?"

"Your father . . . and one of your brothers."

"My what?!"

11

Kevin

I stared at the caller ID—ANDRE TYSON. Wasn't sure whether to let the voice mail pick up or answer. Something inside me told me to answer and deal with Charisse's wrath later because she'd no doubt unleash her fury once she found out. I'd made it my mission to reunite father and daughter ever since we had announced our wedding. Charisse's unresolved issues with her father had been a major stumbling block in her relationships with men, including me, whether she wanted to admit it or not.

No matter how hard I tried, I couldn't fully penetrate the enormous wall she'd built around her heart over the years. The rigidity seemed almost palpable. I could almost touch it. Could I blame her, especially given all the hurt she'd endured over the years? She'd been searching for someone to fill a role only one man could truly fill. The time had come for them to revive their long-stalled relationship and make peace. Forty-one years was long enough.

"Hello?"

"Yes, uhhh, I'm looking for Charisse. Is she home?" he asked, his voice bass deep.

"No, sir. This is her fiancé, Kevin. Kevin Douglass." Okay, so I half lied. Wasn't sure if we were still getting married, but I'd claim it until she made her decision final one way or the other.

"Ohhhh . . . so you're the lucky man her mother told me about, huh?"

"Yes, I sure am."

"Do you know when she'll return home? I really need to speak with her. It's important."

"No, sir. I don't know when she'll be back, but, uhhh, I'd like to speak with you if you've got a minute."

"Sure, son. What do you want to talk about?"

It'd been years since a man called me son; I appreciated the sound in a way I hadn't before my father passed away.

"If you've spoken to Mama Tyson, I'm sure she's told you our wedding's in a week. I've been asking Charisse to invite you, but she's been pretty stubborn and seems as if she's drawn a line in the sand."

"Mmm-hmm. I'm all too familiar with those lines. Her mother is the master line drawer. Charisse inherited the stubborn trait honestly."

I laughed, knowing he was telling the straight truth. "Well, regardless of what's coming out of her mouth, I sincerely believe Charisse wants you here. So, I'd like to extend a personal invitation for you to come visit us within the next couple of days and stay with us through the wedding. I thought the time together would at least give you a chance to talk out your problems. What do you think?"

"That's a generous offer but I don't know if that's a good idea. This rift between us runs long and deep. Much has happened that she's not aware of or doesn't understand. I'd sure love the chance to make her understand, but when she digs her heels in, she won't listen to me. She won't listen to anybody. Got that from her mother too."

"That's what I'm here for. I'll help her listen to reason so you guys can work this out. What I need you to do is agree to a visit. What better gift could I give her . . . than you? And, sir, the truth is . . . we've hit a bump in the road. Nothing we can't work out, but she's trying to run scared. I don't think she and I will have the best chance at forever if she doesn't resolve her issues with you. I want forever."

"And you think a conversation with me will fix *all* that?"

"No, sir, but we've got to start somewhere. Right now, I can't even get her to acknowledge she's got a problem."

"I think I understand. And this bump in the road you've hit?"

"Well, sir, I believe that's a story for drinks when you get here. Will you come and stay with us?"

He let out a long, contemplative breath. "Yeah, I think you may be right. It's time Charisse and I had it out once and for all, especially now. . . . I'll call you back as soon as I make my travel arrangements and let you know when I'm coming in."

"That's great, sir. I look forward to meeting you."

"Well, you be careful when you break it to Charisse. I'm gonna pack a black suit in case of emergency."

"Emergency?"

"Yeah, your funeral."

As I hung up the phone and rested back in my chair, the reality of my phone call hit me.

What did I do?

She yelled, "Hello," and my heart thumped. Mr. Tyson had already called back to say he'd booked his flight and would be arriving with his eldest son, a brother Charisse had never met, the next day. I'd have plenty of time to help them work out their differences *and* save my wedding. I'd convinced myself that once Charisse mended her relationship with her father, she'd realize men made mistakes, even big mistakes, but that didn't mean they weren't redeemable. Didn't mean they weren't good people. Most of all, she might consider how good she'd feel to forgive.

I greeted her in the hall and started our much needed conversation by trying to help her understand the Kristen issue, knowing damn well I'd embarked on a steep uphill battle. She wasn't ready to even *consider* forgiveness, not yet. So, of course, I poured a gallon of gasoline on the nearly out-of-control fire by telling her I'd invited her father for a visit. I figured she'd go ballistic—and just as I predicted . . .

"My what!" she yelled. Flames jumped in her eyes. I'd spent thirteen-plus years with the FBI, arrested drug dealers, led sting operations against some of the most dangerous criminals involving more firearms than an NRA convention, and my inner bitch had never punked out on me as it had when I dropped this news.

Man up! I thought to myself. *You da man! Shake it off.*

I swallowed hard. "Baby, I think it's time you and your dad work things out. There's no better time than the present."

Too bad she didn't listen to *a word* I said.

"My what!" She shook her head feverishly and waved her hands in refusal. "No, no, no, no, no. Get your ass on *that* phone and tell him not to come. What in Satan's pajamas would make you do that to me? We might not even be getting married and you add him to this craziness? Call him and cancel. Now!"

"You're too late. He's already booked a flight. He'll be here tomorrow."

"Tomorrow?"

"Yep."

"I can't even believe this shit. I don't even want to deal with *you* right now. I can't do this, Kevin. What were you thinking?"

Tried to approach her but she was like a cobra snake ready to strike if I took one wrong step. "I believe you're scared, and your fear has a lot more to do with your past than your present. No, I didn't tell you the whole truth about Kristen and I'm sorry. I will spend the rest of my life making up for the pain I caused you if you let me. But I'm not your father. I'm not going to leave you . . . and I didn't cheat on you."

Tears streamed down her face at the sound of those last six words. For a brief moment her expression softened and I thought I'd taken a step forward. But before she could blink, I sensed the wall go back up. "This isn't about you cheating on me or leaving, don't you see? You lied to me. You concealed the truth about you and Kristen to—"

"To give our relationship a chance. Can you honestly tell me you would've given me the time of day if I told you about us?"

She paused. "No, I can't, but you didn't give me the chance to choose. Now you have a child, and I don't get to choose. You invite my father here and don't let me choose. Well, guess what? Marrying you is a decision you can't force me to make. I don't care how this visit with my father goes or how much you beg." She looked out the window as if she was contemplating something and her scowl disappeared . . . briefly. She huffed, "Anyway, which hotel is he staying at?"

"Well, this is the thing . . . they're staying here."

Her neck snapped and she rolled her eyes. "I'll tell you what. I'm gonna take a long, hot bath and pretend you didn't say what you said. We'll discuss this later."

"Okay, baby. Tell you what, why don't I go throw some food on the grill, open up a good bottle of wine . . . for me. Grey Goose for you. I'll even make you a burnt hot dog. Look at it this way, things can't get any worse."

"Don't even go there!" she said, trotting up the stairs.

I walked into the kitchen and started to wash my hands when the doorbell rang.

Charisse yelled, "Oh, that's probably Nisey! She's staying here for a few days. David walked out on her after they found out the baby is Richard's, so please don't ask her where he is or how he's doing!"

"Okay!"

I ran to the door yelling, "Just a minute!" mentally preparing myself for Nisey's scorn. When I opened the door, my mouth fell open and my heart hit the floor with a resounding thud.

I'm in deep shit now.

"Mama Tyson! What are *you* doing here?"

12
Charisse

Kevin had stepped on my last nerve! Did he not comprehend English? I all but signed a blood oath telling him I didn't want my father at the wedding. So not only does he invite him to the ceremony that might not happen, he invites Mr. Tyson to stay at *my house* for a few days so we can kiss and make up. Whatever. Kevin would've had an easier time inviting the devil here to shake hands with Jesus. If I didn't need him as a buffer, I would've kicked his behind out of *my* house. Yeah, I said *my*. His name wasn't on the deed *yet*.

I stormed up the stairs and started my bathwater. Every move I made was accented by a loud, protesting stomp, bang, thud, or slam. I wanted to grab myself a drink to calm my nerves, but I wasn't ready to see Kevin's face quite yet, still had a strong urge to give him a left hook across the jaw. So, I decided to call my sounding board—Lamar. He'd find some way to make me laugh and calm me down—or side with me against Kevin (unlike Nisey, who'd have been all rational). I needed to engage in some healthy group rage.

"A hundred bucks says you can't guess who's coming to visit me tomorrow," I snapped, and let out a long sigh.

"I'm sorry, who is this?"

I chuckled. "Oh, you've got jokes now."

"I had to say something to take the edge off of your voice. You sound stressed. And if we're talking about stressful visits, your mother must be coming."

"If only. No, my father. He's flying in tomorrow with one of my brothers who I've never met. Can you believe Kevin invited him?"

"Say what? How the hell did that happen?"

"I dunno. I guess my father called while I was at Nisey's and they had a little chat."

"Oh, I figured that's where you went this morning. So, what you gonna do? You've been running from your father for like forty-one years. Maybe you *should* face him."

"Not you too!"

"What did you expect me to say? I mean, look at who you're talking to. Where would I be if my kids didn't forgive me for everything I did?"

Friggin' voice of reason.

We hate him.

"What if I'm not ready to forgive? What if I'm not ready to deal with any of this . . . this *crap*?"

"Well, I hate to break it to you, but you can't take a time-out on this one. Besides, this has gone on long enough, don't you think? I mean, the man is sick and wants to make things better . . . even if he can't make them right." Lamar paused to let me ponder his statement. "Charisse, nobody's telling you to love the man or even accept him back into your life. But you should talk to him, tell him how you feel, and listen to what he has to say. You never know. He might have a legit reason. I can't imagine what it'd be, but the possibility exists."

I hated to admit it, but Lamar was right. I mean, look at him and all his kids. They forgave him after all of his ho-hopping. I forgave Lamar for his wrongs, I should at least extend the same courtesy to my own flesh-and-blood father. Truth be told, I was scared of how I might react. The rage I experienced all those years he didn't demonstrate an ounce of concern for my well-being, the years he wouldn't even speak to me or send me a simple birthday card to acknowledge my existence in the world. Could a father hurt his child more?

All of a sudden, he's diagnosed with cancer and wants to come back into my life forty-one years later, after *my mother* had done all the hard work, after she'd help mold me into the strong, successful woman I'd become. His audacity is what really pissed me off. Fucking day-late and dollar-short Johnny trying to step up and be Daddy when he didn't even understand the first thing about who the hell I am or what I'm about. He didn't want to be a part of my life for the hard shit. Once my mother and I were coasting, here his ass comes.

The more I thought about it, the angrier I got and the more I realized I needed to engage in a discussion with him. I'd give him more pieces of my mind than could fit in his brain. He could walk up in my house if he wanted to. He didn't know he'd be walking into a lioness's den, and I was fully prepared to chew him up and eat him alive.

"You're right, Lamar. Let him come. I've got something for him when he gets here," I snapped, probably taking the conversation in a direction that Lamar had seriously not intended for it to go. "But I might need to run away from home after we're done."

"You can always run to me. As a matter of fact, if you want to . . . you can stay forever."

No, he didn't say *forever*. "Lamar, why do you say such things?"

"Because I mean them." After taking in a deep breath, he said, "Listen, Charisse, I need you to hear me out. I realize you're going through a lot right now and I don't mean to add to your troubles, but did you ever think maybe you're finding out about Kevin and his child one week before your wedding for a reason? Maybe all this confusion is a sign that he's not the right man for you."

"And *you* are?"

"Well, you've had time to witness how much I've changed. A big reason I'm still on the right track is because of you and the kind of woman you've been to me. Kevin's skeletons are just falling out of the closet. What if the news about this surprise son is just the tip of the iceberg? What if he's got more women and more babies?"

Woo! He hadn't said anything but a word. What if this disclosure wasn't the end of the skeletons, the end of the drama? If Kevin had, by his confession, planted the seed of doubt in my mind, Lamar had watered, fertilized, and harvested that seed like a mofo.

"You're right, Lamar. But he's got a long-ass way to go to get to *eight*!" I said, referring to the kids Lamar had fathered during his ho-hopping youth.

He laughed. "Okay, maybe you're right. But I find it funny how you're running to me and not him. Interesting, don't you think?"

Shut *me* up.

"Anyway, back to the subject at hand. Talk to your father, clear the air. And look on the bright side . . . at least your mother's not here."

Amen, hallelujah, praise the Lord! That my mother was tucked safely in Winston-Salem with James was my *only* consolation. The only person who held a bigger grudge against my father than me was she. Sure, they'd spoken on the phone on occasion from what I gathered, but I hadn't ever seen them in a room together without Mom spewing some of her signature venom. They were like oil and water. No . . . more like a lit match and a bundle of TNT. Getting them together would be disastrous.

13
Charisse

Thinking about what Lamar had said made me realize that I still felt incredibly drawn to him. Those feelings I'd so easily repressed when things were heavenly between Kevin and me had begun to bubble to my emotional surface. What if Lamar was right? What if all that had happened was a sign that Kevin and I weren't supposed to get married? Look at all my relationships in the past—Sean, Jason, Marcus, and the list went on. In every case, I'd ignored all the red flags, trying to give their cheatin' asses the benefit of the doubt. And *every* time my tolerance blew up in my face like an atom bomb. What made Kevin any different from the rest? I tried but I couldn't give myself a good answer.

Most men are natural performers, posers. They put on acts to get what they want and later knock you upside the head with the hammer of truth when you least expect it. There I was, standing around with a big-ass knot on my head, screaming, *Please, not the hammer!*—but my heart, the stupid organ that it is, wouldn't allow me to let Kevin go.

I looked out of my bedroom window and noticed

grill smoke rising from the deck. Made my stomach growl for burnt hot dogs. I threw on a pair of my loungy pajamas and ran downstairs to get my grub on. As I rounded the corner into the kitchen, Kevin shot me a painful expression, like the face of a child in the seconds before the doctor wields the needle near his ass to give him a shot. In a moment too fast for me to even collect my thoughts, my mother's voice sang . . .

"Heeey, baby!"

"Mommy?! What are you doing here?" I cut my eyes at Kevin and he ran for cover on the deck.

Sweet Jesus Almighty!

The situation had devolved so far beyond a nightmare that it defied definition. I'd officially arrived at the gates of hell. I didn't know why she'd carried herself up to DC from Winston-Salem, but I had to get her ass out of my house and back to North Carolina sometime the next morning or World War III would erupt in my house when my father arrived.

I winced as she walked over to me and gave me a hug and kiss on the cheek. "Is that any way to greet your mama?"

I'd started to ask her why she came when big dollops of tears welled in her eyes and she commenced to sobbing in a way I'd never before seen.

"Mommy! What's wrong?" I watched her intently for a minute and handed her a tissue from the side table.

Took her a good few minutes to pull herself together so she could speak. Nothing in the world is worse than watching your mother cry and feeling powerless to help her. I couldn't stomach seeing her so sad. One thing was certain in my mind, I knew heart-broken when I saw it. Mommy was heartbroken.

"It's James," she said, sniffing and wiping her eyes. "I wasn't completely honest with you when we spoke yesterday. Truth is, James moved out a week ago . . . into some active-living community."

"What!"

"I guess he calls himself tryin' to teach me a lesson. Said he'd come back if I agreed to marry him. Nothing but blackmail. I don't negotiate with terrorists!"

I sat on my chaise and prepared myself for the drama. Kevin came in with a drink in his hand and copped a squat on the end of the sofa farthest from Mama and out of my reach. Smart man.

"I saw him with another woman today and I just couldn't take it no more."

"Wait a minute." I said. "James with another woman? Mommy, that doesn't even sound right?"

"It's true. I caught him squeezing her melons."

I started to laugh because her words probably hadn't come out the way she intended. Definitely needed to get some clarification.

"*You* . . . caught *James* . . . squeezing another woman's . . . b-*breasts*?"

"Nooo! I'd be in jail fo' sho. Her melons . . . in the fresh-produce section in the Piggly Wiggly. That man always picked the sweetest cantaloupe. Mhm-mhm-mhm."

"Ohhhhh! I was about to say."

"Might as well have been squeezin' her breasts the way they was talking though. I was standing there minding my own business, picking some fruit, and here they come walkin' up on me. James *know* today is my shopping day. So, Miss Thang says, 'Thanks for the riiiiide, James!' Dragged her words out just like that, 'riiiiide.' I bet he did give her a riiiiide!"

"So wait, this happened this morning?"

"Yeah. This morning. Then she said, 'James, aren't these the *firmest* cucumbers? I like 'em this siiiize.' Held it up in his face, palming it all suggestive like. Titties half hanging out."

I couldn't help but laugh a little bit because it did sound a little over-the-top.

"Then she said, 'Oh, James, feel on this melon. Ain't it riiiiiipe?' James rubbed all up on her shoulder, giggling like a damn second-grader. Ta he he he. Ta he he hell! I just couldn't take no more!"

Oh, no! "What did you do, Mommy?" I asked, almost scolding her as if *she* were a second-grader.

"I . . . I beat 'em both down with a bag of grapes! Beat the hell out of 'em too. Grape seeds and grape juice flying everywhere. Took two store clerks and a stock boy to get me off of 'em."

"You didn't!"

"I sho did! He knows he brought her on purpose. Trying to make me jealous. I was aimin' for James but she got in the way, call herself protecting 'im, so she got her ass whooped *too*. Some heifer named Sophronia. What kinda name is Sophronia anyway?"

Kevin, who had taken a sip of his cocktail, spewed the contents in his mouth across the floor. My heart started beating fast. What were the odds that there was another Sophronia in Winston-Salem besides Kevin's *mother*?

Sweet Jesus, let there be more than one.

"Sophronia?" Kevin asked.

"Yeah, that's what James said. They called the police on me so I didn't stick around to find out her last
name. Told 'em I had to use the bathroom, hauled ass
to my car, and drove home. Picked up some clothes
and drove straight here. James tried to catch me running out the door, but he couldn't. Remember, he had
that hip-replacement surgery two years ago, so I was
too fast for 'im."

"Oh. My. God. You ran from the police?"

"Hell yeah. What you expect me to do, wait for
them to slap the cuffs on me? Not today! So here I am.
Stayin' with you for a couple of weeks until the heat is
off. I'm too old to go to somebody's jail!"

Lord have mercy! My mama was on the run from
the po po. And if I wasn't mistaken, she'd beat up Kevin's mother . . . with fruit. I'd started to ask if things
could get any worse, but every time I thought they
couldn't, they did.

Kevin looked at me, his eyes wide and guilty, knowing he'd thrust us in the middle of the drama for all
times. I could only shake my head when I thought about
the next order of business now that I *couldn't* send
Mommy back to North Carolina. How in the hell was I
gonna tell this woman that my father would be arriving
to stay in the same house (where she'd be hiding from
the police) the next day?

14

Kevin

Mama Tyson was off the hook, but I didn't comprehend the true extent until she told her tale. When she called the name Sophronia, I instinctively knew the woman was my mother. No doubt in my mind. Wouldn't be the first time flirting with somebody else's man had gotten her into trouble, and unfortunately this incident probably wouldn't be the last. She'd lost her mind since my father passed away. Seemed as if she was working hard to replace a man who couldn't be replaced. Only one Sherman Douglass would satisfy her longing, and he had died.

The way Charisse cut her eyes at me, I was sinking deeper in quick shit—couldn't even use *sand* to describe it. If I hadn't invited Mr. Tyson to stay with us, at best this visit from Mama Tyson could've been a minor inconvenience. Now, I'd created a medium-size nightmare that would only get worse if Ma showed up. Thankfully she had no reason whatsoever to come to DC before the wedding, if Charisse and I walked down the aisle at all. With all the drama going on in the house, waking up the next morning with all of my extremities intact seemed like a reach. Part of me wanted to run, but I couldn't leave my baby alone in the midst of this mess. I thanked God Nisey was visiting. Charisse and I would need all the buffers we could get.

Speak of the devil, no sooner than the thought crossed my mind, the doorbell rng.

"I'll get that! Must be Nisey." I jogged to the door and opened it. When she laid eyes on me, her expression transformed into the meanest facial contortion I'd seen in a decade. I couldn't help but smile at her though.

"What the hell you smiling at?"

"Believe or not, I'm actually happy you're staying with us."

"Us? She ain't kicked you out yet . . . *Daddy*?"

Ouch! Okay, so maybe I'd lost a few cool points. I fully believed I'd earn them back before long, so I took the hit graciously. I was a good man who'd made a mistake, at least that's what I kept telling myself. I was determined to right my wrongs.

"Where's Rissey?"

"In the room with Mama Tyson."

"Mama Tyson? What's she doing here?"

I whispered, "Well, apparently James moved out. I'll let them tell you the rest."

"Papa James moved out? Oh, no!" She turned, tossed me her car keys, and wagged her finger. "And you. You ain't harrrrdly off the hook yet. We're gonna talk later. You got me? Now make yourself useful and get my bags out the car while I go in here and find out what's going on."

"Yes, ma'am." I needed Nisey as an ally, so whatever she wanted, she was gonna get. "I'll get your bags in a second. I wanna . . . walk you in first." In reality, I didn't want to miss out on any conversation, especially if the topic of my mother came up again.

Nisey glided in the room carefree as if she hadn't been hipped to a thing. "Mama Tyson! I'm so happy you're here. This is a surprise! What brings you to DC?"

Charisse had strolled over to the bar and poured herself a double shot of Grey Goose. She downed the entire drink, took a breath, and said, "Mama beat James with a bag of grapes for squeezing some woman's melons. Now she's running from the law."

Nisey appeared as if her brain had gone into overload. "Whaaaat! Nuh-uhhhh!"

"Yuh-huh!" Charisse said.

"I'm ashamed of you, Mama Tyson! You know better than to be beatin' Papa James up with a bag of grapes." Nisey took a seat next to her and patted her knee. "You shoulda used a bag of apples . . . or potatoes."

Mama Tyson laughed. Leave it to Nisey to find something funny in all this drama. We all gave her the eye.

"What?" Nisey said, trying to play coy.

"Nisey!" Charisse admonished. "Don't encourage her."

"Hey! I love Papa James, but if he was squeezing some heifer's melons, he deserved to get his ass whooped," Nisey said. "As long as they been together? Please. They woulda had to tase my ass up in there. Men suck!" she said, glaring at me.

I dropped my head. My hope of gaining an ally slowly faded as I realized Nisey might be on the brink of a man-hating spree . . . and I was one of *them*. I'd be pretty much screwed without her support. Everything I needed to accomplish over that week depended on my ability to make things right with Charisse, help Charisse and her father reconcile their differences, keep Mr. and Ms. Tyson from killing each other (at least long enough to get one or the other back home), keep Mama Tyson from doing time, and somehow get Nisey to like men again, so if I didn't accomplish any of the former, she'd still pity me enough to help smooth things over with Charisse.

Yeah, a lot had fallen on my shoulders, but thankfully mine were broad and strong. Nothing to do except lift my chin up, be a man, and make miracles happen. If I wanted to be with Charisse, I didn't have much choice.

I grabbed Nisey's keys and ran outside to retrieve her bags. Thought I ought to check on Ma, a phone call I was not looking forward to *at all*. Mama Tyson and Ma hadn't met each other even though they lived in the same town. The wedding was to be their first meeting. How would I tell her the woman who beat her ass was Charisse's mother? Only in Charisse's crazy-ass family would I even have to deal with someone beating my mother with fresh produce.

"Hey, Ma! How are you doing?"

"My baby. I'm so glad you called. You won't believe the day I've had."

Wanna bet? "What happened?"

"One of my new neighbors here, sweet man, took me to the grocery store today, and some crazy woman assaulted us with a bag of grapes. Then she ran when we called the police. These old, sorry po-lice can't even find her. Can you believe that?"

"You all right?"

"Yeah, I'm fine. We're both fine."

"Who was the woman?"

"I don't know her but James does. Said they used to live together."

"What set her off? Had to be something."

She got quiet for a minute and carefully chose her words. "I don't know. Why do crazy people do half the stuff they do . . . except 'cause they crazy. We were minding our own business picking out some fresh vegetables and fruit, next thing I know, wham! Took two clerks and a stock boy to pull her off of us. Sho hate to think some crazy woman's still running around."

"Sounds more like a lovers' spat than a crazy woman. Did you file a report?"

"I was gonna file one, but James, he's such a nice man, said the whole thing was his fault. He knew today was her shopping day and he came anyway. He asked me not to. What do you think? Should I?"

"I don't think much of anything would happen to her anyway. Probably not even worth the time and trouble. Since you seem to be doing okay, I say stay out of the situation. And leave *him* alone. He's obviously got some unfinished business."

"I hear you, baby, but I like James. He's the first man I've really . . . you know, since your father passed."

"Nothing *happened* between you two, right?"

"No, nothing. Just talk. Why you askin'?"

"Just wondering. I gotta watch after my ma, right?"

I hesitated for a moment and decided it was too soon to tell my mother the woman's true identity. I'd wait a couple of days until things calmed down.

"So how's Charisse doing? Have y'all figured out what you're gonna do about this weddin' business?"

"No, she's still undecided. Taking some time to think things through. She hasn't had much time because we've had a lot of drama going on. Her father's coming. Nisey's staying with us. And her mother surprised us with a visit today."

"Oh, Lawd! Y'all got a house full of folk. Huh. I was hoping I could come a few days early so I can visit my grandbaby. I can stay at your condo."

"No, Ma! It's a bad time right now. Give us a few days to let things settle down and I'll send for you. Besides, I need to let Charisse meet him first if we're still going through with this wedding, which I pray we are."

"Charisse meetin' the baby ain't got nothin' to do with me. Javon's my grandbaby whether y'all get married or not."

She had a point there, but I couldn't let her come when the fight with Mama Tyson was so fresh. After she had a few days to cool off, I'd ask her to come.

15

Kevin

I grabbed Nisey's bags from the car and took them up-stairs. When my phone rang, Kristen's name flashed on the screen. For some reason, I hesitated in answering, had a bad feeling, but I ignored my intuition as stress. I'd been meaning to call her and set up a date to spend time with Javon but hadn't gotten around to it.

"Hey, what's going on?" I said. My voice fell flat.

"He lied!" she said, her voice trembling. "Everything's a lie, Kevin."

I sat on the bed, my voice full of concern. "What's wrong? What's a lie?"

"My husband. He never wanted to reconcile. All this time he's been building his case against me. He's gonna divorce me and take the kids by proving I'm an unfit mother," she said, in the midst of her sobs. "He wants all of them . . . including Javon, said the process server would deliver the papers to me next week."

"Are you serious? How'd you find out?"

"I overheard him on the phone with his mistress. Bitch. I can't even believe this shit. They've been planning this for months now, ever since he found out Javon isn't his, spiteful bastard."

"What are you gonna do?"

"I'll be damned if I let him take my children. How dare he do this! We *both* had affairs—*both* of us. I threw out the evidence of his affair because I believed we were truly reconciling, played right into his fucking hands. I've got to get something on him or I'm gonna lose my babies."

"He can't take Javon. I'm his father."

"Greg's name is on the birth certificate."

"What!"

"I know. I know. Of course we can prove you're Javon's father, but it'll be a hell of a lot easier to do if he's in my custody. What if the judge gives him custody pending the results of the paternity test?"

"Shit."

"I realize the timing couldn't be worse, and Charisse doesn't want you within ten feet of me, but you've got to help me, Kevin. I don't have anyone else to turn to."

What choice do I have? That's my son.

"Of course, I'm gonna help. We'll get something. Keep your eyes open, and don't let on that you know about his plan. Just play it cool. We don't want him making a move before we're ready."

The weight of the world rested soundly on my shoulders and burdened my tired mind and body. I craved relief in the form of a good night's sleep, which would give me the clarity I needed to deal with the next day's drama. I walked into the bedroom to find Charisse lying in the bed, staring at the ceiling. Struck by how she wore the pain in her soul on her face, I wanted nothing more than to curl up next to her, wrap her in my arms, and let her know everything would be okay. We'd work out our problems. Only one minor complication. How could I convince her when I didn't quite believe it myself?

"You okay, baby?" I asked as I cautiously approached the bed.

She turned her head toward me for a moment, stared in silence, returned her glance to the ceiling, and said, "No, I'm not okay. How did things get so messed up so quickly? We were happy yesterday, and now? Do you think this is a sign that maybe we aren't supposed to get married right now?"

I took in a deep breath. "A sign? I don't think so. If anything, what's happening is a sign that I should've told you the truth sooner, so we could have worked through our problems sooner. I believe in my heart that we will get past this though. If we can get through this week, we can survive anything."

"And if we don't survive this week?"

"Failure isn't an option for me. Is it an option for you?"

She stared at the ceiling again, said nothing, the most heartbreaking silence I'd ever experienced. Had she lost the will to save our relationship? I had to believe she'd trust in me again. Hopefully, after a few days passed and our lives settled down.

"Tell me something, Kevin. Exactly, what all did you and my father discuss?"

"We didn't talk for long at all. When his name flashed on the caller ID, something told me to ask him to come so you guys could work things out. So, I asked. That was about the extent of the conversation. Why?"

"Did he tell you he's been diagnosed with cancer?"

"Cancer? No. He never said a word. What kind?"

"Prostate. I'm not sure how bad his condition is. My mother told me when I was at Crate and Barrel with Lamar."

"That explains why he agreed so quickly. I only had to ask him once."

"Really?"

"I think he really wants to make things right. You should give him a chance. Just hear him out."

"Figures he'd wait until he's dying. Just like a man. Wait until the last and worst possible moment to deliver the worst possible news," she said, giving me the side-eye glance.

"My dad and I didn't always get along, but I'd give the world to bring him back today and tell him I loved him no matter what happened between us. You're getting a chance to do what a lot of people would kill for the chance to do—make amends before your parent is gone."

She rolled her eyes back, tears flowed down her cheeks, and she sobbed.

I wrapped my arms around her as she cried out

all of her pain and hurt. I wanted to make love to her in the worst way, to reconnect with her as we had before things fell apart. Although I wanted to feel the warmth of her body against mine, she only needed my love. She only wanted to be held and feel secure in something. So, for the moment, my arms would have to suffice.

The sunlight shone through the window blinds as a stark reminder morning had come far too soon. Before turning over or opening my eyes, I prayed Charisse and I would survive the day without any carnage once Mama Tyson and Mr. Tyson saw each other.

I rolled over to kiss Charisse good morning, but she wasn't there, and her side of the bed had gotten cold. I tapped on the bathroom door and walked in, but she wasn't there either. Thought maybe she'd gone downstairs, so I threw on a robe and went to the kitchen to find her. When I walked into the hall, I noticed Mama Tyson's door was still closed, but Nisey's door was open. She was in the kitchen starting breakfast.

"You seen Charisse this morning?" I asked.

"No, I thought y'all were upstairs making up. Is her car gone?"

I opened the door leading to the garage and found her car missing. She'd run off again. Only Nisey, her usual hideout partner, was staying with us. I automatically assumed the worst.

"Is her car still here?" Nisey yelled.

I ambled back into the kitchen, my face scowling, which Nisey noticed without fail.

"What the hell's wrong with you?"

"Her car's gone, and you're here. I'd lay ten-to-one odds on where she went."

16

Charisse

Nisey sure wasn't helping me smooth things over between James and my mother with her "beat him with a bag of apples" talk. The last thing I wanted was for Mom to give up on James. He was the best man either of us had ever known. I figured the moment was perfect to change the subject and tell Mom about Kevin since he'd left the room. Fortunately, my overly perceptive mother didn't even give me a chance to confess.

"So, Charisse. Now that we've put all my business on the table, let's talk about yours. What the hell's going on between you and Kevin? Y'all are constantly exchangin' looks. There's more tension in here than a pussy during a Pap smear."

Nisey laughed.

"You could tell? I thought I was hiding it pretty well."

"Baby, you know you can't hide nothin' from me. Now what's going on?"

"Well, I just found out yesterday Kevin and his partner Kristen had a child together," I said to her resounding gasp. "They hooked up before we got involved, but he lied to me about their relationship. Told me they were 'just partners.'"

"Oh, Lord! And he's known all this time and didn't say anything?"

"No, he just found out. But he wasn't going to tell me about it . . . at least, I suspect, not until after the wedding. After I was stuck and couldn't just up and run. I caught them meeting at the park."

"Sweet Jesus Almighty. So, whatchu gonna do? Y'all still gettin' married?"

"I don't know, Mama. I don't know what to do. I'm still trying to figure how I should react. At the end of the day, he lied to me. And he didn't tell some 'after a few weeks this will all be forgotten' lie, rather he told an 'after eighteen years you won't owe any more child support' lie."

She looked at me as if to say, *And?* "Baby, sure as the sun rises every morning, a man's gonna lie. Lying is what they do, even though it ain't what they do best. Sorriest liars on the planet, for sho. Have they been together since y'all met?"

"No, they got together before we did, but if he had told me about their relationship before we got involved, I never would've given him a chance. No way."

"Well, sounds to me like we've gotten to the root of the issue, haven't we? He's in your life now. You need to ask yourself if you can imagine your life without him. If you can, maybe walking away ain't such a bad thing."

My life without Kevin. The thought scared the shit out of me. Not because I'd imagined living without Kevin, but because somewhere, in the deep recesses of my spastic mind, I'd started to imagine a life *with*

Lamar. Kevin had unlocked a door and allowed the burglar inside to clean house.

No sooner than Mom released that lion from the cage, Kevin came back and took a seat next to Mommy, careful to stay out of my reach. Seemed like another good time to change the subject.

"Mom, since it seems you're gonna be staying with us for a few days, I need to tell you something . . . and you're not gonna like what I've got to say."

"What is it? Can't be no worse than this mess with James, right?"

"Ummm . . . yep. I'd say this is worse than the mess with James. Would you like a drink before I tell you?"

"Charisse, you know I don't drink that mess."

"Well, now might be a good time to start."

"Will you just tell me already?"

I swallowed hard and let it rip. Just like removing a Band-Aid, I figured the news wouldn't hurt so much if I spoke quickly and rambled a bit. "Okay, so Kevin invited Dad to DC to stay with us until the wedding . . . he's coming here tomorrow with one of my brothers."

She sat silent for a moment, then cracked up laughing. "Woooo! You almost had me with that one! Lawd, don't ever let nobody tell you you ain't funny!"

"I'm not joking, Mommy. Dad will be here tomorrow."

Her faced turned stone and cracked as if she'd glimpsed Medusa. For a minute I thought I was gonna have to call 911.

"Charisse," she said, trying to sound calm, but her face betrayed her panic. "You have to call him and persuade him not to come. Call him. Right now!"

"Mommy, I can't. He's bought the ticket, and he's determined to fly here, come hell or high water. We're gonna have to deal with him."

"Why would he come here?"

I pointed at Kevin. This mess was his fault. Damn do-gooder. If a hole had opened in the floor, I'm all but certain Kevin would've dived in headfirst to end the misery sooner. He'd just expressed himself to the top of Mommy's shit list, a position I'd occupied more times than I cared to remember. The view ain't pretty.

"Mama Tyson, I just thought with the wedding, this would be a good time for them to work out their differences. I-I had no idea you'd be coming here."

I cut my eyes at him to let him know I was still undecided.

He continued, "And, honestly, I think this distance between them hurts her even more than she says. More than any of us realizes."

"Listen here, that's my baby and *I'll do* what's best for her," Mama Tyson snapped. "You need to mind your own damn business! She don't need to talk to that man! He can't come here. He absolutely can*not*!"

She rolled her eyes at Kevin as she stomped out of the room and upstairs to the guest bedroom and slammed the door.

Kevin looked shocked and saddened, as if he couldn't do anything right.

"Give her a little time to cool off," I said, hoping to ease his despair.

I collapsed in the couch, threw my head back, and

closed my eyes. Mommy had gotten awfully dramatic. I mean, I understood why there was so much bad blood between them, especially given all of my father's extracurricular activities and the *extra* babies he had by other women within a year of fathering me. Then he had the nerve to confess that shit to my mother. Some things you ought to keep to yourself; some confessions aren't meant to be made.

I understood her anger toward him, but so many years had passed and she'd spoken to him rationally on enough occasions that I didn't expect her to be that upset at the news he'd be arriving. What was all the stink about? Right then, the idea struck me that more might be going on than Mommy was letting on. She behaved almost as if she was hiding something.

With that thought, I walked upstairs and got ready to knock on her bedroom door so I could ask. Before my knuckles touched the wood, I overheard her talking to someone on the phone.

"Promise me, Andre. Promise you won't tell her. Please!"

I opened the door and stepped in.

"Mom . . . is there something you're not telling me?"

"What did you hear?"

"Enough. What don't you want Dad to tell me?"

"I don't appreciate you sneaking up on me, listenin' in on grown folks' conversations."

"Grown folks? I'm forty-one!"

"I don't care how old you are. I want you out of here—now!"

"But—"

"But nothing! Leave!"

I backed out of the room and stood in shock. No, my mother had *not* kicked me out of my bedroom in my house where *I* pay the mortgage, as if I'd reverted back to my twelve-year-old self.

Okay, so, yes, she did.

I didn't understand why she'd acted so crazy. Clearly she and my father were keeping a secret they didn't want me to find out. I dug deep into my memory banks for some kind of clue, but I couldn't think of anything. I knew who might be willing to offer me one though—Aunt Jackie. I decided to give her a call in the morning. In the meantime, I was emotionally spent and just needed some sleep.

My head was twisted with thoughts of my father, Kevin, and my crazy-ass mother, who'd just flipped on me for some godforsaken reason of which I was yet unaware. All I needed was a little peace. No more talking or contemplating or discussing or deciding, just some peace. Unfortunately, when I finally got in the bed, Kevin wanted to talk, asking me if I was "okay."

What the hell was "okay"?

He had a baby by a woman who for all intents and purposes had become the bane of my existence. *Not okay*. My estranged father couldn't give a gnat's ass about my life until he got prostate cancer. *Not okay*. My mother broke up with the only man I'd remotely call a father, beat him with grapes, ran from the police, and was hiding a secret from me. *Not okay*. I guessed it was safe to say shit wasn't *okay*. And I didn't know when they'd be okay again. Damn sure didn't seem as if *okay* was anywhere on the horizon.

So after filling the sound void with some pointless conversation and finding out what all Kevin had said to my father, I blubbered in Kevin's arms until sleep at last replaced my tears.

17

Charisse

My eyes open. Sleep hasn't lasted for long. My heart races. I'm suffocating, can't fill my lungs. Sadness, panic, and fear completely overwhelm me. Kevin sleeps deeply, drawing in long, quiet breaths. I slip out of bed knowing he'll never wake up. I want out of my prison. I'm trapped. Need to feel free. In my house, the walls close in on me. Out of the house, I can run. I throw on a sweat suit, quietly escape, jump in my car, and drive. As if on autopilot, the Beemer steers itself to Lamar's house.

I knock and he opens the door; his smile is both welcoming and wanting. He's dressed in black silk boxers. His lips move. They say, "What are you doing here?" I say nothing, just gently lay my hand on his chest, run my fingertips across his nipples, and push him back so I can move in. I close the door behind me.

Before he can ask me why I'm at his house again, I say, "Kiss me." He says, "But—" and I say, "Kiss me," again. This time he obliges, pressing his thick, soft lips against mine as I watch the hazel in his eyes disappear behind his lids. He begins to undress me; my clothes disappear into the darkness.

Our tongues dance a slow wine, as his hands run down my back and cup my soft, ample ass. For so many months, I'd longed for his touch. I want him to feel wrong, but the longer he holds me, the more right he seems. Warmth surges through my body. Our mouths relent and the tip of his tongue teases me from my neck to my breasts. He grips both, gently squeezes them together, as if trying to take both of my nipples in his mouth at once; his moist tongue slides across them. The sensation forces a low, sensuous moan.

He pushes my hand against the stiffness in his boxers. I pull his boxers off, grip him like a microphone, and slowly sink to my knees to take him into my mouth. I tighten my suction against his walls, taking all of him in, and he cries out my name. When he can take no more, he stands me up and walks me to his bedroom, turns my back toward him. He kisses the nape of my neck before he bends me forward.

His hand explores the soaking-wet folds throbbing between my legs. I gasp softly as his fingers enter me. I wish it were more. He pauses briefly to put on a condom and searches my folds with the tip of his manhood. When he finds my sugar walls, he surges in, thrusting harder and harder with each delicious stroke, crying out my name in total ecstasy. No man had ever filled me so completely. My soft moans turn to uncontrollable screams as each stroke brings me closer and closer to climax. His breaths grow heavier as he whispers, "I can't hold it any longer. I'm coming. I'm coming." Neither could I. We scream out as one and collapse on the bed, soaking wet and so satisfied. I turned to find his face.

He looks into my eyes and says, "I love you, Charisse. Please marry me." I open my mouth to tell him I love him too, but no words come. I lose my breath and the room goes dark.

I bolted upright in bed and combed my fingers through my hair to try to get my bearings. The face of the form lying beside me was shrouded by a pillow so I moved it out of the way.

Kevin.

Thank God!

I'd dreamed the whole scene. The sweetest and most vivid dream I'd recalled in my adult life. A dream I'd half wished were true. This shit with Lamar was getting out of hand, but my feelings for him were clearly stronger than even I wanted to admit. I longed to be near him, to hold him. I quietly slipped out of bed and threw on a sweat suit, jumped in my car, and sped to Lamar's house before the impulse passed. Lamar, to me, represented freedom from the problems that plagued me at home. I wanted to be free from all the confusion.

When I arrived at Lamar's place, the sun had just ascended over the horizon. Yeah, I'd gotten to Lamar's place early as hell, and he was so not a morning person, but he hadn't established rules on when I could and couldn't show up. Moreover, he hadn't been in a relationship for ages, so no way was he getting his freak on. I mean the night before the man had hinted, in a big way, that he wanted to marry me. With all the drama going down at Chez Charisse, a life with him and his eight kids had begun to seem more than tenable—maybe even desirable.

I knocked on the door and Lamar answered, wearing the same black silk boxers I'd seen in my dreams. The moment seemed like déjà vu. He asked, "What are you doing here?" just as in my dream. I paused for a minute and opened my mouth to say, *Kiss me*, just as in my dream, then a high-pitched voice called from upstairs, "Lamar, is everything all right?"

Okay, that shit definitely *wasn't* in my dream. My mouth froze open so wide you could've parked a bus inside with room for a U-turn.

"Oh. My. God! You have a woman over? Didn't you just suggest you wanted to marry me *yesterday*?"

"Wait, Charisse. I can explain."

I sneered. "Blah. Blah. Blah. Where have I heard *that* bullshit before? The real Lamar is back in full effect. Haven't changed a fucking bit, huh?"

"Will you stop and listen for a minute? She's—" he tried to say, before I cut him off and took off running to my car. I jumped in and sped off, leaving my second set of skid marks from an angry escape in less than a week. He called and sent multiple texts, but I shut off my phone and drove to my favorite park.

Even though Kevin's rendezvous with Kristen had sucked some of the serenity out of my spot, I'd still find some peace of mind. I decided to sit there until I felt better about something, anything. I turned my phone back on, figuring Lamar would've given up. He understood me well enough to know I wouldn't talk until I got ready. As soon as a signal came through, so did a call. It was Aunt Jackie. I'd already planned to call to see if she'd tell me the secret Mom and Dad were hiding from me. Talk about perfect timing.

"Aunt Jackie! I'm so glad you called."

"Hey there! How's my favorite niece?"

"Don't you mean your only niece? I'm . . . living. That's about all I can say. Everything's a mess."

"Baby, things can't be all that bad."

"Ha! Wanna bet?"

"Oh, Lord. Well, you know I want you to tell me everything, but first I need to know if your Mama's in DC with you. James called here frantic. He's been looking everywhere for her. Said she didn't go home last night."

"She's okay. She's here with me. Drove here yesterday after she caught James squeezing Kevin's mother's melons. Trust me, the situation sounds a lot worse than it is . . . except Mom's on the run from the police now and doesn't want to go back home. Oh, and we haven't told her the woman is Kevin's mother yet, so don't say anything to her."

"You're kidding me, right? I think I need to sit down while you explain—and don't leave a thing out."

Before I realized it, more than an hour had passed. I'd shared everything with Aunt Jackie in excruciating detail, from Kevin's love child to Mommy's running from the law. I figured if anyone could help me find a way through, Aunt Jackie could.

After all, she was a psychiatrist by trade and we'd all lost our damn minds. She was required to have an answer.

"Well, damn," she said. "I don't know what to tell you."

"Aunt Jackie!" I whined in desperation. "You gotta give me something . . . anything."

"I mean, of course everything can be worked out in time, sweetie, just not today. I think your major priority has to be figuring out your relationship with Kevin one way or the other—because your wedding is less than one week away and I need to know whether I should return your gift," she said, laughing.

"So not funny, Auntie."

"I'm kidding . . . well, only about the gift part. This mess with your father needs to be dealt with, of course, but Andre isn't going anywhere anytime soon. He's like your mama, too stubborn to die before he's good and damn ready."

"Do you know if they're keeping a secret from me?"

She paused. "Even if I knew something, you know it ain't my place to tell you. What I will say is . . . your mother and father will be trapped in the same house for almost one week. If you keep pressing on a lemon hard enough, eventually you're gonna get some juice."

"Okay. I hear you loud and clear."

So they *were* hiding something. I'd get the truth out of one of them sooner than later. Most likely, my father. For all their big talk about women gossiping, men couldn't hold a secret in a steel-reinforced bucket. Eventually, the truth would find its way out. My mother, on the other hand, would be a steel trap if she had something on the line. She'd obviously been able to conceal the secret from me for a long time. To me, that meant she had a lot to lose.

What in the hell is so bad she'd beg Dad not to tell me?

The possibilities nagged at me something terrible. I think stewing on the possibilities was a welcome distraction from the other truths that had slapped me in the face. On top of everything else, I'd lost my second-best friend . . . and maybe more.

As I leaned back in my seat and stared through my sunroof, a text came through:

On my way to pick up your father.
We'll be home in an hour.

The moment of truth. Just one more hour and I'd have to face my life again. Have you ever wanted to cry because bawling seemed just slightly better than driving your car off an embankment into the Potomac River? I was *so* there. Mentally and emotionally. The best I could hope is that I'd contain my anger toward my father, and my parents wouldn't kill each other. If we managed that much, the day would be salvageable.

18
Kevin

The time to pick up Mr. Tyson and his son from the airport had come and Charisse still hadn't come back home. I was pissed, not so much because she hadn't returned home, but more so because I was certain she'd gone to Lamar's place. I'd grown more than a little sick and tired of her running to him every time something had gone wrong between us. Lamar had become Charisse's crutch, and as long as she had him to run to, she'd never tough out the difficult times with me and address our problems together from the jump. Derek always accused me of being jealous of Lamar, and nothing could be further from the truth in my estimation. I resented Lamar and Charisse's relationship because Lamar had always disrespected my relationship with Charisse.

Given that I was pretty pissed and didn't want to exacerbate an already bad situation by giving her the fifth degree over where she'd been all morning, I sent Charisse a text rather than call her with an attitude. Since I'd contributed to the nightmare we were in, I didn't have a leg to stand on if I wanted to put her on blast. I realized Charisse wouldn't even *think* of cheating on me; no way would she sleep with Lamar. I just wanted her to need me more than she needed Lamar. That hadn't been the case since she found out about Kristen—or even before really—but that's what I wanted.

As I got ready to leave the house to pick up Mr. Tyson, Nisey sat on the couch in the family room talking to whom I could only assume was David on her cell phone. Nisey, regardless of how ghetto and aggressive she could be, was actually a decent woman, and I believed David would go back to her sooner rather than later. Didn't sound at all as if Nisey was ready to accept him back.

"Don't worry about where I am. You make sure you get the rest of your stuff out of my house before I get home."

I tried to tell her I was on my way out, but she held her finger up, asking me to wait.

"I've got to go," she snapped. "I've got people waiting on me."

She rested her elbow on her knee and leaned her head into her open palm. "Don't worry about what people. Bye!" she said finally, looking up at me. "Sorry. You were saying?"

"I'm about to run out and pick up our guests. I haven't seen Mama Tyson all morning. You want to go up and let her know he's on the way?"

"Yeah, after I hide the fruit. You know Mama Tyson's off the chain, right? It's gonna be a mess up in here today. You sure know how to start some drama, don't you?"

"I guess I've made a mess of things, but you have to know how much I love Charisse. I never expected anything like this to happen. I'd sell my soul to erase that night with Kristen."

"Well, I ain't gonna allow any soul-sellin' up in here today. Truth be told, I thought you were one of the best things to ever happen to Charisse."

I smiled.

"Don't smile. I said I *thought*! We all need a re-minder of the good we initially saw in you because you fucked up something terrible. I mean, you know her history. You of all people know how much she's been hurt and what a hard time she has trusting men. She honored you with her trust and you lied to her."

"I know."

"Frankly, I think it's a testament to her faith in you that she didn't already throw your shit out on the front lawn. In my humble opinion, you have a small window of time to make things right. I mean, I can talk to her, but I ain't stickin' my neck out for your ass if you aren't gonna be completely honest with her from this point forward. Any more skeletons in your closet? Stray kids? Fatal-attraction ex-girlfriends? *Anything* else you'd like to share?"

I had to laugh. Nisey's crazy . . . but she was right about Charisse. If I didn't have a chance, she'd already be gone.

"No, Nisey. I swear on my daddy's grave I don't

have any more secrets, and I'll spend the rest of my life making this up to her if you'll help me get her back."

She rolled her eyes. "Hmph! We'll see. Anyway, shouldn't you be heading out?"

"Oh, man, let me go. Thanks, Nisey."

"For what?"

"For not giving up on me yet."

As I pulled into the arrival area at Reagan National Airport, I slowed down and scanned the length of the curbside to see if I could pick out Mr. Tyson from the crowd. The only people standing around were groups of little old white ladies sporting WHAT HAPPENS IN VEGAS, STAYS IN VEGAS T-shirts. I pulled my truck to the side, turned on the flashers, and waited. After about five minutes, they appeared. I recognized Mr. Tyson right away because he resembled an older male version of Charisse—a tall, fit man with pepper-colored hair and his daughter's cocoa-brown complexion. He wore a pair of stylish glasses, and the middle-class man's uniform—beige Dockers and a polo shirt. Her brother looked exactly the same except he had coal-black hair and looked about twenty years younger.

All of a sudden, I got a case of the nerves, like an African man on his way to ask a father for his daughter's hand in marriage with one too few goats. I stepped outside of the car and waved. "Mr. Tyson. Over here!"

He removed his sunglasses and smiled as he walked toward me. His son smiled and pulled both of the wheeled suitcases.

"Kevin?" Mr. Tyson said, reaching his hand out.

"Yes, sir! I'm glad to finally meet you."

"Please call me Andre, son. This is Trevon, my oldest. Everyone calls him Trey."

"What's up, Kevin," he said with a head nod. I returned the favor.

"All right. Y'all can have a seat while I get your bags in the trunk."

I took a moment to assess my feelings as I threw their bags in the trunk and to prepare for the journey home. They seemed decent enough but my nerves were shot. I wasn't sure what to expect once we got in the house and Mama Tyson or Charisse saw us. Whatever transpired, I was certain the day would be memorable . . . full of Kodak moments.

"So, how was your flight?"

"It was okay," Trey answered. "We hit a little turbulence, but for the most part everything was smooth."

"Well, I hate to break the bad news to you, but I think the turbulence is only getting started. Mama Tyson and Charisse can be a handful."

They both chuckled.

"We can handle them," Trey said. "I'm looking forward to meeting my sister. I've seen so many pictures of her but never met her in person."

"Is this your first time in the DC area?"

"Unfortunately, yes," Mr. Tyson said as he fidgeted with the seat controls, attempting to lean his seat back. "This visit is long overdue."

Trey said, "So how did you and Charisse meet?"

"Wow. That's a long long story." I realized that I

couldn't tell the truth, that I'd saved her from being raped when she was thirteen. So I kept my account simple. "Well, we met in high school. Her cousin Lee and I played football against each other. We got re-acquainted when I arrested her ex-boyfriend more than a year ago. He tried to get her caught up in a real-estate-fraud scheme."

"Man," Trey said. "So how long you been an FBI agent?"

"For about almost fourteen years now."

"Is that right?" Mr. Tyson said. "Only place I've ever seen a black FBI agent is on TV or the movies."

I chuckled. "Funny you said that. I think your daughter used almost those exact words when she met me."

Mr. Tyson appeared uncomfortable so I changed the subject.

"So, Trey, what do you do?"

"I'm a Marine."

"Oh, okay, like father, like son, huh?"

"Charisse told you?" Mr. Tyson asked. "Knowing my daughter, I wouldn't expect her to talk about me at all."

"Don't worry. You still know your daughter pretty well. She only told me the bad stuff," I said, hoping Mr. Tyson would take the joke in the spirit in which it was intended.

Mr. Tyson chuckled.

Our getting-acquainted small talk continued until I turned into Charisse's subdivision. Mr. Tyson's eyes widened at the sight of all the pristine McMansions lining the streets of his daughter's neighborhood.

"Charisse lives here?" Trey said.

"Yep," I replied. "Bought the house all by her lonesome too."

"This is a beautiful neighborhood. She's done very well for herself. Very well indeed," Mr. Tyson said with a hint of pride.

I pulled into the driveway and opened the garage door. Charisse's car was still missing in action, which sent a surge of anger through me, but I figured she'd be showing up any minute—at least I hoped.

"Here we are." I opened the door. "Looks like Charisse is still out, but her best friend, Nisey, and Mama Tyson are here."

"Where's Charisse?" Mr. Tyson asked.

"Uhh, she ran out this morning," I answered, clearly uncomfortable, "to take care of something. She should be home any minute now."

"I suspect she's avoiding me."

"Dad," Trey interjected, "she's letting us stay at the house with her. I don't think she's avoiding you."

"Exactly, Trey. Let's go on in," I said as I twisted the doorknob and opened the door. "We're home!"

19

Kevin

I overheard Nisey yelling in the family room. "Why the fuck do you keep calling me, David? You made your feelings clear when you packed up your shit and left. We don't need you, so get the rest of your shit before I change the locks and donate your stuff to Goodwill! Bye!"

She mumbled, "Sorry bastard! I don't know who the hell he thinks he's playin' with. He must not know 'bout me. I don't need him anyway. Fuck a man!"

I shook my head and announced my presence. "Nisey!" I yelled, hoping to end her tirade.

She stomped into the foyer with a glare scary enough to frighten a rattlesnake.

"Uhh, Trey, Mr. Tyson, this is Nisey, Charisse's best friend in the world."

Mr. Tyson said, "Hello, Ms. Nisey."

Trey seemed at a complete loss for words. His eyes locked onto Nisey as if he'd been struck by a lightning bolt. Too bad Nisey was in a man-hatin' state of mind. Trey could've been on fire and she wouldn't have noticed him.

"Hi, it's nice to meet you both," she said flatly. "Please excuse me. I need to run upstairs for a minute."

No, she didn't even glimpse Trey's face, but the sentiment was clearly not mutual.

Mr. Tyson chuckled. "Well, she seems like a fire-cracker. Not hard to understand how she and Charisse are such good friends."

I thought, *Hmph, a firecracker? More like dynamite.* "She's going through a rough time right now, which is why she's staying with us."

"Sounds like she's single . . . or soon will be," Trey said with more enthusiasm than he probably meant to reveal.

"Yeah, she's definitely single."

Just then I heard Charisse's car pull up in the driveway. She'd realize the gang was all inside once she saw my truck in the driveway. I didn't have a clue as to what her state of mind might be, whether she'd come in swinging and ready to rumble or subdued, but the time was upon us regardless.

The knob turned, the door opened, and Charisse walked in, looking surprised to see everyone still standing in the foyer. She quickly scanned all of us and, with the emotion of a turnip, said, "Dad, you're here."

"Charisse!" he said, much happier to see her than vice versa. He held out his arms toward her. "Why don't you give your old man a hug?"

She ambled over with an expression as cold as the Ice Queen's and gave him a weak hug. When she glanced over his shoulder at Trey, her face brightened and her demeanor warmed. "Wow, you look just like Dad."

"This is your brother Trevon, but everyone calls him Trey. He's the oldest. Chris, the youngest, is a year younger than you."

She gave Trey an affectionate sisterly hug and smiled from ear to ear. "So you're my big brother."

It struck me just how dysfunctional the scene was. Charisse was forty-one and meeting her big brother for the first time. I began to understand why she had so much animosity.

Trey said, "Yeah, I've got you by eleven months, and you've got Chris by a year."

Charisse's eyebrow wrinkled as if she'd tried to do the math. She cut her eyes at her father.

"Let's all go in the family room and take a load off. I'm sure you guys must be exhausted from the flight," Charisse said, leading the way. "Where's Mommy and Nisey?"

"Nisey ran upstairs and I haven't seen your moth—" I started to say before Mama Tyson appeared at the end of the hallway dressed in a high-cut skirt, low-cut blouse, and stilettos. Mama Tyson was looking like a hot mama—breasts sitting up so high she could've rested a coffee cup on them. I'd never seen her wear such a provocative outfit before; she usually dressed church conservative.

Charisse stood in horror as Mama Tyson strolled into Mr. Tyson's line of sight. The same lightning bolt that hit Trey when he first laid eyes on Nisey was nothing compared to the one that struck Mr. Tyson. An instinctive smile blasted through his cool veneer and he mumbled, "Umph. Umph. Umph," the way you react when you're looking at a *Playboy* centerfold, not looking at Mama Tyson.

And we were worried about them not getting along. Based on Charisse's vivid expression as she looked at both of their faces, she'd probably be more concerned that they'd get along *too* well.

"Andre!" Mama Tyson said, smiling as if she'd bought a winning Powerball ticket.

"*La belle* Ella," Mr. Tyson said. He grabbed her arm and ran his fingers down the length to her hand and kissed her gently on her fingers.

While the gesture certainly helped relieve the nervous tension in the room, the sexual tension had been kicked up about a hundred notches.

"Still smooth as you want to be . . . and handsome too."

"I think I'm gonna be sick," Charisse mumbled to me through her gritted teeth.

Nisey finally descended from her room in a much better mood . . . so I thought. Everyone gathered in the family room and kitchen, taking seats where they could find them. In a moment of awkward silence, my phone rang. The caller ID read Kristen. I ignored the call and she called again, and again. Charisse's expression turned agitated and she said, "Who's calling?"

"Someone from work. They can wait," I said, knowing full well I was the worst liar in the world, talking to the world's best lie detector. She didn't believe me any further than she could throw me. I couldn't tell her the person calling was Kristen, not in front of the family.

She'd go off for sure. So I did what I promised myself I wouldn't do again. Lied.

"I'm gonna take this call in the office. It's Derek. He needs some help with a case."

"Mmm-hmmm. Derek. Okay," Charisse said.

I stepped in the office and answered the phone on the next ring. "Kristen, what do you want? Right now is not a good time."

"I'm sorry, Kevin, but it's urgent. I checked my husband's phone a few minutes ago and he has a 'meeting' at the Gaylord listed on his calendar for tomorrow."

The Gaylord, a swanky hotel at the National Harbor, was a social hot spot, a place where one usually went for conferences, vacations, or dates. Not much else happened over there.

"And?"

"Well, he wrote STK, his mistress's initials, in the slot. Do you think you can help me? The meeting's at seven in the evening. I need you to get pictures for the divorce hearing and you can leave right after. I promise."

"This is *not* a good time. We have family visiting from out of town."

"You know I wouldn't ask if I had anyone else to turn to. He doesn't know your face. It'll only take a couple of hours at the most. No more. I promise."

"All right, I'll see what I can do. In the meantime, please don't call me, ringing my phone off the hook again. Charisse is already suspicious. Just send me a text if you need to talk and I'll call you back when I'm free."

"Okay. Thanks, Kevin."

I realized my ass had plunged into even deeper shit. Charisse was already onto me, and I'd need to cover my tracks until things cooled off enough for me to explain everything to her. I sent a text to Derek and asked him to ring my phone several times so his name would be on my caller ID; I'd delete Kristen's number. Charisse was a better detective than me, and she'd be checking my phone the moment I fell asleep.

I set the phone on vibrate as Derek's phone calls came through, then turned up the volume and went back to join the group.

"You finish your business?" Charisse said.

"Did you finish your business when you left the house this morning without telling me where you went?" I asked, to gently remind her I didn't have the only tainted record in the house.

"We'll discuss this later," she snapped. Nope, the issue wasn't over . . . far from it.

20
Charisse

After I received the text from Kevin, I headed home, albeit slowly. I wasn't looking forward to facing my father. Seemed it had been easier to remain pissed at a distance than work things out face-to-face. How could he possibly defend himself? What could he say? "Oh, sorry. I sucked at being your father" or "Catch you in the next twenty years. Sorry I fucked up so badly on the first forty."

In my mind, he had no excuse for not being a father to me. I don't care how complicated his life was at the time. No question my father had his issues. He'd had more women than even he could handle. But he'd never tried to be a father to me until I was too grown to let him. What had kept him from *me*, especially when he'd been a decent father to my brothers? I didn't understand. And if my father and I were gonna make amends, he'd have to answer for his absence in my life for all those years. He'd need to give me a damn good reason why he played Daddy for them and not for me.

When I pulled up to the house, I noticed Kevin's

Range Rover in the driveway, which meant my father was inside. I couldn't deny my nervousness at seeing him again even on my own turf.

Truth is, I think my father intimidated me a little too. I was raised old school. The father is the head of the family, no matter how many rotten, stinking things he did to hurt his family. He was large and in charge. You respected him no matter what. My father's stint in the Marines didn't help soften his persona. Old-school corps. "Pain is a sign of weakness!" he'd once said during a rare visit when I fell off my bike and scratched my knee as a child. No sympathy. Lucky I got a Band-Aid.

Yeah, I'd grown up, but I'd never outgrown my parents. And I'd never outballs my father, no matter how much I wanted to or how hard I tried. So, regardless of how hurt or abandoned I felt, I'd contain my hostilities to a respectful level.

After parking my car, I felt Kevin's Range Rover in an attempt to gauge how long he'd been in the house. The hood still felt warm, so I figured he'd only been inside for a few minutes at best.

I walked in the door, and damn if the crew weren't still standing in the foyer.

My eyes locked on my father's face. The naive little girl buried inside me wanted to be happy, jump into his arms, and yell, "Daddy!" like a four-year-old whose father had just come home from a long day at work. The memory of all our lost years came rushing back into my mind as if a dam had broken. How would I ignore the missed birthdays, the nights when "Good night, Mommy" wasn't followed by "Good night, Daddy." All the days I'd been told Dad was on his way to visit me, and I sat by the window waiting on his face to appear—and it never did . . . or would. My heart still ached, and as much as I tried, I couldn't conceal the pain. My emotions were all over my sleeve, and my lackluster greeting toward him no doubt said what my mouth didn't (for a change).

When compared to the cheerful greeting I gave to Trey, I'm sure my father realized, as everyone did, that I'd shown him all the affection of a wet dishrag. After we all exchanged greetings and hugs we all headed into the family room. That's when Mommy sashayed down the hall looking like Lady Marmalade.

What the hell is going on here?

I wanted to ask her what on earth she was doing in her freakin' dress getup. I knew damn well she wasn't trying to seduce my father . . . not in *my face*. But when their eyes met, the temperature in the room increased about fifty degrees, and I had an almost uncontrollable urge to throw up. Her "display" only increased my determination to find out what she'd been hiding.

"Andre!" Mommy said, his name oozing out in a syrupy-sweet tone that made my head and teeth ache.

"*La belle* Ella," my father said, the sound of which made my face scrunch in anguish.

La belle? No, he didn't, sounding like Pepé Le Pew.

I'd prepared myself mentally for World War III, not the puke-worthy lovefest happening before my mystified eyes. Hearing Mommy compliment Dad on his "smoothness" sent me over the edge. I leaned over to Kevin and said, "I think I'm gonna be sick."

Have I been zapped into the twilight zone?

If I thought things hadn't gone downhill up until then, they officially landed at rock bottom when Kevin's phone started ringing off the hook. I had a sneaking suspicion Kristen was responsible because none of his boys ever rang his phone over and over like that. Only women did that dumb shit. He tried to play it off, of course, and say Derek called, but you can't pull wool over a sheep's eyes. I'd planned to check his phone later. Not that I'd made a habit of checking his phone. But on this occasion, I sensed he was lying to me and I wanted to do a gut check for my own edification.

As much as part of me wanted to forgive him, I had an almost compulsive urge to gather evidence, like a squirrel collecting nuts. Even if I had no intention of using the information immediately, it'd be stored away and unleashed at the appropriate time.

Just as the idle chitchat ended and the awkward silence settled in, Nisey trotted down the stairs. When she saw Mama in the Hoochie of the Year outfit, her mouth gaped open. She looked at me—I shrugged. Hell, I had no idea what Mama was up to either. Then Nisey and I both looked at my father, who was staring at my mama's legs. An acidic bile crept up in the back of my throat.

"Well, lookie lookie. What is going on in here? Mama Tyson! You're looking awfully *lovely* today."

Well, Nisey had the *awful* part right.

"What?" Mom said, looking all innocent, as if she always wore miniskirts and low-cut blouses.

"Let me find out!" Nisey said, as she moved toward the empty seat next to me at the kitchen table. She whispered, "What the hell is going on with your mother? If I didn't know better, I'd think she's trying to hook up with your father."

Shudder the thought. I still wanted her to marry James, but for the first time since we'd met, James was acting like a *man*. Not a take-care-of-house-and-home man, but a do-something-stupid-and-piss-your-woman-off man. I glanced into the family room. Trey and Kevin were having some male-bonding conversation. Mom and Dad were huddled in the far corner of the couch. Every time Dad made her giggle like a schoolgirl, she rubbed up on his knees. I shook my head.

Now I believed with every fiber of my being that Mommy's *Sybil* performance had been inspired by more than some flirtatious urge. Much more. "I overheard Mom begging Dad not to tell me something the other night on the phone. They were keeping a secret from me. Aunt Jackie confirmed as much during our call. I think she's laying it on thick so Dad won't tell."

"You think so? But why would they keep anything from you at this point? Your father already admitted to the affairs and told you about his kids—the evidence of which is sitting on your love seat. No one could question whether you're the man's daughter because you couldn't resemble him more if you tried. So, what's the big secret?"

"I don't know, but, whatever it is, it must be pretty serious for Mommy to be putting on this performance in an effort to keep it hush-hush, you know what I'm saying?"

Nisey glanced over at my mother and father talking and then toward Trey and Kevin. "I didn't notice before because I was so pissed after talking to David, but your brother is kinda fine. He married?"

"Is he married? Let *me* find out!" I said with a big grin on my face.

"It ain't even like that, Rissey, so don't even go there. I ain't hardly trying to meet anybody new right now. I couldn't be good for anyone in my state of mind. I'm asking out of pure curiosity."

"Mmm-hmm! Curiosity my ass. But for your information, he's divorced from what I understand. His wife apparently couldn't get used to being a Marine wife."

"A Marine? Oh, hell no! Marines are crazy . . . and they're all players. I can't fool with them."

Well, I couldn't much argue with her. I'd never met a Marine that wasn't a player. Trey seemed to have a good spirit though. I had enough functioning intuition to tell he was a good man, even if he might be a reformed player like Dad and Lamar, the original player crew. I'd get the scoop from Kevin later on. He was an FBI agent so he'd be a pretty decent judge of character.

"So, anyway," I said, changing the subject, "you

spoke with David, huh? What did he want—or do I even need to guess?"

"He wanted to talk things out, of course, but I don't have anything to say to him. When the going got tough, he picked up his crap and got going."

"As I recall, he had a little help . . . as it went sailing out the bedroom window and across the front yard at the hands of somebody sitting at this table," I said, extending my arms like wings.

"I only threw it out the window *after* he started packing. That's like firing somebody after they quit. I just co-signed."

"With fourteen golf clubs serving as big-ass exclamation points!" I said, motioning my arms as if I'd hit a line drive across the green.

We cracked up laughing. This was our friendship at its best. Both our lives were in complete disarray but we still found humor in the supremely ridiculous.

I stood up and walked over to the Sub-Zero. "I think I'm gonna throw some food on the grill. Want something to drink?" She didn't hear me because she was too busy scoping out Trey. I stared at her until she sensed me eyeing her.

"Oh, I'm sorry. Did you say something?"

"Mmm-hmm. You know curiosity killed the cat, right?"

"Yep . . . and satisfaction brought him back!"

21
Charisse

We finished dinner and the "itis," the near-crippling disease that sucks every ounce of energy from your body when your stomach is overfilled and oversatisfied, had crept up on all of us. Kevin, Nisey, Trey, and I leaned back on the deck chairs and stared up at the starry sky, while Mom and Dad holed up on the couch watching *The Jeffersons* reruns. For a brief moment, we had peace and calm.

I tried my best to talk to Dad, but Mom wouldn't let me get a word in edgewise. She'd clearly made it her mission to distract Dad and keep us from saying a single meaningful word to each other. So, I gave up on Dad and targeted Trey. Being with him felt strange to say the least. We shared the same DNA but didn't know anything about each other. We had no memories of each other, no "tell them about the time when we" or "remember the time when we" stories to share. We were brother and sister, yet no closer than two strangers who might pass each other on the street. I felt robbed. A surge of anger jolted through me as I looked in my brother's eyes, deep brown and lazy like mine, yet I had no clue what lay behind his or what was in his heart. I had a second brother whom I still hadn't seen. My life had been defined by family and relationship dysfunction. What would Trey say? What could we talk about?

As the older son, he might be able to shed some light on my father and who he was as a person. He might even have a clue as to what the big secret was about. So, as Kevin and Nisey gathered up the dishes and cleaned up the kitchen, I decided to get to know more about Trey—and maybe my father.

"So, Trey, this is kind of crazy, but you and I are both over forty and meeting each other for the first time. It's like I don't know what to ask first. 'What've you been doing with your life . . . for the last forty years?'"

He laughed. "I know, but hopefully we'll have the rest of our lives to catch up. I'm just happy to finally meet you. When Dad said Kevin offered to let us visit, I couldn't let him travel without me. I'd always wanted a little sister. Chris used to get on my nerves growing up. I'd have traded him for you in a heartbeat."

"Sounds like the typical little brother," I said with a light chuckle. Trey turned to me, and my expression turned serious. "I guess you know about Dad's cancer, right?"

"Yeah. I was with him when the doctor diagnosed him. We caught it early, thank the Lord. He had the surgery a few months back and he's been taking some radiation to keep things in check. Seems to be working okay. But cancer is cancer. Anything can happen. We have to keep a close watch."

Almost instinctively, I breathed a sigh of relief; the cancer wasn't terminal. The revelation allowed me to release my fear and re-embrace the anger I'd built up for him since my youth.

"You guys close, you and Dad?"

"We are *now*, but we haven't always been, that's for sure. He roamed in and out of my life for most of my early childhood. Always getting shipped out somewhere. Didn't come to visit me half the time when he came to town. I stayed in trouble at school though, lived in the principal's office. Always fighting and hanging with the wrong crowd. I call my behavior simple rebellion; my mom claimed I'd been trying to get attention from Dad. He always showed up when I got into trouble. She died in a car accident when I turned twelve and I've been with him ever since."

His mother died? Well, that explained a lot. No wonder Dad had stayed in California, although he could've brought Trey to the East Coast. Then again, Chris lived nearby. Still no excuse for ignoring me though.

"I'm sorry to hear about your mother. Mom never told me."

"Ha! I'd be surprised if your mother talked about Dad much at all. They used to fight like cats and dogs for real. She'd seriously get under his skin, used to hang up on him and he'd be too mad to function. Then he'd call her back and hang up on her. They never seemed to let go of each other though. Refused to leave each other alone."

I couldn't have planned the conversation any better

if I tried. I wanted to know what they fought about. Did their arguments have anything to do with me? I had a million questions to ask, but I tried to play it cool because Trey might freeze up if he thought I seemed too anxious to know.

"Yeah. They've always been like oil and water—with today being an obvious exception. They fought all the time . . . mostly over money," I said, lying like a cheap rug. In truth, my mother never held an extended argument with my father in my presence. I usually witnessed the initial explosion, and then they'd shoo me out of the room and curse each other in loud whispers.

"They never fought about money while I was around, but they sure as hell fought about you—a lot."

"About me? What about me?" I asked, my heart pounding in anticipation of hearing the truth about the big mystery.

He checked the patio door to make sure no one was eavesdropping and said, "Well, according to Dad, your mom—"

"Her mom what?" Mommy interjected, creeping up on us like a damn ninja. She was straight about to get on my last nerve.

"Ms. Ella," Trey said, looking uncomfortable as hell. She'd busted him and they both knew it. "I, uhhhh, I was just telling Charisse that Dad really looked forward to seeing you on this trip."

"Is that right?" she said, her voice dripping with skepticism.

"Of course he couldn't stop talking about his baby girl either."

"I see," she said. I suspected she realized her interest would be better served if she changed the subject. "So how's Chris doing? The last your father told me, he got sent to Japan."

"Yeah, Okinawa. This is his last year in the Marines. He joined when he was eighteen and he's got twenty years in now, so he's gonna retire. Unfortunately, he won't be back in time for the wedding, but he very much wanted to be here. I brought some of our family photo albums so you can check out our family pictures."

"Wow, retired under forty? That's what I'm talkin' about! Can we look at the pictures now?"

"Sis . . ."

Awwww . . . he called me Sis.

"I'm afraid the jet lag is setting in. How about we check them out tomorrow."

"All right. That's a bet," I said, watching him rise from his seat and head inside. "Good night. I think I'm gonna turn in myself."

"Yeah, I think we all need to turn in," Mommy echoed as she escorted me to the stairs. She whispered, "Charisse, baby. I can tell what you're trying to do."

"That's funny, Mom, because I was gonna say the same thing about you!"

"Leave it alone, baby. Why can't you leave it alone? Ain't no good gonna come from you dredging up the past. Let lying dogs sleep."

● ● ●

Later that night, when the house quieted, everyone settled into bed, and Kevin had fallen into a deep snore-worthy slumber, I got out of bed to take care of one final mission—checking Kevin's cell phone. I crept into the closet, where his pants hung on the door. My hands trembled slightly, as they always did when I was about to cold bust someone. I hit the power button and checked the caller ID. The only name on the screen was Derek.

Derek.

Derek.

Derek.

Want to talk about someone feeling like a natural fool? Kevin had been telling the truth and I didn't believe him. What the hell had I been so afraid of? Why had I engaged in such loony behavior? Not just with Kevin, but with almost every man I'd ever been with. I convinced myself that while my instincts were spot on when it came to sensing shit in other people's lives, they sucked when it came to my own. As I shook my head in shame and placed my finger on the power button, a text came through.

See you tomorrow. Gaylord Hotel @ 7 pm. Kris.

Ain't that a bitch? Meeting at the Gaylord, huh? The Gaylord had become a favorite hookup spot for married people and singles alike. People went there to find a lover or meet a lover. Period. Why he planned to meet that bitch there, I didn't know, but I'd sure as hell find out one way or the other. When I went to return his cell phone, his pants dropped on the floor and his wallet fell open. As I reached down to pick them up, I noticed a picture of Javon. Kevin hadn't bothered to share it with me.

Cute little booger.

Sweet face and his daddy's eyes. No mistaking who his father was. I wondered if maybe Kristen was right. *How can I possibly compete?*

Of course the moment was fleeting; my anger resurged within seconds.

I slipped back into bed, eyes peeled on the ceiling, and spent half the night plotting Kevin's demise.

22
Kevin

After I successfully deflected Kristen's phone call from
Charisse, we joined the rest of the family. The worst
seemed to be over since it'd become quite clear Mr. and
Mama Tyson wouldn't be at each other's throats as
everyone had feared. Well, maybe at each other's lips,
but not in anger.

I thought it best Charisse and I stay a safe distance
apart until she cooled off, so I took a seat next to Trey
on the couch, disturbing him as he stared at Nisey,
who sat near Charisse at the kitchen table.

As Trey and I got to talking, we realized we had
a lot in common . . . including having gone through
a difficult divorce. Trey's ex had had a tough time
adjusting to life as a military wife and all of Trey's
deployments and had sought the comfort of other men
to help ease the lonely nights. Apparently, she hadn't
been discreet about her behavior either. He returned a
day early from one deployment to surprise her and she
surprised him in bed . . . with not one but two men.
One hittin' her ass from the back and one receiving
a blow job in front. Talk about some shit that would

make a man lose his mind. And Trey is a Marine too. His job is to kill people painfully and quickly. Period. That they left the house in the back of an ambulance and not a coroner's van was a testament to Trey's common sense and self-control. We both recognized that while women were plentiful, genuinely good women were hard to come by . . . and after some time, Trey made it clear he had set his sights on Nisey.

"So, man, tell me about Nisey. What's her story?"

"Well, what can I say? She's a single mother holding it down on her own. She and Charisse work at the same real estate firm."

"Oh, okay. Cool. She can do real estate from anywhere."

My eyebrow rose. Sounded to me as if Trey had already started thinking future and he hadn't half known her for two minutes. Wasn't sure what to make of him, so I kept talking. Nisey had become like a sister to me so I wanted to look out for her.

"She practically lived with this dude David for a year or so, but they recently broke up . . . as I'm sure you heard."

"Did one of them cheat?"

"Naaah, nothing like that, but I think that's something for her to tell you about, not me."

"Ohhh, okay. I got you. So, you excited about the wedding?"

"Man, I want nothing more than to marry your sister, but I ain't gonna lie, we're having some issues right now."

I conveyed the whole Kristen ordeal, including

how our hookup happened long before Charisse and I got together. Charisse's issue, as I explained, was not my son or that I'd slept with Kristen. She couldn't stomach that I lied about the nature of our relationship.

"She'd never have given me a chance if I told her about us. You know how women are . . . and she *couldn't stand* Kristen. But from day one, I wanted Charisse, not her."

"I hear you, man. I ain't passing judgment on *anyone*. Sounds like you can work this out though. Be different if you cheated, but you didn't."

"Exactly. I just wish Charisse would view the situation that way."

Just then Nisey and Charisse called everyone to dinner. They had put their feet and some more stuff in that meal. Afterward, we all sat around with our stomachs bulging to the point of causing paralysis.

My whole reason for bringing Mr. Tyson to DC was to give him and Charisse time to talk out their problems, but Mama Tyson had been blocking like a mofo. Stevie Wonder could see that she'd tried her best to keep them apart, but I couldn't fathom why. Certainly, it would be in her best interest to let them kiss and make up . . . unless of course she'd played a part in putting the wedge between them in the first place. More and more, things had shaped up to appear as if this was indeed the case.

After dinner, Nisey and I cleaned up the kitchen together. I packed the leftovers in plastic Ziploc containers and tucked them into the refrigerator, while she stuffed dishes into the dishwasher. She checked out the window to ensure Charisse and Trey were tucked safely on the deck and out of earshot. I got the feeling she wanted to ask about Trey, but she hesitated. Nisey wasn't the type of woman who showed her hand too soon. She and Charisse operated the same way. So I let her off the hook and offered her a small bone.

"You know, Trey asked about you while we were talking earlier."

The corners of her mouth turned up slightly. "Hmmm. He did? What did you tell him?"

"I told him you were married with six kids waiting for you at home."

She slapped me on the arm. "Shut up! For real, what did you say?"

"I told him you were a single mom, holding it down at home, and that you recently broke up with your boyfriend."

"Is that all?"

"Isn't that enough?"

She sucked her tongue.

"Oh, I told him you were a real estate agent and he was glad to hear it. Said you could do that anywhere."

"Nuh-uhhh. For real?" she replied like a schoolgirl who'd just found out the popular boy had a crush on her.

Just as we had finished cleaning the kitchen, Mama Tyson headed for the patio door, to where Trey and Charisse were still talking. She eavesdropped for a second before barging in on them. Nisey and I rolled our eyes. Poor Charisse couldn't get a break. Not two minutes later, Trey came in the house and announced he was turning in. The rest of the crew soon followed. Charisse had set up Trey's and Mr. Tyson's guest rooms in the basement, which was fully finished with two full bathrooms, a living area, and kitchenette. She could've rented the place out as an apartment if she so chose, but she didn't need the money or the headache.

In our bedroom, Charisse's demeanor had turned rather cool. I realized she was still salty about the earlier phone calls, but she'd check my phone soon enough. Hopefully, her snooping would put to rest any crazy thoughts she'd had. I wanted to spend the next day getting our wedding back on track. I'd get ahold of Charisse's things-to-do list and tie up the remaining loose ends, prove to her I wanted the marriage to work, then spend the rest of my life making her happy.

Few things struck fear in a man more than a woman who smiles in his face with scorn in her eyes. Like a dog baring his teeth just as he's about to bite the hell out of somebody, he appears as if he's smiling wide for the camera about the mouth, but the evil-wicked slant in his eyes tells you that if he sinks his teeth into any part of your body, it will be leaving with him and not with you. That's the feeling I had sensed around Charisse from the moment we cracked our eyes open to greet the day, that she wanted to walk away with one of my limbs in her teeth.

Oh, she smiled with a sweetness unseen since Shirley Temple, but I sensed something was wrong . . . very wrong.

23
Kevin

First on my agenda, I inspected my cell phone. Knowing Charisse had checked it at some point during the night, and realizing I'd told Kristen to text me if she needed anything, I feared a message might've come through that caused Charisse to quietly plot against me. But when I turned on the phone, the only calls were those I'd received from Derek (by request) the previous day. Confident I didn't have anything to be concerned about, I took the wedding-things-to-do list from her purse and tucked it in my back pocket. As Charisse slipped into her favorite jeans, the ones that made her ass look particularly squeezable, I decided to feel her out (so to speak) and check to see if she might give me some clue as to why she'd been so bitchy all morning.

"So, baby, what's on the agenda for today?"

She sat on the bed and combed her hair back into a ponytail. "I'm not sure. Mom's probably going to spend the day trying to keep me from talking to Dad if we stick around here."

"Oh, you noticed too, huh?"

"How could anyone *not* notice? I thought I'd take

them on a tour of DC today, let them check out the monuments since this is Dad's first time in the city. What do you have planned today?" she asked, her eyebrow raised.

I'd planned to surprise Charisse once I made some progress on tying up the final wedding details, so I kept the details of my activities vague. "Well, I have a few errands to run today. Things have been so crazy, I haven't had a chance to get much done."

"Errands, huh?" She didn't even bother to disguise that she didn't believe me.

"Yeah. Errands. I have some things I need to take care of. I thought I'd go work out later too. I haven't been in a few days."

"Work out, huh? I *bet* you are."

"Charisse, what's with all the attitude? Is it your time of the month? You need me to make a chocolate run?"

"No you didn't pull the PMS card."

"If you've got a problem, talk to me or get over it. I'm getting tired of walking around on eggshells when I haven't done anything wrong."

She shook her head and rolled her eyes. "You haven't done anything wrong, huh? Is there anything you need to tell me?"

"Is there anything *you* need to tell *me*?" I snapped.

"Don't answer my question with a question. I'm giving you the chance to speak now or forever hold your peace. So, for the last time, do you have anything to you need to say to me?"

"No . . . I don't!" Okay, I *could've* and probably

should've told her about the meeting with Kristen, but, the way she'd been acting, I refused to give her the satisfaction of knowing she was right. I'd tell her eventually, but when *I* got ready and not before. I loved her, but all the tiptoeing around her feelings was getting old . . . quickly. I hadn't done anything wrong . . . except not tell her the whole truth about Kristen. Granted a child from another relationship was no small thing, but Javon's presence in our lives wouldn't exactly spell the end of the world either.

"Okay, then," she said. "If you don't have anything to say, then we're cool. I'm sorry for snapping at you."

I tried to give her a hug, but her arms hung as limp as cooked spaghetti. Her eyes even appeared a bit misty, but I couldn't for the life of me imagine what she could be upset about.

"Are you okay? What's wrong, baby?"

"I'm fine . . ." Her voice trailed off. "I only wish we could turn back the clock. I'd do so many things differently if I had the chance. Anyway, since you're gonna be in the streets today, I'm going to treat everyone to dinner while we're out. Maybe after you've finished your *workout*, you can meet us."

"Definitely, just text me and tell me where you're gonna be."

"Will do."

From securing the photographer, the expensive one Charisse had wanted from the get-go, to double-checking on the floral arrangements (painful to say the least), to picking up our custom platinum bands, I got on my game and did everything I'd resisted doing out of stubbornness. If Charisse would just chill out and remember the love that brought us together, we'd be happily married and flying to an all-inclusive honeymoon to an island paradise in just a few days.

Although I loved her, I wasn't willing to keep begging for her forgiveness. If she truly loved me and wanted to spend the rest of her life with me, she'd stop her campaign to eternally punish me for my mistakes and accept one of the hundred apologies I'd offered over the past few days. Listen, I never claimed to be perfect. Didn't mean we couldn't have a long and happy marriage. Didn't mean she wouldn't eventually accept Javon as her own.

I realized being a good man didn't give me license to hurt or lie to her either, but if she wanted our relationship to work, she'd have to find a way to let the pain go and forgive so we could move forward.

Just as I started toward the National Harbor to meet Kristen at the Gaylord, a call from Derek came through.

"Hey. What's up, man?" Derek asked.

"I'd have an easier time telling you what's down. My spirits for one. Things are crazy right now. Beyond crazy."

"Why don't you check with your wifey and see if she'll let you off of your leash long enough to get some drinks tonight. I'm sure you could use one or two right about now."

"Naaah, man. I can't tonight. I'm about to meet Kristen over here at the Gaylord and help her out with something. Afterwards, I'm gonna try and meet up with Charisse and her family. Her father's in town."

"Hold up! What the hell are you helping Kristen do at the Gaylord? Hold her legs up in the air?"

I laughed, but Derek knew I didn't roll like that. "You trippin', dude. Hell no. Man, some shit's going down with her husband. He's trying to leave her and take the kids, including Javon. So we've got some business to take care of."

"Whaaat?"

I explained their history. Both had cheated before, but Kristen stopped and her husband didn't.

"I didn't want to get involved, but she didn't have anyone else to turn to. It's only gonna take an hour to deal with this mess, then I've got to catch up with Charisse and the family."

"What did Charisse have to say about your helping Kristen? I know she's pissed."

"She doesn't know. I didn't tell her."

"Kev, you like playing with fire, don't you?"

"I ain't playin' with fire. I'm a grown-ass man. I don't have to tell her everything I do," I said, knowing I didn't mean a word. Yes, I'd been playing with fire, but compared to cheating, helping Kristen catch her husband cheating so she'd be protected during their inevitable divorce amounted to nothing—comparatively speaking.

"Mmm-hmm. Whatever you say, man. I hear you."

"Listen, I've got to go. I'm at the hotel. I'll holla at you when I'm done. A'ight?"

I drove my truck to the hotel's valet stand and

walked over to meet Kristen at the Comfort Suite, which sat adjacent to the Gaylord. We'd plan our strategy before getting into position.

After pushing my way through the circular doorway, I noticed Lamar standing at the check-in desk, accompanied by a younger woman. I hoped to hell Lamar had finally found his own woman, so he'd leave Charisse alone, but she looked like a female carbon copy of him. Figured they must be related. I scanned the lobby and Kristen hadn't arrived, so I attempted to skulk to the seating area before Lamar noticed I was there.

No such luck.

"Kevin?" Lamar said, as if he hadn't been in my house making coffee a couple of days ago. I turned and painted on a fake smile because I didn't want Lamar to know how much he irked me.

"Hey, what's up, man?"

"Nothing much." Lamar looked at me curiously in a moment of awkward silence. "Oh, I'm sorry. This is my cousin Tracy. She and her fiancé are checking in today. He's heading here from Chicago for business."

"Ohhhh, pleasure to meet you," I said, somewhat disappointed.

"You too," Tracy replied. "Excuse me please. I'm gonna run to the ladies' room."

"So," Lamar asked, "where's Charisse?"

"Oh, uhhh . . . she's sightseeing with her family today."

"So what brings you—" Then Lamar looked behind me and smiled. "Oh, I see."

I turned around and saw Kristen approaching. Of all the bad timing in the world, Kristen had the worst. Wondered why I always seemed to be spotted with her at the worst possible moment.

She smiled at Lamar as she approached. They'd met once before when Kristen and I worked the case against Charisse's ex-boyfriend Dwayne, so they'd already been introduced.

"Well, well, well. Kristen," Lamar said smugly, as if he'd caught me midstroke. "Two times in one week. What a coincidence."

My eyebrows wrinkled. I had no idea where they would've seen each other before, but I wanted to ask. Before I got a chance to, Kristen shot Lamar an uncomfortable look and made her escape.

"Lamar, good to see you again," she said before turning to me. "I only wanted to tell you I'm here. I'll wait for you over there." She pointed at a seating area near the bar. Then she paced toward some empty seats.

"Likewise." Lamar gave me the side-eye glance. "Well, I'm taking my cousin out to dinner at McCormick and Schmick's so I'll catch you later. Don't hurt yourself now."

"Man, whatever." I wanted to explain to Lamar that the situation wasn't as it seemed, but the more I tried to explain, the more Lamar would assume I lied anyway. I had no doubt he would mention our meeting to Charisse, even if he played as if he were letting it slip out on the sly. So, I seriously needed to hurry up and finish so I could tell her the truth before Lamar did. If I hadn't been a knucklehead and had told her the truth from the beginning, Lamar would be the least of my concerns. I hadn't planned to have to deal with this wrinkle in the plan.

I walked over to Kristen. "What's going on?"

"Well, he's definitely here already. I checked the valet area and saw his car parked there. He usually goes to the sports bar, but knowing him, he'll be trying to impress her with his wallet so he may have taken her to the club. I don't know."

"All right then. Guess the time has come to get this party started." I slipped on my shades and headed across the street to the Gaylord.

As I eased through the Gaylord lobby, the richness of the hotel never ceased to amaze me. Crowds of people moved in and out of the conference areas toward the glass atrium, where they soaked up scenic views of the Potomac River. Normally, I would've been among them, but I had a job to do.

I spotted my target sitting at the bar beside a beautiful, thick, chocolate woman reminiscent of Charisse. She couldn't have been more different from Kristen, a polar opposite in terms of body type, but equally beautiful about the face. She sat with her shapely legs facing the crowd and drew many stares as gawking brothers passed by. Her dress put the *little* in *little black dress*. Greg leaned over to kiss her on the lips; I stood behind a large palm and photographed them with my camera phone. With so many tourists moving around, no one noticed.

I checked my watch: 7:30. I'd only been watching Greg for a half hour and already had enough to suggest his relationship was questionable, but with Javon's future in the balance, I wanted to get as much evidence as I could to ensure Kristen would get her fair share . . . and the kids if their divorce became contentious. No sooner had the thought crossed my mind than the adulterous couple moved toward the elevators leading to the hotel suites upstairs. I went to the front desk and asked the clerk, "Excuse me. Can you tell me which room Greg Thomas is staying in?"

"Oh, I'm sorry, sir. I'm not allowed to release that information. I'd be happy to call his room and tell him you're here for a visit."

"N-no, that won't be necessary." I reached into my pocket, pulled out my FBI badge and credentials, and flashed them long enough for her to spot the letters FBI and my name. Her eyes widened.

"Actually, I'm here on official business, but he may not want to speak with me, if you know what I mean. Letting him know I'm here would be a bad thing."

"Oh, no, sir. I understand. It's not a problem. He's in Roooom"—she scanned the computer screen—"690. Up these elevators to the sixth floor and to the left."

"Thank you, ma'am," I said with a wink.

Now, isn't that ironic? Room 6–9–0.

As I walked toward the elevator, a text from Charisse came through on my phone:

We decided on a restaurant.
The fam is sitting down to eat.

I stopped to respond before going upstairs:

Where are you?

She wrote:

Standing right behind you.

My eyes widened as big as motorcycle wheels and I slowly spun around on my heel. "Charisse! What are you doing here?"

"Funny," she said, her eyes red with fury, "I was gonna ask you the same thing!"

24
Charisse

Kevin left the house to run his "errands" and go meet his little girlfriend, while leaving me at home with a houseful of crazy people. I gave him the chance to tell me the truth, to confess his extracurricular activities, and all he did was try to turn his dirt-doing around on me. Hey, I didn't do anything wrong . . . nothing happened between Lamar and me. Okay, so maybe I *wanted* something to happen at first, but hearing that woman's voice proved to be the wake-up call I needed to remind me of Lamar's suppressed inner player.

When he and I attended college, I'd been some kind of crazy about that man. The ultimate slick willy, OP (original player), and consummate juggler of women (usually five or more at a time), I should've known better than to believe anyone as adept at ho-hopping as Lamar would let that lifestyle go so easily. No way. He's like a dandelion. When it grows, it may appear to be a flower, but it's still a destructive weed at the root. How crazy would I have been to let Kevin go for Lamar's philandering ass? I would've looked like an überfool running behind him.

As I started making up the bed, someone knocked at the door.

"Come in."

It was Nisey. She came in and shut the door behind her. "So what's on the agenda for today? I need to get out of the house."

"I thought I'd take everyone sightseeing today. Dad and Trey haven't been to DC before. Besides, Kevin's gonna be running 'errands' so . . ." I said, adding air quotes.

"What does 'errands' mean?" She mimicked me.

"I checked his phone last night. He and Kristen are meeting at the Gaylord tonight at seven."

"What! You've got to be fucking kidding me. After everything's that's happened?"

"That's what I said. Couldn't believe him, but I suspected something was up when his phone blew up yesterday."

"So, what you got planned? I know you ain't lettin' this shit ride. Because if you do, I sure the hell won't. I just finished talking to his ass and he swore to me he had no more secrets or surprises."

"Oh, he did, did he? You know me better. He doesn't know, but we're all meeting at the Gaylord tonight. I'm gonna treat the family to McCormick and Schmick's for dinner, and while you guys are eating, I'll be at the Gaylord killing Kevin."

"Damn. What's up with men these days? I don't even know." She took a seat on my bed. "You know,

I've been meaning to ask where you disappeared to the other morning. Kevin about lost his mind looking for you."

"I went to visit Lamar. He's been gassing my head up about wanting to marry me, saying this thing with Kevin might be a sign that Kevin's not the right man for me . . . and maybe he is."

"Hmph. I'm not sure about that, but he's certainly changed a lot for the better. I'm straight tripping on the fact that he's actually talking marriage. This is Lamar we're referring to."

"Ha! Changed a lot? I'll give you a sign . . . how about a woman called downstairs at five a.m. asking if everything was okay when I knocked on the door."

"Nuh-uhhh! Did he tell you who she was?"

"No, because I didn't stick around long enough to listen. I mean, come on. Like you said, this is Lamar."

"True that," she said.

"In two days, I went from having two men who wanted to marry me to zero. That should be a new Guinness world record."

"Well, everything happens for a reason. And we understand how God works. Something better must be on the horizon."

"Yeah, that's what we said about Kevin after Dwayne got arrested."

"Keep the faith," she said. "So, on yet another subject, when are you gonna sit down and talk to your father. Seems like you've hardly spoken two words together."

"Only because Mom won't let me within two feet

of him. She's definitely hiding something major, but as long as she's playing talk-blocker, there's no way we can have the discussion we need to have. And the wedding's Saturday. They won't be here much longer."

"Is the wedding still on?"

We all piled in Kevin's truck and headed out on our sightseeing tour. Mom sat in the passenger seat next to me. Trey and Nisey sat behind us, and Mom ensured Dad got in the third-row seat way in the back of the truck. As far away from me as he could possibly be. I played some oldies but goodies on my iPod, mostly Earth, Wind & Fire tunes. We sang "September" as we drove through the city. I took them to the Mall, where we went to the Lincoln Memorial. We walked up to the Washington Monument, but the line was three-people deep all the way around. Dad and Trey settled for pictures.

They refused to leave the city without seeing the White House. Dad kinda got teary-eyed thinking about Trey and Chris serving in the military under a black commander in chief. He recalled participating in the March on Washington, watching Martin Luther King Jr. deliver his "I Have a Dream" speech. Who would've imagined over forty-five years later . . .

Of course no trip to DC would be complete without taking Dad to visit the Iwo Jima Memorial near Arlington Cemetery. While he and my brother were in Marines heaven, Mom's face screamed bored and not a little bit tired. Honestly, Mom had always seemed to resent Dad's career. She thought it'd given him license to cheat on her. Women could hardly resist a man in uniform, and Dad had always traveled somewhere, never stayed home. She'd even confessed she suspected Dad had shacked up with one of his women when he claimed to be on "special assignment."

Mom's anger toward Dad simmered just beneath her disgustingly flirtatious surface. She wouldn't be able to keep this act up for too much longer and seemed increasingly on the verge of erupting. While I would like to have stoked that fire, I couldn't afford any scenes that day. The time neared six o'clock and we needed to get to the National Harbor so I could make some scenes of my own.

We arrived at the restaurant not thirty minutes after I basically pushed everyone from the memorial. I had no idea what Kristen and Kevin had planned, but I needed to catch them together before they disappeared into a hotel room—the thought of which made my temper flare.

Did it ever dawn on me they could have a completely legit reason for meeting? Hell no. My mind went directly south because I was touched in the head and scared to death to get married, particularly because of my track record in previous relationships. Kevin knew I was crazy too, so if he had the *slightest inkling* he might get caught, he should've fessed up right away. If I thought he was touched in the head, you know, *mucho loco*, I sure woulda told him what the hell I was doing, even at the risk of his getting pissed. Being forthright would've been the smart thing to do and could've saved us both a lot of heartache.

We had a short wait before the hostess seated us. A perky blonde, she spoke with a pronounced lisp that made her sound as if someone let some air out of her head whenever she opened her mouth to speak.

"Ssssso, here's your table. Please be seated and enjoy your time here. Deidre, your waitress, will be out to take your orders in just a moment." We thanked her for the hospitality and waited for Deidre to show up. Ten minutes later she finally breezed by our table to take our drink orders.

"Hi, my name is Deidre," she said with a deluxe ghetto attitude, as if she dared us to place an order and earn her keep. I didn't know from whence they hired this heifer, but whoever was responsible needed to be fired their damn self and never hire personnel for the restaurant industry in life. Ever again.

"So," she said, then heaved a sigh so deep it nearly sucked all the joy from the room, "I guess y'all gon' order drinks or what?"

I thought, *Naaaaah, we're gonna sit here parched and dry-throated because your ass got the wrong job.*

"Could you give us a minute?" I said. "We're still looking over the menu."

She sucked her teeth and blew out an aggravated breath. "A'ight den. I'll be right back."

She whipped around without glancing up, and I knew she walked away because all twelve of her ghetto hoop earrings jangled. One pair contained the word *payed*. As in she "payed" for earrings with a misspelled word.

Just as Ghettiqua started back toward us about five minutes later. Nisey said, "Ummm, Rissey. We got company walking this way. Check the door."

I turned, and damn if Lamar and some high-yellow heifer weren't walking toward us. Talk about balls. I'd felt certain he wouldn't introduce his new piece of ass to *me* of all people. Lamar wore a big, mischievous grin on his face, made me want to smack it off. No, he wasn't bringing his ho to our table.

He stood next to my chair and bent forward to kiss my cheek. Everyone's eyebrows rose, including mine. I wanted to run because if I had seen *my man* kiss *her* that way, I would've straight beat his ass and gunned for hers.

"Hello, everyone. I'm Lamar, a good friend of Charisse's from college. This is my cousin Tracy. She's visiting from Chicago."

The choir sang, "Hiiiii!"

I said, "Your cousin?"

"Yes, my *cousin*," he said, emphasizing the word *cousin*, "as in my aunt's daughter. Her fiancé should be here in a little while."

Awww, damn. Boy, did I feel stupid. You'd think after years of hasty anger exits, I'd learn to cool my hot temper and listen to someone for a change. Nope! Fortunately no one else at the table was aware of my faux pas, except Lamar and Nisey . . . who did the unthinkable.

"Why don't you guys join us for dinner? I'm sure they wouldn't mind pulling up an extra table," she said, winking at me.

During the commotion Ghettiqua created as she pulled the table and chairs next to ours, her ass lodged squarely on her shoulders due to the actual work she had to do, I whispered to Nisey, "What the hell are you thinking? Kevin would kill all of us if he caught Lamar here. Did you forget he's armed twenty-four/seven?"

"Oh, you mean the Kevin who's on his way to meet Kristen at the Gaylord right this minute?"

I gave her the evil eye.

"Hey, at least now your man count is back up to one."

25

Charisse

Of course my dad and Trey took to Lamar like a weave to glue once Lamar announced he'd served in the Marines. They were like one big happy family, acting as if they'd known each other for years upon years, laughing and joking, talking about boot camp and gunnies, Parris Island, and a bunch of navy carriers I'd never heard of. They threw the word *squid* around once or twice in reference to some navy guys.

For me, the situation felt kinda surreal because they liked Kevin, but they sure weren't interacting with him in the same ultrafriendly way. Good thing for Kevin my father's opinion about men (or anything else) didn't account for much to me. Mom's opinion didn't influence me as much as she'd have liked it to. I'd ignored enough of her guidance over the years to let her know I had a mind of my own. But her opinion always mattered. I wanted to get her insights and respected her point of view, and more often than not, her opinions helped form my own, even if I didn't follow her advice to the letter.

Speaking of Mom, she sat tight-lipped almost the entire time. She remembered Lamar from my college years and had never liked him much, said he reminded her of my father . . . and not in a good way. So, that they all got along so swimmingly didn't score him any cool points with her, even if he'd hit a slam dunk with my dad.

Nisey, on the other hand, hung on Trey's every word, and he couldn't keep his eyes off her. He'd been attentive toward her, ensuring she had everything she wanted or needed. Kept her wineglass filled, picked up her napkin when it fell to the floor, and helped her order her meal (and she let him help as if she needed it). The simmering connection between them almost made me envious, but I'd be lying if I said the sight wasn't a happy one despite the that I liked David. Sure, I empathized with his dilemma, but he should never have run out on Nisey. When you love someone, truly love them, you stay and at least try to work out your problems, no matter how much trying hurts or how difficult things might be.

That's when it struck me. Perhaps I'd become the proverbial pot calling the kettle black. Of course the difference between my situation and David's was that Kevin had gone to an illicit meeting with his piece of ass and had lied to me about the nature of their relationship, whereas Nisey had been completely honest with David and he understood the situation from day one.

I glanced down at my watch and the time read nearly seven thirty. Fortunately, all the chatter had slowed down the meal, so everyone had just received their entrées when I made my escape.

"Excuse me. I'm gonna run to the ladies' room for a second. Be right back," I announced.

Lamar excused himself and trotted behind me.

Shit, I thought. *Now I'm gonna have to apologize. He's got me cornered.*

"Hey," I said. "Funny meeting you here."

"You didn't give me a chance to explain."

"I know, Lamar, and I'm sorry, but we'll have to talk about this later. I've got to get to the Gaylord."

"Ohhhh, no. You cannot go to the Gaylord right now. Uhhhhh, I think you ought to know Kevin's there with Kristen. Tracy and I saw them earlier."

"I know. I'm going to meet up with them now; however, they don't know I'll be joining the party."

"I'm coming with you then."

"No, I need to go by myself. This is between me and Kevin."

"I understand, but there's something I need to ask."

"What's that?"

"Now that you know the truth about Tracy, is there a chance for us?" A wanting expression was on his face. "I mean, for us to be together?"

I gazed into those beautiful eyes of his, the thought of Kevin with Kristen lying heavy on my heart, and said, "Yes. We have a chance. But I've got to break off my engagement with Kevin first. Let me deal with one thing at a time."

A wide smile emerged on his face. He gently gripped my face and pressed his lips ever so sweetly against mine.

"I love you, Charisse."

Hells bells!

●   ●   ●

The second I walked into the lobby, I spotted Kevin photographing some couple at the bar. Well, I figured he must be taking pictures of them because no one else was sitting in the direction where his phone was pointed. Had to be them. I didn't recognize the man, but the woman looked familiar. A quick scan through my memory banks and I remembered she was the same woman who came to my house with Kristen after I caught Kevin with Kristen at the park. Why in hell would Kevin be taking pictures of her?

When they left the bar and headed toward the elevators, Kevin followed squarely on their heels, making a brief stop at the guest services desk. I thought about following him to keep an eye on what he was up to, but a flashback of Lamar's kiss and *I love you* made me want to hurry up and get this scene over with. So, I walked up behind him and sent him a text:

> We decided on a restaurant.
> The fam is sitting down to eat.

He wrote:

> Where are you?

I wrote:

> Standing right behind you.

He turned around and looked at me as if I were the walking dead. I sniffed to see if I could smell something foul, certain I'd scared the shit out of him. He asked why I'd come. I said, "Funny, I was gonna ask you the same thing!"

"I'm, uhhhh . . . I'm—" he stammered.

"Let me save you the trouble of lying to me again. I know you're meeting Kristen here. I saw her text."

"What text?"

"The one I deleted when I checked your phone last night. So, where is she?"

"Listen, you need to let me explain."

"All right. Say what you have to say."

Okay, this is the point where I'd usually sprint and ignore every single lying word he had to say. But since the lesson with Lamar was still fresh in my mind, I waited to listen as I mentally prepared to get my sprint on as soon as he finished.

He looked at me curiously because staying and listening was completely against my character. He stepped back as if he wanted to put some space between us in case I took a swing. "I'm here to help Kristen, not screw her. Her husband is threatening to divorce her and take the kids, including Javon. She believed if she could prove he was having an affair, she'd have a better chance to keep them."

"But Javon's yours."

"Well, her husband's name is on the birth certificate, not mine."

"Oh." The situation seemed a little clearer, except one thing.

"Exactly. So I'm here to get pictures of them together. And that's all."

Okay, well, that explained why Kevin had gone to the Gaylord, but it didn't explain . . .

"I understand everything you're saying, except . . . that woman can *not* be his mistress."

"Why?"

"Because that's Kristen's friend."

"Her friend?"

26
Kevin

Not until Charisse revealed that Kristen's husband's mistress was a friend of Kristen's did I start putting two and two together. How could I not see it before? I'd dismissed Charisse's suggestion that Kristen's feelings for me ran deep as a product of her overactive imagination, not truth. Charisse told me Kristen's cold attitude toward her had been all the evidence *she* needed to confirm Kristen had fallen in love with me. Fool that I was, I ignored her.

I'd ignored far too many incidences where Kristen was concerned, including her insistence on accompanying me every time I was due to be in the vicinity of Charisse.

I remembered when Dwayne's case first came across my desk. Kristen and I reviewed the file and saw Charisse's name. I told Kristen I'd met Charisse during high school, and that of all the women I had met in my life, Charisse felt the most like the one that had got away. I daydreamed about her all the time, anticipated the moment we would again cross paths, and prayed she'd be single when that day came.

From the moment I shared my feelings with Kristen, her attitude changed big-time. She'd either attempted to avoid conducting surveillance involving Charisse or she insisted on accompanying me no matter where I went or what I was doing, even when other investigative and administrative issues needed to be taken care of.

The day I literally ran into Charisse's car, our first meeting since high school, Kristen snapped at me, asking me what I was thinking. When I told her I'd been thinking of Charisse, she copped a major attitude and hardly spoke two words to me for the rest of the day.

When I mentioned I planned to attend the singles' dinner at Lamar's church so that I'd have an opportunity to talk to Charisse about Dwayne (and be near her), Kristen showed up at my door dressed and ready to go. I told her I wanted to go by myself, and she accused me of trying to take over the case, insisted she be allowed to attend. Later, she blamed her nasty attitude on the difficult separation from her husband and claimed the drama had begun to take a toll.

By sheer coincidence, I'd received a call from my mother, who had been trying to sell a piece of property from my father's estate. Once she finally found a buyer, she called and asked me to come home and handle the sale for her . . . not twenty-four hours later, I spoke to Lamar and found out Charisse's mother had suffered a stroke. Kristen again insisted she be allowed to accompany me to North Carolina, on the outside chance there was a major break, of course. When I told Kristen I planned to stop by the hospital for a few minutes to deliver some flowers to Mama Tyson, her face cracked and she walked around with her ass on her shoulders all morning until I agreed to let her go with me. Manipulative bitch. In the gift shop, she complained I'd spent too much money on the lavish get-well bouquet.

On Charisse's fortieth birthday, when Dwayne took Charisse to the Skydome in Crystal City to celebrate, I nearly reached my breaking point, wanting so much to tell Charisse about the past we shared and reveal my feelings for her. But she seemed enthralled with Dwayne—at least until Dwayne disappeared and I swooped in to ask her to dance. My confession dangled on the tip of my tongue when Dwayne reappeared, cut in on our near kiss, and whisked her away for the rest of the night. Seeing them together made me sick to my stomach. Kristen showed up a moment later and bought me a drink to ease my angst. Before I realized what had happened, I'd gotten too drunk to drive. Kristen took me home, and when I woke up, we both lay naked in bed.

I thought it strange that the drink would've been so strong. Although I was far from a lush, I thought I could hold my own. Didn't matter. What happened, happened. I couldn't relive the night and undo what had been done.

"Kristen's friend?" I asked.

"Yeah. She came to my house the night I caught you two at the park with Javon."

"Why didn't you tell me? What did she say?"

"I don't know, Kevin. I'd been drinking . . . a lot, and I guess part of me believed the things she said to me. You hurt me so much," Charisse said. "She said you didn't tell me about what happened between you two because you had fallen in love with her. She said that because you and she are both FBI agents, you shared a life that I could never understand."

"She's crazy. Baby, I didn't tell you because I was afraid to lose you, not because I'm in love with her. Please. I did a stupid, stupid thing. I've never had romantic feelings for her. From the day Dwayne's case landed on my desk, my whole world revolved around you."

"You can't expect me to believe that, Kevin. The evidence of your romantic feelings is named Javon. Clearly, you had some thoughts that weren't centered around me. And look at her. Look at me. I mean, she's every man's dream."

"You're *my* dream, Charisse. I realize now that you were right all along. Kristen's been playing games with you and Greg because she wants to be with me."

"Well, duh. I've been warning you about Cruella for ages. She's in love with you. You didn't believe me, called me crazy and jealous."

"No, I did not."

"Well, you thought it. Don't act like you didn't."

I chuckled and tucked my phone in my pocket. "One thing's certain. I'm damn sure not running around here trying to get more pictures of her husband. She's clearly setting him up. I'll be damned. All this to be with me."

"Don't get too full of yourself, chief. Probably

more accurate to say 'all this because she's a crazy bitch.'"

"Well, at least you know nothing is going on between us."

"What are you gonna do about Kristen now that you know what she's capable of? Don't forget she carries a gun like you do."

"I'm going to let her think that I've got the evidence she needs while I figure out what to do next. My only concern now is Javon. She clearly ain't altogether in the head. I don't want her putting him through any drama, and I can't risk pissing her off before I can prove he's mine or I might never get to be a part of his life."

I sent Kristen a text telling her I'd gotten the photos. She expressed her undying gratitude, which about made me sick. *Old fake bitch.* I didn't make a habit of using the B-word when referring to women, but sometimes the term was the most appropriate—and speaking about Kristen was one such time.

Charisse and I headed back to McCormick & Schmick's to join the family. For the first time in days, I thought I had reason to be hopeful about Charisse and the wedding. The Kristen issue had been addressed. Charisse clearly understood Kristen never stood between me and my love for her—and she never would. I loved Charisse and only Charisse. If I'd wanted Kristen, I could've had her, but nothing about Kristen, not even her beauty, appealed to me because she had a funky attitude. On the other hand, everything about Charisse appealed to me . . . except for her quick temper, but I'd even started to get used to her outbursts. I thought I'd give hope a boost by making another confession.

"So, you want to know how I spent my day?"

"I don't know. Do I?"

"Yes, you do." I reached into my back pocket to pull out her things-to-do list. "Here. Check this out."

She grabbed the paper from my hand and opened it. "Wait. This is my list." She scanned the page from top to bottom. "Why is everything crossed off?"

"I took care of all outstanding issues."

"Everything?"

"Yes. Everything. I dropped thirty-five hundred on the photographer you wanted and even finished ordering the floral arrangements."

"You did?" Her eyes brightened and a smile emerged. "I can't believe this, Kevin!"

"Believe it, baby." I opened the door to the restaurant. "Now, if you'll still have me, all we have to do is—"

I froze in my footsteps, mouth gaping open, when I spotted Lamar and his cousin Tracy kicking it with Trey and Mr. Tyson as if they were one big happy family. I know my face was jacked up. Somebody was gonna get cussed out, and for a change, Charisse would be lucky to escape *my* wrath.

27

Kevin

"I had no idea Lamar would show up here, Kevin . . . and Nisey invited him to sit with us, not me," Charisse said.

"Did you tell him, 'Thanks, but no thanks'?"

"No, I didn't. I was leaving to catch you and Kristen together . . . or at least that's what I thought at the time."

"So, it's okay for you to disrespect me, knowing how I feel about him, because you suspect I might be doing something wrong? If the shoe was on the other foot, you would've cussed me out and asked questions later. You act like it's cool for you to condemn people even when your only proof is your suspicion. But if *you* make a mistake, it's 'Let's forgive, forget, and move on.' I've got news for you, Charisse. You don't get to have it both ways. Not today."

She started to argue but relented. Her eyes said she realized I'd only told her the truth and nothing but the truth. You know she didn't apologize though, too stubborn to acknowledge she was in the wrong. So she said, "Listen, dinner's almost over. Let's get through the evening and we can discuss this when we get home."

"Fine!" I snapped.

I didn't understand why she kept entertaining Lamar. He clearly had an agenda, and his top priority was to break us up so he could have her to himself. How could she not comprehend this? Maybe the problem wasn't that she *couldn't* see it, maybe the problem was that she *didn't want* to see it. Even more significantly, maybe she welcomed his presence and contemplated a relationship with him. Not only was that a battle I couldn't fight, it was a battle I refused to fight. As much as I loved Charisse and wanted to spend the rest of my life with her, our relationship, our marriage, couldn't work if any part of her heart was invested in Lamar. As the night unfolded, more and more, I questioned her loyalty to me.

"Well, well, well, look at what the cat drug in," Nisey said snidely as Charisse and I approached the table.

Charisse smiled uncomfortably and asked the waitress for another chair.

"Hey, everybody . . . Nisey," I said, my voice going from fluffy to flat. I shot her a look to make it plain that I was in no mood for her attitude. Unfortunately, Nisey was slow on the uptake . . . or just plain didn't care.

"Hey! There's my son-in-law-to-be. Come on and have a seat. Glad you made it. Lamar, Trey, and I were just boring the ladies with old Marine war stories."

"So, where've you been, Kevin. You missed all the fun," Nisey said.

My eyes narrowed as I turned to her. "I actually took care of some last-minute wedding details today."

Nisey raised an eyebrow to Charisse, her eyes asking if I was telling the truth. Charisse nodded.

"Ohhh, okay."

Shut you up.

With Charisse and Nisey chilled out, I tried to suffer silently through the rest of dinner . . . that is, until Lamar went on the offensive and tried to use the opportunity to get a dig in and make me look bad.

"Hey, Kevin," Lamar said. "Imagine meeting you twice in one day. I didn't know you were coming here. Where's Kristen?"

Mama Tyson's eyebrow raised, Charisse's chin fell to her chest, and my ire had been stoked. I'd had enough of Lamar's bullshit. I waited for Charisse, my future wife, to speak up for me since she knew the truth about my activities.

She said nothing. Just gulped down her wine.

Despite what happened, I still tried to hold it down in front of the family.

"Kristen went home to cook dinner for her husband. She and I had some FBI business to take care of." I turned to address the rest of the table. "Kristen's my ex-partner. She and I met at the Gaylord on a business matter."

"Ohhh. So, how old is your son now? He looks like he's a big boy," Lamar said casually as he shoveled a forkful of pasta in his fat mouth.

Every mouth dropped open and everyone exchanged uncomfortable glances. Lamar smirked, knowing he had opened a can of worms I couldn't close, putting me securely in the hot seat. While Mama Tyson, Trey, and Nisey hardly reacted at all—as they'd already been told the truth—Mr. Tyson was somewhat taken aback.

"Kevin, you didn't mention you had a son."

Although I had nothing to be ashamed of, I stammered for a second, leaving enough of an opening for Lamar to sneak in another sucker punch.

"Oh, I'm sorry. I thought everybody knew Kristen is your baby's mama. Go figure."

"Lamar!" Tracy said, cutting her eyes at him, shaking her head no to urge him to stop. Charisse placed her elbow on the table and laid her forehead in her hand.

I shook my head and stiffened my back. "Javon's doing fine, Lamar. How are all of your kids, Lamar? Is it still eight or do you have more on the way? We all know how you like to juggle the ladies. I don't know how you keep everybody straight."

Lamar's eyes narrowed.

"Eight kids? Dang!" Trey said, his eyes wide.

Mr. Tyson slid his chair back as if he was preparing to excuse himself to go to the restroom when Nisey whispered, "Don't leave now. This is gettin' good."

Lamar, mirroring me, straightened his back and said, "Well, at least Charisse didn't find out about *my* kids two days ago. Maybe if you had some honesty about your shit, your fiancée wouldn't need to leave your bed early in the morning trying to find a *real* man."

Her father glanced at me and said, "A little bump in the road?"

Enough was enough. He'd plucked the proverbial straw that broke my back. Brothas have been killed for less than that. I turned to Charisse, waiting for her to say something, anything.

She said nothing.

So I did.

"You know what! Fuck you, Lamar, and the hole you slithered out of. I don't have to take this shit!" I jumped up and rocked the table, toppling an empty wineglass. "Charisse, I can't even believe you could sit here and let him get away with this. Who are you gonna marry, *him* or *me?*"

Charisse eyebrows scrunched together betraying her anger at the insult. She had some kind of nerve. She let Lamar spend the night humiliating me in front my future family, yet had the audacity to get an attitude because I questioned her loyalties. What did she expect?

"You know what? Never mind. *You* want him? *You* can have him. The wedding's off . . . and I'm out!" I gritted on Lamar and stormed out of the restaurant.

Yeah, I walked out in a huff, but when I got about ten feet from the door, I realized what I'd said . . . and done. Talk about Charisse and her temper? I'd definitely taken things too far, but no way could I back down with Lamar still there. I turned to look at the door, half wanting to go back and apologize. Another part hoped to see Charisse run out the door after me. But I didn't budge, and apparently neither did she—as evidenced because the door never opened. So I wandered around the parking lot until I found my truck and left. After sending Charisse a text telling her I'd left the valet ticket for her Beemer at the hotel's front desk, I turned off my phone so I could lick my wounds in peace.

28
Charisse

Ain't that a bitch?

Or should I say, *Ain't she a bitch?*

When will men ever listen? I'd been telling Kevin that Kristen was in love with him, but he wouldn't listen to me, insisted I was being dramatic. Now, here he was explaining how Kristen had involved him in some kind of wild-goose chase. It was as if the Red Sea had parted and the skies cleared when Kevin said Kristen asked him to follow her cheating husband and I realized she supplied the mistress. She'd set up Kevin and her husband. Her little visit to my place had no doubt been part of the master plan, intended to shake my faith in Kevin's love for me at my most vulnerable moment, plant the bug in my ear about Lamar, and use Javon to worm her way back into Kevin's life. We'd all fallen victim to her lies and deceit.

After finally telling Kevin she'd come to my house after I caught them at the park, he asked why I hadn't told him sooner. Good question. So, why didn't I say anything? It's simple really. Because I believed her. Up until the moment at the park, Kevin had been the most perfect man I'd ever committed to. He was everything I'd dreamed I could want or need in a man, and my love for him scared me as nothing else had before because . . . I guess the truth is, I never felt worthy of him.

From the attempted rape when I was thirteen, to the player after player I'd attracted in almost every relationship since, my relationships with men had been a study in dysfunction and heartbreak. Hell, my own father didn't even want me, at least that's what I'd spent the last forty years believing. I'd succumbed to my misguided notion that I meant *little* or *nothing* to the men in my life, and if that was the case, how could I mean *so much* to Kevin? This perfect man. This loving man. This caring and considerate man. This marriage-worthy man. How could I, this broken shell of a woman with the scarred soul, possibly be worthy of such perfection?

The worst blow came when I found out Kevin wasn't as perfect as I believed. I feared our fairy-tale relationship might be more like same shit, different day.

When Kristen came to my house that night, I took her words as God delivering me a sign that, indeed, I was not worthy. Little did I know, the devil was working triple-double overtime to scare me away from the best man that ever happened to me, and I almost let him get away with it. Almost.

Finally admitting the feelings of worthlessness to myself, if not Kevin, I realized I'm worthy of a happily ever after with Kevin—or any good man. My self-worth is not determined by how men have treated me or whether my father played a role in my life. I'm the one who determines my worth, both in how I feel about myself and how I treated others.

Sure, I'd made a lot of mistakes in my lifetime, but I deserved happiness.

And, no, Kevin wasn't perfect, nor should he have to be. My biggest mistake was putting Kevin on such a high pedestal that I set him up for a long and hard fall from grace. Kevin's only role in my life should've been enhancing my own happiness, and he excelled in that role. To expect constant perfection was unfair.

Keeping it real, the happiness and inner peace I'd gained in my relationship with Kevin is probably what drew Lamar to me. He wouldn't have wanted the self-loathing version of me I turned into after my relationship with that Sir Kiss a Lot Marcus and before I'd acknowledged my cousin Lee's betrayal that led to the attempted rape and decimated my trust in men. Sure Lamar helped, in a small measure, to restore my faith in men. But Kevin had done most of the heavy lifting, and he'd earned my hand in marriage as no other man had before.

So when I explained my reasons for not sharing Kristen's Jedi mind trick attempt with him sooner, he said, "Baby, I didn't tell you because I was afraid to lose you, not because I'm in love with her. I did a stupid, stupid thing."

Stupid is right. He should've realized the truth would come out sooner rather than later. Yes, I probably would've gotten upset, but, to be honest, I wouldn't have written him off. How could any sane woman write off a beautiful hunk of man like him?

Once we both realized the extent of her deception, I asked, "So what are you gonna do about Kristen now?"

He said, "I'm not sure. I'll come up with something. For me, the main issue isn't Kristen, my main concern is Javon."

Well, I had no doubt Javon belonged to Kevin. Looking at his picture in Kevin's wallet, the resemblance was striking. Kevin couldn't deny him on his best day. No, no. The judge need only take one look and Kevin would be expressed to child-support city. But knowing Kevin, he wouldn't leave Javon's fate in the hands of crazy Kristen and her mentally unstable ass. Given her *Fatal Attraction* attitude, I'd begun to think it would be in Javon's interest to live with Kevin. On the other hand, if doing crazy shit behind men made a woman an unfit mother, 95 percent of the female population would be banned from bearing and raising kids. Regardless, Kevin definitely needed to wield a bigger hand in his son's life, and he'd find a way to make that happen.

During our short walk to the restaurant to rejoin the family, Kevin told me he'd spent the day finishing up our things-to-do list for the wedding, an enormous gesture on his part. The effort hadn't been lost on me. So, I decided to tell him after dinner I wanted to go through with the wedding.

As we walked inside, I'll be damned if in all the excitement I completely forgot Lamar had joined us. Thanks to *Nisey*. When I saw Kevin's expression at seeing Lamar yukking it up with my father and Trey—and sitting in the seat where Kevin should've been—I ain't gonna lie, I wanted to haul ass up out of there and stick my head in the ground until the night ended. Kevin was pissed and he had every right to be; I just couldn't make the situation right at that moment. My dad and Trey had already taken a liking to Lamar and would've thought I'd gone psycho if I just interrupted their conversation and told Lamar and his cousin they needed to leave. Kevin had to understand that. So I figured we could just be grown-ups and get through the evening, which wouldn't last much longer anyway. They'd nearly finished dinner. The next day, I'd sit Lamar down and make it clear to him that my relationship with Kevin came first, and if he couldn't respect that, we couldn't be friends anymore.

As we approached the table, leave it to Nisey to start some shit with her "look at what the cat drug in" comment. In all fairness, she didn't know the truth. If I had held my silence about Kevin and Cruella's meeting until I found out the truth, she wouldn't have jumped off the Kevin Hate Fest. Note to self: don't speculate on infidelity issues with your family and friends until you're certain of the facts.

Oh, but when Lamar got started, the whole night went downhill . . . *fast*.

"Hey, Kevin. Imagine meeting you twice in one day. Where's Kristen?"

Oh, hell no! Here we go!

I couldn't believe Lamar even took the conversation

there, and we hadn't even been seated for two minutes. Talk about stuck between a rock and hard place. Lamar's behavior was partly my fault because I'd given him hope that we might have a future. I couldn't exactly cuss him out for believing me. I hoped beyond hope that my parents' presence would encourage Kevin to be the bigger man and let the comment go. Just as I would expect from him, he stepped up to the plate and took a great swing.

"Kristen went home to cook dinner for her husband," he lied. Kristen's husband was busy cooking hot, butt-naked sex with her friend at the Gaylord. "She and I met at the Gaylord on a business matter."

My nervous stomach settled a bit after that comment. Kevin would've been well within his rights to cuss Lamar out after that comment; but he took the high road and tried to avoid confrontation. My respect for him grew tenfold. Unfortunately, Lamar parked his ass squarely on the low road and had no intention of budging whatsoever.

"Ohhh. So, how old is your son now? He looks like he's a big boy," Lamar said casually as he shoveled a forkful of fettuccine in his mouth.

Did he say what I thought he said? I went into shock. What the hell was Lamar trying to prove? Didn't he realize that by trying to call out Kevin, he was embarrassing me too?

"Kevin, you didn't mention you had a son," my father said.

Kevin shrugged, nodded, and stammered just long enough for Lamar to lob another cheap shot.

"Oh, I'm sorry. I thought everybody knew Kristen is your baby's mama. Go figure!"

I wanted to say, *Go to hell!* But I couldn't speak.

No—he—didn't! I sat in utter disbelief as Lamar showed his ass. Even if he believed Kevin had been cheating with Kristen as I did, this dinner with my parents and with his own cousin present was not the time or place to dredge up anybody's dirt. It struck me; Lamar didn't speak up at the most inopportune moment to *help me.* He wanted to *hurt Kevin* . . . and he hurt me in the process. He didn't seem to care, nor did he appear to have any intention of stopping. Just as I finished processing what he'd said in my mind, Kevin took a detour on the low road and I realized things would only get worse . . . much worse.

"Javon's doing just fine. How are all of your kids? You still got eight or do you have some more on the way. We know how you like to juggle the ladies. I don't know how you keep everybody straight."

My eyes widened and my face felt flush. I thought, *Lord, please let me pass out. Let me fall out on this floor.* The whole "don't throw stones if you live in a glass house" saying seemed quite appropriate to the occasion. Lamar's the one who took it there. What was Kevin supposed to do? I sure wasn't mad at him. I just wanted the night to end.

The tension grew so uncomfortable that my father tried to make a run for it. I'd have been right behind him. That's when Lamar dealt the final blow that would drive Kevin out of the fight . . . and out of my life.

"Well, at least Charisse didn't find out about *my kids* two days ago. Maybe if you had some honesty about your shit, your fiancée wouldn't need to leave your bed early in the morning trying to find a *real* man."

My father glanced at Kevin and said, "A little bump in the road?"

Kevin shrugged.

I didn't know what my father's comment meant, nor did I care, because by the time I finally resolved to call Lamar outside and bomb his ass out, Kevin said, "You know what? Fuck you, Lamar, and the hole you slithered out of. I don't have to take this shit!'

Kevin's display sent me into another wave of shock. I'd never seen him lose his cool to this extent, and I didn't know what to think. Everything happened so fast, insults slinging back and forth, I was much slower on the uptake than usual and didn't react as fast as I should've. But I knew Kevin had lost his monkey mind when he said, "Who are you gonna marry? *Him* or *me*?"

No the hell he didn't go there with me! I thought, *If you have to ask, maybe I need to rethink my selection.* I hadn't handled the situation in the best manner, but lest we forget, none of the drama would've happened if he hadn't lied in the first place. Before I could crank my neck and roll my eyes, Kevin yelled, "The wedding's off!" and he stormed out the door.

Dad said, "Charisse, maybe you should go after him. You need to learn to appreciate a good man when he's staring you in the face. Stop giving him such a hard time."

Oh no he *didn't*. My fiancé had stormed out on me, and here he comes, Daddy dearest, trying to inject some wisdom. He sure picked the wrong time to start playing his role. I'd contained my contempt toward him during his entire visit, but my anger began to spill with this remark. He had some nerve trying to advise me on knowing a good man, as if he'd ever served as any kind of example for me. *Please*.

"Is that right?" I said, twisting my neck with *all kinds* of attitude. "And tell me, *Father*, how would I know a good man? From *you*?"

Who said that?

He shot me a heated glare.

"I mean, since you want to go there, let's go there. Who was my example of a good man when I was growing up? Whose job was that, huh? Who was there to teach me the right way a man is supposed to treat me and love me? Who let me know that at least *one* man in this world valued me if no other man did? Sure wasn't you!" I snapped. "And you have the nerve to say I don't know a good man when I see one? Tell me something *I don't* know! If it wasn't for James steppin' up to do your job, I never would've either."

My father's gaze drifted around the room, anywhere and everywhere except on me. He grabbed his napkin from the table, dabbed his eyes, got up, and walked away.

I scanned all the dumbfounded faces until my

eyes locked on Lamar with this Steve Urkel "Did I do thaaaat?" look on his face, knowing exactly what the hell he'd done.

I shook my head. "How could you do that, Lamar? How could you?"

29
Charisse

A pregnant silence hovered around the table. Trey craned his neck, and when he spotted our sorry waitress, he waved her over. "Check please!"

I'd buried my face in my hands when a text came through on my cell phone.

Valet ticket for your car at Gaylord front desk.

"Shit!" I said.

"What?" Trey asked.

"Kevin took his truck, left my car. I'm not going to have enough room for everyone."

My laser glare burned a hole straight through Lamar.

"Uhhh, listen everybody," Lamar said. "I apologize for my behavior tonight and ruining your evening. I don't know what came over me. Please let me take care of the check and help you all get home. I've got room for three in my car."

Although my first inclination was to throw gasoline on him and set him on fire, I accepted his offer so

I could get everyone home. It would also give me a prime opportunity to initiate a much needed heart-to-heart with Lamar—once and for all.

Everyone herded into the house appearing pretty wiped out from sightseeing all day and the night's drama. Everyone turned in except Trey and Nisey, who got cozy as the flames danced in the deck fireplace. Wasn't hard to see they didn't need the fire to keep warm. The heat from their attraction was undeniable. Although I'd become hopeful they could find love in each other that they hadn't shared in their past relationships, both of them were on the rebound. I could only hope that neither would end up hurting the other.

Tracy and Lamar watched television downstairs while I slipped into some comfortable pajamas, not that I couldn't have kept my outfit on. I just needed a minute to collect my thoughts and pull my speech together.

No question, meeting Lamar again had been a blessing. He'd supported me during one of the worst relationships in my life—Dwayne. Lamar helped keep me grounded and reminded me that I could trust my own intuition when I'd been struggling to decide whether Dwayne was a good man or another bum I'd attracted. He helped me to realize that even the worst of players could have good souls and could be redeemed if they were sincerely motivated to change. He had indeed become a good man any woman would be lucky to have. As that thought crossed my mind, I heard a knock at my door.

"Come in."

Mommy poked her head inside. "Hey, baby. You got a minute?"

"Sure. What's up?"

"That was some scene at the restaurant tonight, huh?"

"Yeah. *Scene* is right. Right out of the drama that is my life."

"You know, I never did like that Lamar, even when you were in school, he had *player* written all over him—and over all his ways. Reminded me so much of your father. But with the obvious exception of his performance in the restaurant, he's changed a lot and for the better . . . at least from what I can tell."

"He really has, Mom. He's always quick to say I'm part of the reason he's remained on track. He's a better man now."

"Yes, he is. And it's clear he loves you. Ray Charles could see how he feels, and he's blind *and* dead." She sat next to me on the bed and patted my knee to soothe me the way she did when I was a kid. "But something occurred to me as I watched his display tonight. Seems to me everything Kevin does is to make *you* happy. And everything Lamar does is to make *him* happy . . . and if you should find happiness in the process, then lucky you."

Whoa! Where'd this bit of wisdom come from? Those were among the most perceptive words she'd

ever spoken to me. Totally caught me off guard because what she said rang so true.

"Look at what happened. Any other man in Kevin's
position wouldn't even attempt to sit at the table with
his archenemy who's clearly in love with the woman
he plans to marry. But he put his pride aside for you.
Lamar was trying to score points with your father at
Kevin's and your expense. Seems to me you could do
a lot worse than marrying a man who wants to make
a life out of making you happy. I wouldn't let him get
away if I were you. Maybe your daddy isn't allowed to
say that to you, but I am."

She was right about Kevin. Everything he did was
out of love for me. As wrong as he was for lying to
me and concealing his and Kristen's relationship, in
my heart I realized he might've been more confident
about confessing to me if I didn't cut and run every
time I had to exercise trust in someone. So quick to
write people off, especially men.

And maybe cutting and running was the right
thing to do with *some* of the bums I'd been with. Hell,
not even saying hello would've been *the best* tactic with
most of those boneheads, but Kevin was a good man
and deserved more. Through his every act, decision,
and opportunity, he'd taught me the heart's greatest
lesson—unconditional love.

I nodded in agreement with Mom, something
new and different, and tossed in an observation of my
own. "You're right, Mommy. Absolutely right. But as
I see the situation, we could say the same thing about
James, couldn't we?"

She cut her eyes at me, knowing I'd only spoken the truth, then silently walked out and closed the door behind her.

The old cut-and-run—at least I'd gotten the trait honestly.

Yeah, I had every intention of getting my man back, but I needed to square things away with the one downstairs first. I schlepped down the hall not knowing how Lamar would react to what I had to say. I'd brought this problem on myself, telling him he had a chance at a future when I realized in my heart I only wanted Kevin. The time to pay the piper for my mistake had arrived.

I ambled into the family room like a death-row inmate on her way to the electric chair and said, "Lamar, can I speak to you out front for a few minutes?"

He nodded and followed me out the front door, into the crisp but refreshing air.

"Listen—" I said before he cut me off.

"Charisse, before you start, I've something I need to say."

"Okay, go ahead."

"I'm sorry about tonight. The way I behaved was wrong. When I saw Kevin and Kristen together in the Gaylord, I immediately believed the worst, which gave me more hope than I'd ever had before that you and I might have a future. When you two walked into the restaurant and seemed like you'd made up, I became . . . almost . . . desperate. Like I had to do something . . . anything to give myself a chance. What I did was selfish. I didn't think about your feelings and I'm sorry."

That's the Lamar I'd come to know. He's a good man, no doubt. He just wasn't the best man for me.

"I appreciate your apology. The thing is, even though I can't deny that I love you and your friendship has been among the most important of my life, I am deeply and completely head over heels in love with Kevin, and I want to spend the rest of my life with him. For better or for worse. If he'll still marry me."

"Oh . . . I wouldn't worry about Kevin. From what I saw in him at our first meeting, he'll never let you go. Besides, if for no other reason, he'd marry you just to keep you away from me. I'm your insurance policy."

I laughed. "Things between us are gonna have to change, Lamar . . . a lot."

"I know, Charisse." He held his arms out for a hug.

He wrapped his arms around me as I leaned my face against his chest and said, "Wow. So, this is what it feels like."

I looked into my favorite hazel twins; they'd gotten a little misty. "What?"

He locked his eyes on mine and said, "Heartache."

30
Kevin

I slipped into the shower hoping the hot water would soothe the ache in my spirit. No matter how bad I felt at that moment, I realized Lamar would've always been the third person in our marriage if I'd let things continue as they had for the past couple of years. He would've always remained a source of tension between Charisse and me, and marriage is hard enough without adding to the difficulties before you even say "I do." Frankly, Lamar was an issue for Charisse to deal with, and she hadn't wanted to do so up until now. Since she hadn't called me to apologize, I surmised she wasn't ready to put Lamar in his place. Sure, I could've made demands, but if she didn't set the boundaries of their relationship by her own will, she would've accused me of trying to control her.

Although I regretted the scene that'd transpired, one truth seemed certain—calling off the wedding would either save our marriage over the long term, or ensure I didn't marry someone whose loyalties rested with another man.

After toweling off and throwing on a pair of sweatpants, I called my mother and told her everything that had happened, which, in a rare event, left her at a loss for words.

"Baby, you okay? I know your heart is aching, but sounds to me like you did the right thing in the end. I mean, you ain't totally blameless here, don't get me wrong. You shoulda told Charisse the truth about that high-yellow heifer from the beginning. But when you get married, you agree to forsake all others . . . and Lamar is one of them 'all others.' You want me to call and talk to her?"

"No, this is something she needs to figure out on her own or anything I say will seem to her as if I'm pressing."

"Yeah, I guess you're right. She's strong-willed for sure, but there ain't no doubt in my mind she loves you. Just give her some time. One thing you ain't got a lot of time to deal with is this Kristen business. I hate to say it, but with everything you know now, are you sure he's even your son?"

"Yeah, I've thought about the possibility quite a bit. I do believe he's mine because he looks just like me, and he doesn't resemble either of them. If I didn't have Javon, I wouldn't deal with her crazy ass again."

"I know *that's* right."

"But I have to make sure my rights are protected."

"How are you gonna do that?"

"Don't worry. I have a plan," I said, sounding a little more confident than I probably was. "Anyway, I don't want to talk about this anymore. It's making my head hurt. I was wondering . . . if I buy you a ticket, will you come and stay with me for a few days? I don't want to be here by myself right now; the house is too quiet. Besides, I'd like you to meet your grandbaby."

"Honey, now you know you ain't said nothing but a word. When you want me to come?"

"I'm going online to see if I can book a flight for you for tomorrow morning."

"You know me—the earlier the better. I don't like to fly when I can't see outside."

"All right, Ma. I'll get you on the first flight out if I can. I'll call you later with your itinerary."

"Okay, baby. You try to get some sleep and don't worry yourself to death over this mess. The Lord's surely gonna make a way. Everything's gonna work out according to His will, and you can't ask for better than that!"

I stumbled out of bed. My heart ached as much as my head. I barely made out the numbers on my digital clock. I rolled over and stared at the emptiness on the other side of the bed. Not since the first few weeks in the very beginning of our relationship, during the brief time when Charisse was still trying to prove she was wholesome-wife material, had we spent a night apart.

Sure, the alarm clock reminded me that I was awake, but seeing Charisse every morning reminded me that I was alive and that I had a witness to my life, someone who cared about where I was going.

This new sense of loneliness overwhelmed me.

What if she'd taken me seriously? What if she never came back to me? What if she realized she didn't need me in her life after all and married Lamar?

What have I done?

While my regret seemed to expand by the minute, I couldn't let my angst paralyze me. I had work to do.

As much as I hated to talk to *her*, I had to call Kristen. I'd use my mother's visit as cover for the business I needed to take care of with Javon. Kristen's game playing had already cost me enough. All this madness would end sooner rather than later. She was an FBI agent so she wasn't a fool. I'd need to be smart about playing my hand. If I showed my cards too soon, Kristen would figure out my plan, rendering the entire situation game over . . . and maybe hindering my ability to be a good father to Javon in the future.

After I spoke to her, I'd call Derek to get some help to solve the Greg part of the Kristen issue once and for all. I took a deep breath and dialed her number.

"Kevin," she said, sounding uncharacteristically happy.

"Hey, Kristen. Look, I wanted to tell you that I got everything we needed last night, so we won't have to worry about court. I don't think Greg's case would even get that far. I have every confidence everything will work out as it should."

"I'm so glad to hear that, Kevin. I can't even tell you how much I appreciate what you did. Your help means the world to me. Hope I didn't get you in trouble with Charisse."

"As a matter fact . . . the wedding's off." I hoped the

news would bolster her confidence so she wouldn't suspect me of anything nefarious. "I think she might be in love with Lamar, and I couldn't lie to myself anymore. Our relationship probably wouldn't work anyway. She and I come from different worlds. She doesn't understand this business."

"Wow, I'm surprised you'd say that, but I feel the same way about Greg, especially now. I can't believe he's trying to do this to me. Looks like we'll have each other to lean on."

My stomach soured as the words oozed out of her mouth like molten lava. "Yes, I'll always be here for you, Kristen. Always," I lied. I could almost hear her smile through the phone. "Listen, my mother's coming into town a little later today. I was hoping I could get Javon for a little while so she can meet him."

She got quiet. "Oh. You don't want me to be there, do you? I don't think your mother likes me very much, but you're free to take him for a couple of hours."

"Nonsense. My mother thought you were *something else*, but I appreciate you giving us a little time to ourselves so we can all bond."

"You're welcome. I'm glad you're back in my life."

"Maybe when she and I are done, we can all meet for dinner," I suggested, knowing she'd refuse because she didn't want to come within two feet of my mother.

"Noooo. I appreciate the offer but that's okay. It'll be your Mom's first night in town. You two enjoy each other."

"All right then. I'll be on the road quite a bit so just send me a text when we can pick him up."

My first order of business had been accomplished—getting Javon alone with me for a couple of hours. For my next task, I'd need to find a way to speak to Greg. Nobody would know the truth about what was going on in their house (and Kristen's mind) the way he would. I couldn't call him up and ask to meet because Kristen would immediately suspect I was up to no good, at least as far as her interests were concerned. Fortunately, Greg and Derek were frat brothers, a status that bonded complete strangers in a way I never quite understood, so I'd need to solicit Derek's assistance to move my plan forward. I also needed to swing by the Walgreens. Had to thank God for the extent to which science has advanced over the past few years. Who would've imagined a day I could walk into my local drugstore and pick up a kit that would allow me to prove whether Javon was my son in three to five days and for less than $50?

God bless America.

As I made a half-assed effort to straighten up the house for my mother's stay, my thoughts drifted to Charisse. I'd held out some deep-seated hope to hear from her. I'd have done a somersault if she had sent a simple text saying *I love you and I miss you.* I didn't need any long, drawn-out apologies—and certainly didn't require a thousand of them the way she had expected from me. One sincere apology would do. One simple acknowledgment that she hadn't respected my misgivings about Lamar and that she'd allowed him to interfere in our relationship would be enough to reaffirm why she was the woman with whom I had wanted to spend the rest of my life. I'd be as ready to marry her as I had been just a few days ago, before all the drama started.

Still, even though I knew I'd done the right thing in putting my foot down on the Lamar issue, I felt uneasy about abandoning Charisse with all the drama going on at the house. She still hadn't had the opportunity to talk things out with her father, and who knew how she'd react when *that* deed was done. With the pain and hurt she'd stored up for so many years, I expected an emotional eruption of volcanic proportions and wanted to support her . . . but she needed to get over her stubbornness and call me first. Couldn't be the first to break or she'd never respect my feelings. I understood Charisse well enough to know only a man as strong-willed as she was could earn and keep her respect. She'd find out sooner rather than later that I was that man.

With the dusting and vacuuming finished, I was getting ready to change the sheets on the guest bed when my cell phone rang. Derek must've been reading my mind.

"So, how'd things go last night? Did you get what you needed on Kristen's husband?"

"Oh, yeah, I got a lot more information on Kristen and Greg than I'd bargained for."

I broke down the whole story to Derek. Told him how I'd run into Lamar and got a few pictures of Greg's so-called cheating. And how Charisse rolled up on me.

"So, wait a minute. Charisse saw this woman with Kristen before?"

"Yeah. Apparently, after Charisse caught us talking in the park, Kristen showed up at her place with this woman she described as her 'friend.' Probably brought her in case Nisey was with Charisse. If Nisey *had* been there, she'd have gone off."

"So, Kristen's trying to set Greg up?"

"Certainly seems that way."

31

Kevin

"Why would Kristen want to set Greg up?" Derek asked. "That doesn't make any sense. He's good people."

"From what I can tell, she thinks she's going to leave Greg because she's under some serious delusion she has a chance with me. She probably needed to get him caught up to ensure she gets full custody of the kids. According to Kristen, Greg is a good father. He'd probably fight for joint custody under any other circumstance."

"I guess. Seems to me she could just ask him for a divorce. He ain't a crazy brotha by any means."

"Don't forget, Derek, we're in the state of Maryland. She'd have a twelve-month waiting period before she can even file for divorce. If you can prove infidelity or abandonment, a divorce can be done in three months. I know that personally because that's how I got my divorce."

"What makes you think this is all about you?"

"Check this. She had the nerve to tell Charisse

she's in love with me. Not only that, she said *I* was in love with *her*. Told Charisse that because we're FBI agents, she and I share a life Charisse couldn't understand."

"Whaaaat? Man, that bitch is cuh-ray-zee! You better hope she doesn't go *Fatal Attraction* on your ass."

"Seems to me like she already has. I've let her know from day one that I wanted to be with Charisse, and she's been hostile toward Charisse ever since."

"Well, I'll tell you one thing. I can't let my frat brother go out like that. I gotta tell him something so he can be prepared."

"I was hoping you'd say that. I need you to get him out to shoot some pool or something so I can meet up with y'all and talk to him, find out where his head is. Dude is steppin' out on Kristen, so they obviously aren't happy. Once we find out what's up, I'll figure out what to do from there. I need to be careful though because if he runs back and tells her anything, I'm screwed."

"I hear you, dawg. How soon do I need to make this happen?"

"Yesterday. I'm going to take care of this paternity test today. I'm picking up Javon so I can get the sample. I need to have proof that he's mine before I go any further . . . and time is running short. Kristen's gonna be asking for those pictures soon. She claims Greg is going to serve her with divorce papers next week. But, if my instincts are on point, *she'll* probably be the one serving *him.* So we need to get him on board or he's gonna lose his kids . . . and maybe more."

"Cool. I'll hit you up when I make the call."

My, how time flies when you're plotting and scheming.

I stopped by Walgreens to pick up the test kit and ran a few other errands, such as grocery shopping. One thing about my mother: as long as groceries were in the house, she'd cook them. Good food was one of the perks of having an old-school Southern mother. I felt sorry for men with city-slicker mothers who didn't cook. Derek practically moved into my place anytime Ma came to town, and she didn't mind one bit. The only thing she loved more than hearing compliments on her cooking was watching someone scarf it down and fall asleep shortly thereafter. If they didn't fall slam asleep, she took it as a challenge that she had more cooking to do . . . or they had more eating to do. More often than not, the latter.

When I pulled into the arrival area at the airport, Ma was easy to spot. She was the only woman wearing a turtleneck sweater on a beautiful seventy-five-degree fall day. Ma dressed by the calendar, not the temperature. After September first, all of her spring and summer clothes got packed up, and all of her fall and winter clothes came out. She'd been anal for as long as I could remember.

I turned off the ignition, stepped out of the car, and waved my hand until she noticed me. Seeing her face always lifted my spirits. Yeah, I was a mama's boy for sure, which had always been a bone of contention between my father and me. While my dad loved his family, he didn't show a lot of affection; an occasional pat on the back or head was about all he could muster most days. I learned to express love from my mother. I vowed that when I got married, my wife and children would never go a day without hearing from my mouth *and* seeing through my actions how much I loved them. My boys used to call me soft. I'd always respond, "I ain't soft. I love hard." This comeback was usually sufficient to shut all the noise down.

Ma walked to me with her arms wide-open and wrapped me so tight, I almost lost my breath. "Look at my baby! I'm so happy to see you." She stepped back to conduct her usual inspection. "Well, you look good . . . but you look hungry. I love Charisse and all, but she don't feed you enough."

"Ma, don't say that. She feeds me as well as I need to be fed." *And gives me the kind of cookin' I can't get from you.*

"Mmm-hmm, whatever you say."

I opened her door and helped her inside before tossing the bags in the back and getting on the road.

"So, when am I gonna visit with my grandbaby?"

"Patience, Ma. We'll pick him up in a little bit. Let me get you home and settled in first."

She turned on the radio to her favorite gospel station, 104.1, rested back against her seat, and rapped her fingers against her knee. Whenever I glanced at her hands, once smooth and soft and now showing their age, I was always saddened, reminded that she wouldn't always be around. I turned my eyes back to the road.

"So, you heard from Charisse? I imagine y'all must be missin' each other pretty good now. Been practically attached at the hip since you got together."

"No, Ma. Haven't heard a word. Not even a text. You know how stubborn she is, so she might take a while to come around."

"She will. I don't doubt it one bit. Out of all your girlfriends and even that silly wench you married, she's the one that's got the most sense. I believe she got enough not to let you go, so give her some time. Everything's gon' be all right. Thank you, Jesus!" she said, raising her hands in a soulful praise.

No sooner had her hands gone in the air than my phone rang. Charisse's phone number flashed across the screen. My heart leapt. I smiled wide and took a deep breath, trying to play it cool for a few minutes before confessing how much I loved and missed her.

"Hello."

"Kevin, this is Nisey. I've only got a minute. I'm in an ambulance with Charisse. You need to get to Holy Cross Hospital as fast as you can. There's been an accident."

"What! What happened?"

"I gotta go. We're pulling up to the entrance. Just get here as fast as you can."

"I'm on my way!"

32
Charisse

I forgot to turn off my cell phone ringer before bed, which would explain why the damn thing woke me up at 7:00 a.m. the next morning. I didn't even bother looking at the caller ID. Only someone who was unaware of my anti-morning-person nature would dare call me at this hour. And if I didn't answer, they'd only call back.

"Whoever this is, it better be important."

"Rissey . . . I mean Charisse. This is David."

I racked my brain but couldn't think of anyone named David who would need to break my sound sleep before the roosters even woke up.

"David who?"

"David . . . Denise's David."

"Ohhh. Why on earth are you calling me at this time of morning?"

"I'm sorry, but I've been trying to find Denise for days. I was hoping she'd be with you?"

I rolled over on my side and laid the phone on my ear so I could pull the blanket over my shoulder. "Did you try calling her?" I asked, knowing damn well he had.

"Yeah."

"What did she say?"

"She said she didn't want me to know where she was . . . except she used a few four-letter words."

"And so you called me of all people to find out where she is? No offense, but I'm her best friend, not yours."

"What else can I do, Charisse? I made a mistake, the biggest mistake of my life, when I walked out on her. I want to make things right, but I need your help to make her listen to reason."

"Listen, David. For what it's worth, I've always thought you were a good guy, but you made Nisey believe you were gonna stay with her no matter what happened with the test results, and she allowed herself to build a life with you based on your promise. Then, when the chips fell, you didn't even pause before you ran out on her. You betrayed her trust, and I've never seen her so hurt about any man. She downed half a bottle of Grey Goose at seven in the morning."

"For real?"

"Yeah, for real. So, what you're asking me to do is tell my best friend, my sister, to take a chance and trust you again. To do something I probably wouldn't do my-self—give you another chance to hurt her again."

"I'm not asking you to make her trust me. I'm only asking you to convince her to meet with me. I'm serious about making things right. I even went to talk to Richard, had a man-to-man talk with him last night. I told him he was the father, but I wanted us to work together for Jamal's sake. We aren't exactly best friends, but we're definitely willing to try and behave like adults."

"Wow, I'm surprised . . . in a good way. I can't believe you and Richard worked out your differences." I paused and let out a long breath. "Okay. Okay. I'll talk to her. I'm not making any promises but I'll try."

"Thanks, Charisse. I really appreciate it."

Well, call me surprised. David came through after all. Kind of shocking given the way he left. I'd never seen Nisey fall apart over a man. Ever. She's the kinda woman who would break up with a man one day and interview multiple suitable replacements the next. She never let a man spend an entire night at her house, let alone move himself in, for all intents and purposes. I mean, David still had his own place, but little by little his things started to appear at Nisey's place to the point where he probably had more stuff at her place than at his own.

And trust me, Nisey understood exactly what the hell he was doing. She wouldn't let a man sneak and move in if she didn't want him to live with her. I've seen enough men try and fail miserably. She'd run around the house triple-checking to make sure no foreign items had been left, and if she didn't have any interest in seeing the fool again, she'd box his crap up and UPS it to his residence the next day to ensure he had no reason to come back. Men were good for that shit, leaving some stray item behind so they could call you when they wanted to kiss and make up.

Once Nisey was through, she was through. I sure wished I came equipped with her emotional "off" switch.

David had no idea how lucky he'd been or how deeply she'd fallen for him, but apparently he was about to find out just how lucky he was because, given the way she'd been looking at Trey, he might've tried to come back too late. Men were masters at realizing what a good woman they had when the revelation came too late to matter.

I washed my face, brushed my teeth, and threw on a robe to go get breakfast and, more important, the coffee started. I grabbed my phone and flipped through my caller ID hoping to see a call or text from Kevin, but he hadn't sent a single word. I glanced at the calendar on which our wedding date was circled with a big star drawn on the inside.

I missed him something terrible and he hadn't even been gone twenty-four hours. I wanted to text him *I love you and miss you*, but I was too afraid he wouldn't respond. Frankly, I wasn't in the mood for rejection.

I grabbed the glass pot from my stainless-steel Cuisinart coffeemaker and started to fill it with water. Then I heard the front door open and close. I put the pot on the counter, brushed my hands down the front of my robe, and walked toward the front door.

Surprise. Surprise.

"Nisey? Trey? Where in the world are you two coming from?"

Each shot me a "cold busted" grin.

"We went out for a walk this morning. It's a beautiful day out," Nisey offered. Didn't she realize to whom she was talking?

"A walk, huh?" I said, scanning them both from head to toe. "So, why are you still wearing your outfits from yesterday?"

They eyeballed each other and smiled.

"Nisey, you can handle this one. I'm going up to take a shower and get a nap. See you later?"

She smiled and nodded.

Trey paced up the steps while a glowing Nisey trailed me into the kitchen. I gave her the eye before I reached up into the cabinet to grab the Starbucks-at-home coffee bag. The far-off gaze in Nisey's eyes suggested she'd already started to move on from David. She stared into the distance until I broke her trance.

"So!" I said, waiting for her to start spilling her guts. If I didn't get the 411 soon, she was gonna need 911. "Heifer, do not make me reach across this counter and yoke you. What's going on?"

She paused thoughtfully. "Rissey . . . Trey is simply amazing!"

She'd never used that term to refer to any other man. He must've put something on her ass.

"Amazing, huh? Sounds like you were out delivering your cookies."

"Nooo!" she said, chuckling. "Not yet anyway. Girl, we drove around downtown, parked near the Tidal Basin, and talked all night long until we watched the sun rise over the Potomac."

"Talked, huh? About what?"

"Everything . . . and nothing. We just laughed and joked. Shared our dreams and fears. He's so smart and funny, just . . . *amazing*!" she said matter-of-factly.

There was that word again. "Wow, so you guys really hit it off?"

"I'd say that's an understatement."

Uh-oh. I smiled until I thought about poor David.

She immediately noticed the change in my demeanor. "What is it? You don't approve?"

"Girl, please. I'm couldn't be happier for you. It's just that . . . well . . ."

"What is it?"

"David called me this morning looking for you. He sounded genuinely sorry that he walked out on you and he wants you back. He even had a long talk with Richard."

A panicked expression hijacked her face. "Wait a minute! David spoke to Richard? About what?!"

"Well, David told Richard Jamal is Richard's son and asked if they could try to get along and act like adults for both Jamal's and your sakes."

Her mouth cracked wide-open. "He didn't!" she yelled.

At this point, I didn't have any idea what the hell was going on with her. Why was she acting as if I'd told her stilettos had been outlawed or something?

"Yeeeaaaah." I hesitated. "He did."

"Son of a *bitch*!"

So eloquent. "Nisey, we do have adult company in the house. What's wrong with you?"

"Please tell me this isn't true. Please tell me David didn't talk to Richard."

"What the hell is going on?" I said in a way that let

her know she'd better come up with an answer quickly or I was gonna kick her ass.

She bolted up from her seat, stomped out of the kitchen, and up the steps. A few seconds later, she arrived with a sheet of paper and thrust it in my face. Then she sat at the breakfast bar and buried her head in her hands.

"What's this?"

"Just read it," she said without looking up.

I scanned the page; it contained the paternity test result. I looked at the paper, then up at Nisey, then back at the paper again.

"Nisey . . . ummm . . . this says that *David* is the father."

"Yep. Sure does."

33

Charisse

Umm . . . okay. Call me crazy, but I thought we wanted David to be the father. My head was spinning. "Why in the hell would you tell David that Richard was the father?"

Her face was painted with a pained expression. "I needed to know whether he was with me for Jamal or because he truly loved me. I honestly didn't know if he'd leave me, but I hoped with all my heart he wouldn't. I'd planned to tell him the truth as soon as he said the results didn't matter. When he started packing, I got too hurt, too angry, to tell him the truth. If he was gonna walk, I wanted him to keep on walking."

"Sweet Jesus Almighty, Nisey. While I'm glad we can get rid of crazy-ass Richard, David is the father and still very much in love with you."

"If he was so in love, he never would've walked out on me the way he did. I mean he could've taken a drive, gone to play golf, or any one of a hundred different things to take a time-out and get his thoughts together, but he packed up his shit and rolled out. Now he wants to waltz back into my life like nothing happened? Well, I'm sorry for him because he came back too late."

"Too late? What do you mean?"

"I mean . . . I have feelings for Trey now, and I can't make those feelings disappear because David's decided he now wants to make the choice he should've made days ago."

"Well, Nisey. You know I, of all people, understand what you're saying. If I were you, I'd make damn certain you take your time and make the right decision, because at least one good man stands to get hurt."

After our conversation, Nisey disappeared into her bedroom, probably to think about what she was gonna do about the David situation. She'd started falling for Trey and she wasn't alone. I personally didn't think she could go wrong with either choice, but the heart wants what the damn thing wants.

I hadn't seen Mom or Dad all morning, and it was nearing 9:00 a.m. Figured they both needed to recover from all the walking we'd done while sightseeing the day before.

I stuck my foot in some cheese eggs, grits, bacon, and homemade biscuits and stored them in food savers so folks could eat when they got ready. Then I settled into my chaise with my second cup of coffee and turned on the television to some nondescript program. The chatter served as white noise because my thoughts were elsewhere. With no Kevin to drive me crazy and no wedding to plan, I had no idea what to do with myself. I'd busted my ass all year so that I could take off from work the month of the wedding. I didn't have any work to do, except to sit around the house and be depressed.

What I needed to do was take my ass over to Kevin's place, do not pass go, do not collect $200, tell him that I'd set Lamar straight, and ask him if he'd still have me for his wife. To hell with pride. Pride couldn't keep me warm at night. Pride couldn't rub my feet, take out the trash, or make a perfect burnt hot dog. Most important, pride couldn't love me as I'd never been loved before. What good would my pride be if I couldn't spend the rest of my life with the man I loved?

So, I swallowed my pride—okay, more like choked it down—and headed upstairs to get dressed, when my phone rang. James's cell phone number flashed across the screen. Lord, if he'd seen Mama in action the past few days, he'd be ready to kill her, my dad—or both. I took in a deep breath and answered.

"James!" I said enthusiastically . . . maybe too much so. I was happy to talk to him though. I missed him even if Mom didn't.

"Hey, baby girl! How are you doing?"

"I'm hanging in there . . . by a thin thread. A lot has happened."

"So I've heard. Your aunt Jackie filled me in on some of what's been going on. How are you holding up?"

"You know me, James. Life has to go the full twelve rounds to get me down. I'll get through it," I said, careful to avoid telling him Kevin had called off the wedding.

"How's your mother doing? I imagine she told you about what happened."

Of course I'd need to respond to this question with a bold-faced lie. I couldn't exactly tell James Mom had been flirting with my father ad nauseam and dangling her boobs and legs in his face since he got off the plane.

"Yes, she told me about the whole sordid affair. Don't worry, James. I know you only wanted her to miss her good thing," I said before I started my big fat lie. "She's really having a hard time and misses you. I've never seen her act . . . quite this way before. Ever."

Well, the last part was definitely true. I hadn't seen her behave like a flirty hot mama before.

"Really?" James sounded relieved and hopeful. I heard a bunch of movement on his end in the background and then a car door slammed. "I'm very happy you told me this news. I guess I made the right decision."

"What decision?"

My doorbell rang and my first thought was that Kevin had come home to me.

"James, can you hold on for a second? Someone's at the door."

"Sure, I'll wait."

I jogged to the front door, so excited to see Kevin's face again, I planned to jump into his arms and tell him how much I loved him. But when I opened the door, Kevin wasn't there.

"Surprise!"

"James?"

Awww hell! Didn't people know how to call anymore? What the hell was I gonna do now that James would be added to the dramatic mix of family already staying at my house?

"Yep, it's me!" He crossed over the threshold and gave me the warmest hug.

"Oh my God! What are you doing here?" I asked in a half "Happy to see you," half "What the hell are you doing here?" tone.

"I had to see your mama. I missed her so much, and I'm sorry about what happened. I woke up at three a.m. and started driving until I got here. Wasn't thinkin' straight. I half thought about going back home until you said she missed me too."

Damn. Damn. Damn.

That's what the hell I get for lying. I'd made my bed. Nothing to do but lie in it.

"Oh, well. I'm so glad you . . . came," I said half-heartedly. "Come on in!"

He walked inside and scanned the house with a prideful smile. He hadn't seen the place since he'd first helped me move in. Back then, the walls were bare and the house still echoed when people spoke. I hadn't had a chance to do much decorating. Over the past couple of years, my house had become a home.

"Wow. I love what you've done with the place. It's beautiful," he said as we worked our way to the family room. "So, where's your mama?"

"Uhhhh . . . I think she's upstairs in the guest

bedroom. I haven't seen her this morning. We all went sightseeing yesterday and everyone was pretty wiped out. Lemme go up and check on her."

"No, that's okay, I want to surprise her."

I wasn't sure if that was a good idea. God knew what she'd be wearing if the previous days had taught me anything. Didn't want James to think he'd been in love with an undercover hoochie mama all these years. Since I'd banished my father to the basement, I wasn't really concerned about James seeing them together. Once Mom saw James, all the flirting shit would come to an abrupt halt, my only consolation.

James reached the top of the stairs. I pointed to Mom's door. He gripped the knob, opened the door, and said, "Surprise!"

Oh, we all got a surprise. The surprise of our lives.

Mama and my father were sitting on the bed wrapped in each other's arms. Thank God they still had their clothes on. Mom got the deer-in-the-head-lights look in her eyes when she saw James's stunned face. They both snatched their hands behind them and backed apart.

"Ella? What the hell's going on here!" James said, breathing heavily. I put my hand on his shoulder, knowing he must be devastated.

"Mom? Dad?" I asked, waiting for some kind of explanation.

"James?" Dad said.

Hold up? How does Dad know James?

"Baby, this is not what you think," Mom said to James, her eyes filled with genuine despair.

James vigorously shook his head no and turned to run back down the stairs. He'd had hip-replacement surgery so he couldn't go too fast. Mama jumped up and ran after him. He got about two steps down, then lost his footing and tumbled helplessly toward the bottom. Almost the entire flight. His head bounced hard against several risers before he landed with a thud at the base. A gash on his temple started to bleed and he lay motionless.

I stood paralyzed. Couldn't move. I heard a voice say, "Call 911! Now!"

Another voice said, "See if he's still breathing?"

Another voice said, "I don't feel a pulse. I've got to do CPR. Tell the ambulance to hurry!"

Someone wailed, "James! Oh my God, James! I love you. Please don't die. Please don't die!"

My knees buckled under me and I started to drown in darkness. Everything went black. An arm wrapped around my waist.

And then . . .

Nothing.

34
Kevin

"What's wrong, baby?" Ma asked.

"That was Nisey. Charisse is on her way to the hospital . . . in an ambulance."

"Oh my Lord! What in heaven's name happened?"

"She didn't say. Just said there's been an accident."

My mind raced as fast as my pulse.

Was she in a car accident?

What if she's dying?

Did she get shot?

I didn't know. From then forward, Nisey would be the absolute last person I spoke to in an emergency. She gave me enough information to worry myself sick and not enough to be useful.

I zigzagged through traffic on the beltway. Thankfully, most people were at work already. I jumped off the exit and cautiously ran several lights, pausing to make sure traffic was clear before proceeding. If I got pulled over, I'd show my credentials and explain the situation. They'd leave me alone.

Once we finally arrived, Ma and I hurried into the

emergency room area and noticed Trey pacing back and forth in the waiting room.

"Trey, where is she?" I asked, forgetting to introduce my mother.

"She's back with the doctors. She conscious now."

Conscious? That meant she was *unconscious* at some point. *What is up with these people?* Trey would be another person I'd avoid in emergency situations.

"What happened!"

"Apparently, she went into shock. The EMTs said that's common when people go through an emotional trauma."

I began to wonder if I'd need to pay someone to tell me the whole story at once. The bits-and-pieces shit was killing me.

"Emotional trauma? What would send her into shock?"

"Someone named James, who I heard is like a father to her, fell down the stairs at her place. He was unconscious and his head was bleeding. She witnessed the whole accident."

"Oh, no! Where is he?"

"He's being treated in the trauma unit. They're supposed to give us an update right here shortly."

"Okay," I said, looking at my mother. "I'm so sorry, Trey. This is my mother. Everyone calls her Mother Douglass. Ma, this is Charisse's brother I told you about."

"Nice to meet you," she said with a slight head nod. "Baby . . . who is James?"

Oh, shit! I'd forgotten to tell my mother about

James and Mama Tyson with all the excitement going on. Frankly, I'd pushed the whole ugly ordeal out of my mind thinking I would tell her in another day or so, once Charisse and I made up. Now, caught between the proverbial rock and hard place, I didn't have any option except to tell her immediately before she ran into Mama Tyson, who had two important reasons to be in the hospital—her daughter and her man. So, I gathered my courage and prepared to confess. "Mom, listen. I've got to tell you something. James, the man who had the accident today, well, he's from—"

Like a doctor dashing for the ER, Nisey came flying from behind the double doors that led to the examination area. She ran straight to me, not even noticing anyone else . . . well, except for Trey, who rushed to her side. "I'm so glad you're here! You can come in the back and see Charisse now. They just want to monitor her for a little while longer before they release her. They won't allow more than two people back at a time, and Mama Tyson's already sitting with her."

"I wanna come too," Ma said.

"Oh. Who's this, Kevin?" Nisey asked.

"I'm Kevin's mother."

I looked at Nisey with a panic-stricken stare, my eyes begging her for help. Nisey's eyes said, *What the hell do you want me to do?*

Quick on her feet, Nisey said, "Well, Mrs. Douglass, maybe you can give them a moment alone and I'll bring you back in a few minutes. They should probably have a minute alone to talk."

Ma glanced at me and I nodded.

"Okay, you're right. I'll wait."

Nisey led me back to Charisse's bed. About twelve beds were lined up, six against each wall. Each was separated by portable curtain dividers. I pulled back the opaque white cloth until Charisse's face came into view; her eyes were closed.

"Baby?" I said.

She opened her eyes and smiled. "Kevin," she said, tears flooding her eyes.

She didn't have to say another word. Somehow an apology didn't even seem necessary anymore. I sat on the stool next to the bed and wrapped her tightly in my arms as she sobbed.

"It's okay, baby. I'm here. I'm here."

She sobbed harder. "I-I'm so sorry Kevin. I love you so much."

After she calmed a bit, I sat back and looked into her eyes, which were heavy with worry.

"Is there any news on James? Please tell me he's okay."

"He's doing okay, baby. They've stabilized him. We're gonna be getting a report in a few minutes."

"Is he conscious?"

"I'm not sure yet. I had to check on my baby first. I'll go get his status in a minute," I said. "So, uhh, where's your mother?"

"She went to the bathroom. She'll be back in a minute."

"Well, I have some news."

"What's up?" Charisse smiled as she rubbed my hand.

"My mother's here. With me. Right now. I picked her up from the airport this morning. Nisey's with her in the waiting room."

Charisse bolted up in her bed, her eyes popped open wide. "Oh my God! Did you tell her about Mama?"

"I didn't have a chance. Everything happened so fast. By the time I thought about telling her, Nisey called me in to visit you."

"Sweet Jesus Almighty," she said, getting out of bed.

"What are you doing? You need to lie down."

"No, what I need to do is get my mother out of here until we get a chance to explain."

"Where're you gonna take her?"

"I dunno. I-I'll tell her we need to find James."

"Okay. Lemme go and keep my mother out of here. She insisted on coming in."

Just as Charisse peeped her head outside the curtain, Mama Tyson reappeared, wiping her eyes with Kleenex.

"Kevin! I'm so glad to see you," she said weakly, reaching her arms out to hug me. Then she glared at Charisse. "Where do you think *you're* going?"

"I wanted to find out how James is doing?"

"You lay down. Mother's orders! I'll go find out how James is doing. They wouldn't let me check on him earlier. Maybe they're done workin' on him now."

"Uhhh, let me go with Mama Tyson," I said. We headed toward the doors leading to the lobby. As soon as I pushed them open, Nisey and Ma were standing directly in front of us. Mama Tyson and Ma, face-to-face. Took about three seconds for them to recognize each other before their eyes narrowed and they gritted their teeth as if they wanted to fight like Mike *Tyson* and Buster *Douglass.*

I said, "Ma . . . meet Charisse's mother, Ms. Ella Tyson."

"You!" Ma snapped, folding her arms indignantly across her chest. "So this is where you ran to. I couldn't hardly recognize you without a bag of grapes in your hand."

Mama Tyson cranked her neck and said, "I couldn't hardly recognize *you* without a bag of grapes upside your head!"

Mother Douglass was about to respond to the insult when she stopped. "Wait a minute! The James that took a fall is *my* James?"

Before I could open my mouth to utter a solitary word, Mama Tyson yelled, "*Your* James! I don't think so. You must be out yo' mind!"

"Well, ain't *you* the pot callin' the kettle black," Mother Douglass said. "Out of *my* mind. They ain't even got a pill for *your* kinda crazy!"

"Yeah, and they ain't got a pill for your kinda *ugly* either!"

"I should have your ass arrested, jailbird. Kevin, arrest her!"

"Okay, Ma. That's enough."

"What!" Mama Tyson said, bobbing from side to side as if getting ready to box. "I'm right here. You want a piece of me? Come and get all you want! I got plenty fo' ya!"

Nisey finally interjected, "Okay. Okay. Let's break it up, ladies. Don't forget why we're here today, okay? Neither James nor Charisse would want you two arguing like this. Now, can't we all get along? For their sakes?"

"Yes. Please," I urged. "Listen, Ma, why don't you come in here with me so you can visit Charisse. Mama Tyson, Charisse told me she'd like to get an update on James's condition."

"Good idea, Kevin," Nisey said. "Come on, Madea. Let's go check on James."

Ma and I headed back toward Charisse's bed, and Ma stepped inside the curtain first.

"Mother Douglass. I'm so happy you're here. Come in and have a seat."

Ma grabbed Charisse's hand. "I'm glad to see you're doing okay, baby. How you feelin'?"

"I'm fine, had a sissy moment and fell out. They're gonna cut me loose shortly."

My cell phone beeped. Kristen left a message saying I could pick up the baby. I smiled, and of course my perceptive fiancée immediately noticed my change in demeanor.

"What's going on, Kevin?"

"I just got a text from Kristen. We're gonna pick up the baby so Ma can meet him."

Charisse's face cracked. "Oh."

"Don't look like that, baby. Everything's gonna be

just fine. Just trust me. I'm working things out for our family, yours and mine."

She smiled.

Mr. Tyson poked his head in just as Ma and I were getting ready to leave.

"You doin' all right, Charisse?" he asked. "You gave us quite a scare."

"I'm doin' okay, Dad," she said, looking at Ma. "This is Kevin's mother, Mrs. Sophronia Douglass."

"Pleasure to meet you, Mrs. Douglass," he said, slightly bowing his head.

She smiled as wide as the Pacific Ocean. "Well, it's a pleasure to meet you too. Please call me Sophie," she said, reaching out for his hand. She winked at Charisse. "Now I understand where you get your good looks from."

I had to roll my eyes at that; Charisse chuckled.

"Let's go, Ma."

"Well, they told me I can take you out of here," I overheard him say to Charisse. "I'm gonna take you up to see James now. There's been a change in his condition."

35
Charisse

When I woke up, I wasn't sure where the hell I was. I only knew I didn't want to be there. Sirens blared and a plastic sheath covered my mouth and nose. I saw a bunch of machines and wires, and Nisey was holding my hand.

"You're gonna be fine, Rissey. We're on our way to the hospital," I heard Nisey say.

Suddenly the memories of the events that prompted my trip in the ambulance flashed through my head. A vision of James falling down the stairs haunted me. I clinched my eyes tight to make the sight disappear, but the more I tried, the more it fought its way through. Felt as if everything happened in slow motion. If I had been a few seconds earlier, I could've grabbed his arm and made him take his time, but I got to him a few seconds late. As I watched, my heart nearly stopped from the panic. Of all the people in the world, why did this have to happen to him?

Please don't die, James, I thought. If I lost him, I'd lose my father—the one consistently good man who'd been there for me throughout my entire life. What would I do without him?

I lay there helpless. I couldn't go anywhere. Couldn't call anyone.

When they wheeled me into the emergency room, they poked, prodded, and questioned me like crazy. How do you feel? *Like shit. How's James?* Are you in pain? *Yes, from all these questions. Where's James?* How's your breathing? *Does it matter? You're still not going to stop asking me questions. Will somebody please tell me how James is doing?*

Finally, a barrage of visitors. Mom and Nisey first. Kevin showed up, to my surprise—with his mother, no less. I couldn't be happier he'd come. I prayed she and my mother would forgive and forget . . . mostly forget. If not, my family might become the newest generation of Hatfields and McCoys. And lastly, my birth father. I called him birth father as if I'd been adopted. In a way, I had. My father had essentially given up on me until I was fifteen and James had stepped into his shoes—wore the hell out of them too. He hadn't been a "figure," he was a father, in every sense of the word. Treated me as if I were his own child.

My father poked his head inside the curtain just as Kevin and Mother Douglass walked out. "You doin' all right, Charisse?" he asked. "You gave us quite a scare."

"I'm doin' okay, Dad."

After I introduced Dad to Mother Douglass, and she and Kevin left, Dad said, "Listen. I'm gonna take you up to see James now. There's been a change in his condition."

"A change?" I said, bracing myself. "He didn't . . ."

"No, he's gonna be okay. He's conscious and talking. They say he has a severe concussion, a few cuts, and a pretty bad knot on his head, but he should have a full recovery."

I raised my right hand to God. "Thank you, Lord. Thank you!"

The tension in the silence between my father and me as we walked up the hall to James's room was palpable. I tried to think of something to say and remembered he'd mentioned James's name in Mama's room. I never realized they'd met. James usually avoided family functions when my father was scheduled to show up, such as funerals, reunions, and such. He always deferred to him, respected his position as my father, even though most of the time James acted more like the father than the one whose sperm helped create me. "Dad, how do you know James? I heard you say his name when he walked in Mom's room."

"Hmph. That's a long story, Charisse. Goes way back. James is a good man though. We never held any grudges against each other because we both loved your mother. I know how special he is to you."

"Yeah. He's very special. Like a real—" I started, before I realized what I was about to say and to whom I was about to say it.

Dad shook his head and started to speak before he cut himself off. We rounded the corner in the trauma wing, and Dad pointed to a room ahead of us. "James is right there—in Room 201."

We walked inside and his bed was shielded by

makeshift curtains, so neither he, nor my mother, who was speaking at the moment we arrived, saw or heard us walk in.

"I swear to you, James. There ain't nothin' going on between us. Nothin'. I was only trying to keep him from telling Charisse what happened. I swear before Jesus, that's the truth."

"Ella, maybe it's time she knew the truth. Ain't you tired of lying? I know I am. She deserves better."

"Maybe it's time I knew the truth about what?" I said as I pushed the curtain aside and walked near the head of James's bed. Mom's eyes got big as quarters, and James looked at her as if he wanted to protect her.

My father's hurt shone through his every expression. "I can't believe you, Ella. So you were playin' up to me so I wouldn't tell your secret? You ain't changed a bit. You were always selfish and you always gon' be selfish."

"You got nerve talkin' about selfish!" she snapped. "You married me. You had a family at home who needed you. Yet, you was runnin' around with every Jane, Betty, and Sue who would open their legs to you. You damn sure wasn't thinking about me when you ran around with all them women. Then you come home and have the nerve to tell me you had *a baby* with one of 'em—a new baby boy!"

"So that makes everything you did all right? I ain't a perfect man, but at least I came home to tell you the truth. All you did was lie. And you've had me, James, and Jackie covering up for you all these years, claimin' you're protecting Charisse when you really ain't protecting nobody but yourself."

"Protecting me from what?" I said.

"Tell her, Ella. She's a grown woman. Tell her the truth right now or I will," Mr. Tyson said.

Mama shook her head no in defiance and stood to walk out the room, cut and run, but James grabbed her arm before she could take a single step. "You need to stay here for this."

"Okay, I'll start. The reason I didn't visit or contact you for all those years, Charisse, is because . . . your mama told me you weren't my child!"

My heart thumped so hard I thought the whole world could hear it. "What! I-I don't—" I said, confused, angry, and hurt all at the same time. My head snapped toward Mama, then back to my father.

"Yes, she told me you belonged to James! She slept with James not long after finding out she was pregnant by me . . . and then she told him he was the father."

I shook my head no. "Is this true? Tell me this isn't true!"

"She didn't tell me until you were already fifteen years old. By then, I didn't hardly believe her. And by the time I believed her, it was too late to make amends with you. You were already too angry with me to give me a chance."

"Mom! Why? How could you do this to me? All those years I thought my daddy didn't want me. All those birthdays I cried because I didn't get a card.

Resenting him, sometimes almost hating him, for not being there to protect me when that boy tried to rape me. All these years thinking I was worthless and didn't matter to the one man on this earth who was supposed to love me unconditionally. You let me believe he abandoned me. Why, Mom? Tell me why!"

36

Charisse

A sea of tears streamed over Mommy's trembling lips. "You wanna know why? Because I didn't want no baby by him! I was so happy we were having a baby, finally. I thought you would make him stop all his damn running around. The day I found out I was pregnant with you was the day he told me he had a child by Trey's mother . . . a baby, a baby boy." She looked at Dad, beating her chest with her fist as if trying to resuscitate her heart. "I was your wife. I was the one you made a commitment to, and you threw it all away. You broke my heart. You broke our family and our future. I didn't want no baby by you!"

She walked to me, ran her hand down my arm, and tried to grab my hand, but I jerked it back. I didn't want her to touch me. I barely processed what she'd said. "I went to a doctor on the other side of town that did abortions. I thought about getting rid of the baby, but I couldn't do it. Something in my heart allowed me to love my baby when I couldn't love its father. Upon leavin' the doctor's office to get somethin' to eat, I met James. He had the kindest eyes I'd ever seen on a man.

Everything about him said love to me. He took me out for coffee and asked me if I was married. I told him no, I didn't have no husband, because I didn't." She pointed to Dad. "He was never a husband to me. Never. Our marriage wasn't worth the paper the pastor signed. I burned the certificate and our marriage went up in smoke. Nothin' left but the ashes of what used to be."

My father stared at her as if for the first time understanding how much he'd hurt her. "Not long after she told me James was the father, I left North Carolina and went to California . . . and that's where I stayed. I kept your mother's secret all these years because . . . truth was . . . I *wasn't* any kinda husband to her. I was young, stupid, irresponsible, and didn't do right by her at any turn. Probably wouldn't have done right *by you* even if I had known you were mine. I didn't even begin gettin' my act together until Trey's mother died. I'd been forced by her death to grow up and be a man . . . and a father."

I turned toward James. "So how long did you think I was your baby?"

He reached out for my hand and I weaved my fingers with his. "Not even a year, baby girl. Your mama told me the truth right after you were born, but it was too late . . . because I'd already fallen in love with you. You were my baby girl, my heart. Always have been. Always will be."

I sat down beside James, laid my head on the bed next to him, and cried until I couldn't cry anymore. Years of anguish and hurt and pain rained from my eyes and cleansed my soul. I'd experienced the deepest pain and greatest joy in my life in a single day. After so many years believing I didn't matter, I received the greatest gifts of my life that day. I'd gained not one but *two* fathers . . . and my wedding was just around the corner—all thanks to Kevin. If he hadn't invited my father to stay with us, I might never have found out the truth.

To call the day emotionally exhausting would be like calling the New York City Marathon a short skip around Central Park. Somehow the term didn't quite capture the full breadth of the complex nature of the journey.

The doctor came in right before visiting hours ended and said James would need to stay in the hospital for observation, but that he would be released in a day or two, news that left me as elated as I'd felt in ages. Even Kevin's visit couldn't top that . . . although he'd come quite close.

Trey had driven Mom and Dad to the hospital in my car, so we collected everyone, including Nisey, and headed home. When we pulled into my driveway, a car was parked on the street in front of my house, but I couldn't place it. I noticed two men sitting up front though. All of a sudden, Nisey said, "Oh, hell."

"What?" I asked.

"That's David's car."

"David? Well, who's that in the car with him?"

"I didn't see—" she said as she craned her neck, trying to peer inside his car. "Richard!"

"Oh, no!" I said, thinking some major drama would

be popping off that night . . . as if there hadn't been enough already.

Trey glanced at Nisey. "Everything okay? You need me?"

She shook her head no. "I can handle this."

"Yeah, and I'll be out here with her," I said, knowing I wasn't about to miss a thing.

Mom and Dad got out of the car and went straight inside, both looking exhausted from all the drama that'd transpired throughout the day. Trey, in a bid to mark his new territory, kissed Nisey on the cheek before heading in behind them.

David's face nearly split in two at the sight of that little display. "Who the hell is he?" David asked as Richard drifted a short distance behind. Apparently, Dick was too busy getting the grocery list from his wife to care about what David and Nisey were discussing.

Nisey's glance fell. "He's Charisse's brother Trey. Why do you care?"

"Why do I care? We're in a relationship the last time I checked."

"Well, you must've checked four days ago because, as I recall, that's when you packed up your shit and left. Now I know you didn't drive here with your little sidekick to have this conversation with me, so what do you want?"

"I wanted you to know that Richard and I have worked things out. I brought him here to show you that he and I have agreed to work together for Jamal . . . and for you. I want us to be a family, Denise. You can't throw away everything we've built together."

Right about then, Richard's sorry ass decided to insert himself into the conversation. Little did he realize his face would be cracked in a couple of seconds . . . a sight I wouldn't have missed for the world.

"Listen," Dick said. "I'm willing to work with both of you for my son, but I ain't gonna have him caught up in your little soap-opera relationship drama. Y'all need to work your problems out or I'm gonna have to assert my parental rights to make sure my son's gonna be all right."

Nisey rolled her eyes. "First of all, you ain't got no parental rights because you're not Jamal's father, David is. So you can just *assert* your ass back to the car. What's going on between us parents ain't got shit to do with you."

David and Richard stood dumbfounded, bearing the same expressions they had when she first told them she'd gotten pregnant and didn't know which was the father.

"Yeah, you heard me right. David is the father. The paternity test results are right upstairs if you need proof. I lied to him because I wanted . . . no, I *needed* to know if he stayed with me because he loved me or because he believed he was Jamal's father. And I got my answer when he left me. Call me crazy, but I don't want to commit to any man who is only with me because we have a child together. I want more and I deserve more. You don't need to be in my house or my bed to be a father to Jamal. Those are special places reserved for *my man* . . . and he's in the house. So if you'll both excuse me, I have some place to be."

"Denise . . ." David said, looking hopeless and helpless as an unfazed Nisey kept walking toward my front door.

"Oh. And David. Next week you'll get your next introduction to fatherhood. We single mothers call it child support and weekend visitation. Come on, Rissey. We've had a long day."

I smiled and said, "You fellas have a good evening."

Later, when the house was quiet, I caught myself creeping into the kitchen for a little midnight ice cream snack. I kept a secret stash of butter pecan Häagen-Dazs way in the back of the freezer behind a box of veggie burgers where no one would ever find it, at least not anybody from *my* family. When I got to the bottom of the stairs, I noticed the kitchen light was already on. I'll be damned if my mother wasn't sitting at the table about to shove a big-ass table-spoon into my treat.

"Heeeey! I was coming down for that. How'd you find it?"

"I knew you had to have some good ice cream stashed somewhere in this house. When I saw those nasty-ass veggie burgers, I figured you were hiding something behind them because I know you didn't buy them to eat."

"Sorry to break the news to you," I said, grabbing a spoon from the drawer, "but you're gonna have to share."

"Make room for one more," Nisey chimed in.

One pint of Häagen-Dazs to split three ways. I thought the scene would get ugly.

"I know you got some Oreos up in here somewhere. Ooh, and some ice-cold milk to dunk them in."

"See, this is why I don't invite y'all over. Always coming up in here eatin' up all my good snacks."

They laughed as we made ourselves comfortable at the table. Mom refused to let her eyes meet mine. I guessed she still questioned whether I was angry at her for not telling me the truth about my father . . . that he hadn't abandoned me as I'd always believed.

"You might not realize this, Charisse," she said, digging her spoon into my ice cream delight, "but I'm not perfect."

"For real? You don't say!"

"Well, knock me over with a feather," Nisey added.

"Hush, child!" Mom said. "Let me finish. What I did to you and your father was very wrong. He ain't often right, but he did say one thing that hit a little closer to home than I cared to admit. What I did was selfish. I put my own anger and hurt before what either of you wanted or needed."

"Mommy, you disappointed me to the core, but I understand what you must've been going through at the time. Lord knows I've been through those situations enough times to relate. I always say, sometimes you've got a right to be wrong."

She shook her head no. "Baby, nothing good can come from doin' folks *wrong*, no matter how *right* you think you are. I'd rather focus on my *right* to be happy, the *right* to make the best decisions for the people I love and for myself. Seems I haven't focused on that enough in my lifetime."

"You're gettin' pretty deep over ice cream, ain't you,

Mama Tyson?" Nisey asked as she dunked a cookie into her milk.

"Watching someone you love nearly die will tend to kick up the serious factor, Nisey. Make you realize how stupid you've been and how much time you've wasted."

We both nodded, knowing she regretted James. One thing was certain, she'd never let him get away from her again.

"Well, Rissey," Nisey said, trying to lighten the mood a bit, "from the looks of your meeting with Kevin in the hospital, I'm guessing we have a wedding to finish planning."

"Hmmm. Well, you guessed wrong." I paused just long enough to see their stunned faces. "Kevin already finished all of the planning. I just have one last item on my list, and he couldn't take care of that one for me."

"What's that?" Mama asked.

"I still don't have a dress."

Nisey said, "Oh! I know the perfect boutique in Chevy Chase. If you can't find something there, then your ass is entirely too picky. We'll go first thing in the morning."

I turned to Mom and flittered my eyelashes. "Moooom-my! Could you do me the tiniest of favors. Please, please, pretty please?"

"I'll do anything in the world for you, baby. All you need to do is ask."

"Could you make up with Mother Douglass so that I can invite her along? This would give us all a chance to bond."

She held her silence for a few seconds before she said, "Except that!"

37

Kevin

In what can only be termed an irony, I asked Kristen to meet me at the airport park where all my trouble began. Ma enjoyed the views of the Potomac River during the day, but nothing could compare to night when lights blanketed the cityscape. I'd bring her back to visit one day soon. While waiting on Javon to arrive, I took the time to explain the plan to Ma. Although she had always taught me to be up-front, upright, and straightforward, she understood why I had to choose a more circuitous route in dealing with Kristen.

"What I want you to explain to me is how you always find yourself involved with these crazy-ass, no-good women. Don't make no sense. It ain't like you didn't have a good example growin' up. Your father and I were married over forty years before he passed."

I smiled. "I don't know, Ma. I guess I always wanted to believe the best in people. I fault you and Dad. Watching you guys all my life made me naive enough to believe if someone said they loved you, they meant it. I don't know, maybe in some ways they're sincere, but they may not always love the same way you do. Love means different things to different people."

"I know that's right," Ma said.

"That's why I'm certain marrying Charisse is the most right decision I've ever made in my life. I finally found someone who views love as I do. That faithful-for-life, down-for-whatever, old-school love that never ends, not even in the worst of times."

Kristen's car pulled into the parking lot and a smile emerged on Ma's face. She reached for the door handle as if she wanted to jump out and run to Javon.

"You excited?"

"You better believe it!" she replied. "Someday when Javon and my other grandbabies that you gon' make with Charisse get grown, you're gonna understand that, as a parent, our job isn't quite complete until we can watch you give birth to, raise, and get tortured by your own kids. This is the beginning of that length of my parenting journey and for me, ain't nothin' better. No, sir. Don't get no better than this. I only wish your daddy was here to see it."

Kristen approached the car, Javon clasping her fingers and smiling as he stumbled on her heels, clearly still learning to walk. Watching them, I didn't want to hurt Kristen or her relationship with Javon. But I refused to leave the fate of our relationship in her hands. I had to do the right thing for everyone involved, including Greg.

"Oh, my Heavenly Father! Look at him. He's beautiful. I understand what you mean. If he ain't you all over again, I don't know who is!"

"It's nice to see you again, Mrs. Douglass. I, uhhh, I only wish we could be meeting under better circumstances."

"Oh, don't you fret about that now. What could be better than meeting my grandbaby. Can I hold him?"

"Sure." Kristen picked up Javon and leaned him toward Ma. He squirmed a little at first, but when the sunlight reflected off her earrings, he got distracted and went willingly.

"He so precious," Ma gushed. "We're gonna walk over to the bench and let you two talk for a minute."

"Did you bring the information that I need with you? I'm supposed to meet with my attorney next week," Kristen said.

"Awww, man, Kristen. I totally forgot," I lied. "I picked up my mother from the airport, and then Charisse was admitted to the hospital this morning. Things have been absolutely crazy all day. Give me a couple of days to let things settle down and I'll get the pictures to you."

"What's going on with Charisse?" she asked, as if to say, *Why do you even care?*

"Well, Charisse's mother's boyfriend, James, fell down the stairs at her place and got hurt. Even though we're not getting married, I still had to make sure everything is okay. I mean, he's like a father to her. I couldn't leave her hanging," I said, hoping Kristen still had some semblance of decency.

"Yeah, I guess I can understand that."

"Anyway, we'll hook up in a couple of days when things settle down. I'd ask you to come by my place but you know how nosy my mother is. I'd rather not deal with this while she's here."

Kristen thought about it for a minute. "I guess that'll be okay. I just need to make sure I'm ready for Greg."

"Don't worry. I've got Greg covered."

"Anyway, I'm gonna run over to Crystal City to do some shopping at the mall. Should I meet you back here in a couple of hours?"

"That's perfect . . . all the time we need."

As my mother and I drove to my place to get the swab for the paternity test, Derek hit me up on my cell.

"Hey, man," Derek said. "I got ahold of Greg. He said he'd meet me at the Game Room tonight at seven. I realize that's a little soon, but he kept talking about how busy he is with the kids. I'm lucky I got him to come out for that long."

"That's cool, man. Did you tell him I was coming?"

"Nah, I only told him we'd be meeting one of my boys for drinks."

"All right then, I'll catch you later. Thanks, man."

"So, Derek set up the meeting?" Ma asked.

"Yep. Tonight at seven. I've gotta say . . . I'm looking forward to finding out what Kristen's been up to."

"Six ball, corner pocket," Derek said, pointing out his shot with the tip of the pool stick. He peered up and saw me approach. "What's up, man? Glad you made it."

The Game Room, a man cave replete with pool tables, full bar, and flat screens tuned in to every major sport, played host to the Kangol, white-patent-leather Stacy Adams, and Hennessy crowd. It appeared pretty empty, but we'd met on a Thursday, so most folks probably had to get up for work the next day. Derek and Greg were standing near a pool table in the back, the perfect location to talk without everyone dipping in our business. I noticed a few empty beer cans sitting on a nearby table, which told me they both had thrown back a few drinks and would probably be pretty chill. The more chill Greg was, the more inclined he might be to talk about his and Kristen's dirt. As I walked up to the table, Greg looked at me as if he recognized me from somewhere, but we'd never met before . . . at least not to my knowledge.

What's up with him?

"Hey, what's goin' on," I said, giving Derek some dap before I reached out my hand to Greg, which he blatantly refused to shake. Left me hangin'.

"*This* is your boy?" Greg said, the tension in his voice undeniable.

"Yeah. Kevin, this is my frat Greg. Greg, this is Kevin, one of my boys from the Bureau."

"Oh, I know exactly who he is."

38
Kevin

You know how sometimes you can't see your own face but you can physically feel how jacked up your expression is? That's exactly what happened to me.

"Hold up. You know me?" I asked, confused as hell.

"Yeah, man. I'm sure you know me too. You and my wife used to kick it, right? If I'm not mistaken, y'all have a child together."

"Wait, wait, wait. Kristen told you about *me*?"

"Yeah. She told me everything. I mean, I know everybody is free to make their own choices, but I don't even know how you can call yourself a man and give up your child for another man to raise."

"What!" Derek and I said in unison.

Greg looked back and forth between us. Now, he was confused.

"Kristen told you *I* gave him up?"

"Yeaaah"—he hesitated—"she practically begged me to put my name on his birth certificate. Said I'd be the only father he ever knew."

All I could do was shake my head. "Man, I don't even believe this shit." I was pissed . . . lyin' bitch.

Here I'd started to give her the benefit of the doubt, and every time I found out something new about Kristen, she actually began to scare me.

"Greg," Derek said. "I think y'all need to sit down and talk."

We all took seats at the table and ordered a couple drink rounds while we exchanged Kristen horror stories. I decided to reveal enough information to make Greg feel comfortable. Listening to the lies Kristen had already told about me, I felt certain more had been going on with this woman than met the eye. Eventually, Greg told me that he was aware we had a relationship in the past.

"A relationship?" I said.

I begged to differ—a one-night stand did not a relationship make. Kristen had, of course, made our one-night sound much more involved. As we continued to talk, we each learned much more than either of us wanted to know.

"First of all, there's no way I'd ever knowingly give up my parental rights to *any* child of mine. I didn't even know Javon was in the world until last week."

"Last *week*? She told me she spoke to you when she first found out she was pregnant," Greg said, obviously astonished. "Can I ask you something? Why do you call him Javon? His name is Greg Jr. At home, we call him GJ."

"What! I call him that because Kristen told me Javon is his name."

"Get outta here. His middle name is Javon, but we don't use it."

"Ain't this a bitch? Is there anything she *didn't* lie about?"

"Sure as hell doesn't appear so."

"She told me you planned to serve her with divorce papers. Is there any truth to that?"

"Divorce papers?" Greg shook his head in disbelief. Seemed as if he realized he'd been living with a stranger. "Man, I ain't gonna lie. We haven't been happy for more than a year now, but I certainly hadn't been planning a divorce. I mean, the reason I'm still living with her is for the kids, and my reason hasn't changed."

He continued, "She and I were going through a divorce when y'all were winding down on the Dwayne Gibson case. When the mediator announced he planned to award joint custody and order the sale of the house with proceeds split fifty-fifty—as opposed to her retaining ownership like she thought—she begged me to give our marriage another chance, for the sake of the kids. So I did."

"Okay, yeah. Now, that's about the time that Charisse and I got together. Seems like once she realized she didn't have a chance with me, in addition to the house and kids issues, she claimed she wanted to work things out with you."

"I thought she might have feelings for you, but she told me you got her drunk one night when she was depressed about me and you took advantage of her."

"Oh, hell no! More like the other way around."

"When she found out she was pregnant, she said you didn't want anything to do with the baby because you fell in love with some chick . . . uhhhh . . . I can't remember her name. Sherry?"

"No, Charisse."

"Yeah, that's the name, Charisse."

"Derek, do you hear this mess, man? She's been playing both of us like a guitar. Just plucking the strings."

All Derek could muster was "She crazy."

"Now, everything makes sense."

"What makes sense?" Greg asked. "What the hell's going on?"

"Man, you might want to take a gulp of that drink first. You ain't gon' believe the next part of this story."

I told Greg how Kristen set him up with the woman he'd been seeing and that the woman was actually Kristen's friend. I surmised that Kristen wanted to leave her marriage, but not without the house and kids. Filing for divorce on the grounds of adultery would've given her the best chance at keeping everything . . . and sinking her claws into me.

"You've got to be fucking kidding me." Greg went through a range of emotions—anger, shock, even sadness. He'd been living a lie for a long time . . . too long. "I should've realized she had some ulterior motive, always showing up at my house to visit when Kristen worked late, titties hanging out, pants tight. *She* came on to *me*. And since Kristen and I hadn't been together in *too many* months, I fell for her game hook, line,

and sinker. I could kick her ass right now. For real."
He started to get up but Derek grabbed his arm and
yanked him back down.

I did some fancy talking and tap dancing to keep
him from running home. "Man, I understand you're
pissed right now, but think about your kids. Striking
out at Kristen will feel good right up until the police
lock you up. Look at the situation this way. Kristen's
gonna leave regardless of what you want at this point.
You need to ensure you get joint custody if that's what
you want. If I were you, I'd go visit my attorney *yesterday*. File the paperwork for joint custody and separation."

"What about the pictures?" he said. "What if she's
got other evidence?"

"Even if she wanted to use them against you, at
this point she couldn't because of a little-known prin-
ciple called unclean hands. Essentially, it means she
can't use evidence of adultery against you in court
proceedings if she is the one who set you up. We can
easily prove she set you up because Kristen and your
mistress threatened Charisse, who can identify her.
And she'd be happy to testify. She's not a Kristen fan
at all."

A wave of relief washed over Greg. "But you're not
going to give the pictures to her, are you?"

"Hell no," I said.

"This still doesn't explain why she put Greg's
name on the birth certificate. What does she have to
gain by doing that?"

"It's simple," I said. "She was pissed I chose Charisse

over her. She told Charisse, not four days ago, she was still in love with me."

"What!" Greg said. "Shit, do you think I can play this off? All I want to do right now is beat her down, for real."

"Be patient. If you really want to hit a woman where it really hurts, *outsmart her*. Stay two steps ahead. That's what we're gonna do. Trust me, in a few days you'll get all the revenge you'll ever need without touching a hair on her head."

39
Charisse

"Good morning, my beautiful bride-to-be," Kevin sang, making a forbidden call before 8:00 a.m. Lucky for him he was so sweet and I was so happy. "Tomorrow's the big day, and you should be getting ready to find a dress. Why do you sound like you're still sleeping?"

"Because I *was* still sleeping. We had a rough week, remember? Plus, I stayed up late last night talking to Mom and Nisey."

"About what?"

"I think Mom's having regrets about James. His accident really put the fear of God in her, made her realize how important he is to her . . . to us really."

"James is a good man. I don't know why she's been so afraid to marry him."

"My father put her through some shit," I said, explaining why my father had been absent all my life and why James had treated me like a daughter. For a while, he believed I was his daughter. "So, you understand? She'd really been through a lot."

"Wow, can you imagine how she must've felt, finding out about Trey like that?"

"Hmmm. It's a stretch, but I think I've got a clue," I said sarcastically before Kevin realized what he'd said and corrected himself.

"Sorry, baby. You know I didn't mean it that way. Anyway, given what has happened, seems to me you've got a new problem on your hands."

"What's that?"

"Who's gonna walk you down the aisle?"

Shit, I thought. *Kevin's right.* "Sweet Jesus. I haven't had a chance to think about it until you mentioned it."

"Well, rehearsal's tonight. You're gonna have two fathers present, so to speak. When the minister asks who's gonna give you away, you'll need to answer him."

All I could do was shake my head. This was not a choice I wanted to make. James would be home later that evening, so he'd be well enough to attend the wedding. My father's revelation was a bit of a game changer. No, he hadn't been in my life, but he hadn't been absent on purpose. How could I blame him now?

"I'm thinking maybe I'll walk down the aisle by myself."

"Well, that'd solve the problem, wouldn't it? Seems like everyone loses though."

"I guess. Anyway, please make sure your mom is ready. We're going to the boutique shortly and I want her to come with us to pick out my dress."

"With us who?"

"Me, Nisey . . . and Mama," I said, mumbling the *and mama* part under my breath.

"I don't think this is a good idea. You didn't hear the argument they had the other day."

"Oh, but I heard. I don't expect too many people in the hospital *didn't*. Mom has promised to stay on her best behavior. If you can get your mother to do the same, we all might survive the next two days in one piece."

"Okay, will do," Kevin said. "Listen, I've got to talk to you about one last issue before you jump off of the phone. It's about Kristen."

"All right, ladies! Let's go. Time is a-wastin'," Nisey yelled from downstairs, trying to rush us out of the house. I'd started to get a serious case of the jitters. With all the drama over the past week, I didn't have time to feel any nerves—now I had too much time. That the ceremony was the next day and I had no dress was frightening enough. My angst had only been compounded by not knowing who would escort me to my groom. Just as the thought crossed my mind, my father stuck his head in my bedroom door.

"Hey, Charisse, you got a minute?"

"Sure, come in. Although we've really got to make it a minute or Nisey's coming after me . . . and that won't be pretty," I said, chuckling.

He walked over and sat next to me with a gift-wrapped package in his hands. "You know, I'm thankful to Kevin for inviting us. So glad we had a chance to clear the air. Please know that just because you weren't with me doesn't mean I didn't think about you every day. I hope that we'll spend more time together now, maybe you'll come visit your old man sometime."

"I'd like that. Dad." I patted his hand. "I'd like that very much indeed."

"Uhhh, Trey, Chris, and I wanted you to have a little something to remind you of us when we head back to California."

I grabbed the package and ripped off the paper to reveal an ivory-colored photo album with OUR FAMILY written on the front. I was saddened a little at first because I wanted so much to be a part of their lives and I wasn't. One person in the family would be missing—me.

As I flipped through the album, page by page, I couldn't believe my eyes. Photographs of me, Chris, and Trey, from infancy through high school and beyond, formed collages of our lives, with my dad in his Marine Corps dress blues. Even one rare photo of my father holding me when I was a little girl. Must've been five or six at the time. His eyes, they smiled at me. I *hadn't been* excluded or forgotten.

"Oh my God, Dad! Where did you get these?"

"Your mother's been sending them to me for years, ever since she told me the truth. Guess she wanted me to have a piece of you in California."

"This is so beautiful!" I said, almost too choked up to speak. I pressed it against my heart. "I'll treasure this . . . always."

He started to leave, but stopped before he reached the door. "Listen. I need to say one more thing."

"Sure."

"While nothing in the whole entire world would make me happier than walking my beautiful daughter down the aisle tomorrow, James has been a father to you in ways that I could only hope to be. I don't want you troubling yourself for one second over your decision, okay?"

I only nodded. If I tried to speak, I'd have fallen apart.

Tears welled up in my eyes. I was so touched by his gesture toward me . . . and James. Although I knew he was trying to make my decision easier, he'd only succeeded in making the choice much harder.

"Rissey, if you don't get yourself down here right now. I'm coming up!"

"I better go. Thanks, Dad." I hugged him and, for the first time in my life, gave him a kiss on the cheek. Made me happy to know it wouldn't be the last.

With Nisey playing chauffeur, we swung by Kevin's place to pick up Mother Douglass and headed for the bridal boutique in Chevy Chase, a swanky, predominately upper-class neighborhood where superb service in high-end stores was a-plenty. None of the merchandise had price tags because if you had to ask how much stuff cost, you couldn't afford it.

We walked into the cozy boutique, which was set up like a cozy upper-crust living room with a platform in the middle. I usually hated mirrors, but I kinda looked forward to trying on dresses. I'd never worn a full-length gown. This would be my first formal event in forty years. My high school boyfriend had decided to take my slutty cousin to the prom instead of me, so I'd never even bought a prom dress. My first wedding took place at the justice of the peace, and I wore a snazzy suit, didn't get a gown. Even holiday real estate events were largely semiformal. I had lots of little black dresses for such occasions, but never got to be the princess.

Becky, the bridal consultant, asked for my size . . . *out loud* . . . in front of everyone. So, of course, I wrote the number on a note and slipped it to her, making her take a blood oath never to tell anyone, especially not my mother. After flipping through a few catalogs, I'd narrowed my designer down to Justin Alexander or Simone Carvalli. Their dresses had a 1940s and 1950s glam look—classic and timeless. One of the dresses reminded me of something Bette Davis might've worn in *All About Eve*. She pulled a few options into the dressing room, and the fashion show began. Nisey sat squarely between Mama and Mother Douglass to ensure they didn't go to blows.

I tried on the first dress, a quasi-low-cut satin number. Didn't take long to figure out Mama and Mother Douglass wouldn't agree on anything.

"That's beautiful, Charisse," Mother Douglass said. "Elegant. Shows off all your curves."

"Well, if she wears that, we're gonna have to worry about the tent in the groom's pants," Mama said. "I think we need to go more conservative."

Five conservative dresses later . . .

"Now that's perfect," Mama said.

"Yeah, if she's going to a convent. Does this thing come with a chastity belt? Lookin' like she's about to take a vow of celibacy. To hell with that, I need some more grandbabies," Mother Douglass said.

Mama broke down and chuckled at that one. "I know that's right. We definitely want more grand-babies. So, when you gon' get pregnant, Charisse?"

Finally, they bonded over something, even if it wasn't a topic I cared to talk about with either of them. "Sheesh, can I get down the aisle first?"

Nisey jumped in, "Yeaaaah, I don't think she needs to go *quite* so conservative."

Two not-so-conservative dresses later . . .

"Rissey, I think this one is perfect. Not too conservative, sexy but elegant," Nisey said.

"I like it too," Mother Douglass said, nodding her head. "That's perfect."

"Mama, what do you think?"

"I think you look like Cinderella . . . good thing you've got a real Prince Charming for a change."

Mother Douglass grinned proudly as if to say, *That's my baby!*

40

Charisse

My wedding day had arrived. I was so excited, filled with the triple A's—angst, anticipation, and alcohol. Not a lot of alcohol, just enough to ensure the bats out of hell flapping around in my stomach were sedated long enough to allow me to get *to* the altar . . . and not bolt for the nearest exit in terror. Nisey, God love her, gave me a stainless-steel flask filled with Grey Goose as a best-friend wedding gift.

No matter how afraid I was of our unknown, I'd felt certain of one thing—if I didn't marry Kevin, I'd regret my decision for the rest of my life . . . and I had already experienced too many regrets.

"Charisse? You dressed?" Mama called from outside the dressing room door. I'd kicked everyone out moments before so I could collect my thoughts and take a swig of my calming elixir. I couldn't handle the constant jabbering from the Impossible Three, Mama, Nisey, and Mother Douglass. They sounded like a gaggle of geese, and my nerves had been stomped on one too many times as they tried to ensure my hair and makeup were just so. I told them Kevin didn't care, and

I certainly didn't. They told me I might not care at the moment, but I'd be crying the blues when I saw the jacked-up wedding photos and my bad hair and makeup were immortalized for generations to come.

"I'm ready. Come in."

Mama walked in first, with Nisey and Mother Douglass trailing closely behind.

"Oh my goodness," Nisey said. "Rissey, you look absolutely incredible."

"Really?"

"You're positively glowing."

I wanted to tell them I wasn't glowing. Between the alcohol and the hot-ass dress I'd probably started to sweat. Each hugged me, careful not to drip their mascara-stained teardrops all over my dress. I posed the question meant to get the party started—and over with.

"Everybody ready?"

"Yes, baby. We're all waiting on you."

I grabbed my bouquet and tipped carefully out the door in my too-high heels. My biggest fear was that I'd break a heel and bust my ass . . . or just bust my ass. Fortunately, Kevin insisted on a carpet runner to minimize the threat. One of the many reasons I so loved that man.

As I entered the vestibule, I thought about the night before and how hard it had been to decide whose arm I'd take to lead me to Kevin . . . and my destiny. Both James and my father had made the decision so difficult. They both loved me and I was the only daughter to each. Walking by myself would cheat us all. After praying on it for a while, I realized the choice was one I shouldn't be forced to make.

So, I didn't.

"Dad? James? You two ready to get me to my groom?"

James smiled wide. "We sure are."

Dad dabbed his eyes with a handkerchief and kissed my cheek. "My beautiful baby girl."

I slipped one arm through my father's and one through James's and we glided down the aisle to the altar as Stevie Wonder's "Ribbon in the Sky" echoed through the sanctuary. When the music stopped, the minister made his introductions and asked, "Who gives this woman to married?"

Together, my father and James said, "We do."

After Kevin and I received our blessings, pledged our undying devotion, made our promises, exchanged our rings, and vowed to endure through the easy and the hard shit, we each said, "I do."

For the second time in our lives, he became husband and I, wife.

By the time they called us for our first dance, my dogs were kicking my ass. The Manolos were no mo'! They sat under the table as Kevin and I swayed to our song, the first song we ever danced to, during my fortieth birthday celebration at the Skydome—"So Close" by Jon McLaughlin. Only this time we weren't so close. We'd made it. By some miracle from heaven. We'd arrived at our fairy tale. Our dream come true.

As we floated around the dance floor, I surveyed

the room to admire my beautiful family. Trey and Nisey had been wrapped up in each other all night long. If our wedding had provided inspiration for anyone, those two would be married sooner rather than later. I could hear the echo of wedding bells around them. I gave them six months . . . a year tops. They'd only known each other a few days but had been goo-goo-eyed ever since Nisey got off her David mess.

James and Mama, on the other hand, couldn't look more distant, even though they were sitting right next to each other. I could tell Mama's mind was somewhere else, and James appeared almost disappointed. After unsuccessfully asking my mother to marry him for so many years, I imagined attending my wedding was as much a sad occasion as a happy one for him. He wanted to have with Mom what Kevin and I had. But none of us could do a darn thing to make her come to the realization before she was ready. After the song finished, I grabbed the microphone from the DJ booth to say a few words.

"Uhhhh . . . excuse me, everyone. I just wanted to take a few minutes to thank everyone for coming. I'd like to make a few very special thank-yous." I turned to Kevin. "First, I'd like to thank my wonderful husband for giving me the one gift I needed but would never have asked for—and the one gift I truly believe no other man would've had the courage to try and give me—my father and my brothers. Their presence here proves it's never too late to be a father to your children and never too late to be a family. I will cherish them forever."

A bashful smile appeared on Kevin's beautiful face and he mouthed, *I love you.*

"I'd also like to thank Mother Douglass and Mommy for all of your love and support through this week and over the years. Without you, we would not be the people we are today—and I mean that in a good way."

The guests laughed.

"Last, but certainly not least, I'd like to thank James Butler for supporting me almost my entire life." I looked Mom directly in the eye. "It takes a special kind of man and a special kind of love to be a father to a child who isn't your own."

Mom's face turned sheepish and she stared at the ground.

I looked at James. "Thank you for setting such a great example for me. Because of you, I could believe a Kevin existed."

James blew me a kiss from across the room, then looked at my mother. She avoided his gaze . . . and stood and walked toward me, holding her hand out for the microphone.

"Well . . . I think Mom would like to say a few words. Here you go."

"Hi. If you know me, you know I ain't one for giving speeches, but today is a special day. Thank you to everyone for coming to celebrate this glorious day with my beautiful daughter and her new husband. How many of you thought *this* miracle would happen?"

I cut my eyes at her. She smiled and the crowd laughed.

"I know in my heart these two have the love they

need to last forever." She leaned over to kiss me on the cheek. "Now . . . for what I really want to say. I've learned a hard lesson this week. You know, life is short and everything we have, everything we cherish, can be taken in a moment's notice. We have to tell and show the important people in our lives that we love them . . . every day. So, I'd like to take this opportunity to say something I haven't said far often enough. James, I love you. And I'd like to know . . . will you . . . marry me?"

Loud gasps sounded across the entire reception hall. Every eye widened, every eyebrow raised, every mouth opened, and every head turned to James, waiting on him to answer.

James scanned all the frozen expressions, shot Mommy the evil eye, and said, "Hell no!"

Mommy's face cracked into a thousand pieces, and a wave of murmurs traveled across the room.

James stood up and trudged toward her with an expression on his face I couldn't quite decipher. He grabbed the microphone from her hand. "All these years I been asking this stubborn-ass woman to marry me, and she flat out refused me at every turn. Ain't no way in this world or any other I'm gonna accept her proposal!" He dropped to one knee, almost in slow motion (hip surgery), and gazed into her eyes. "No, indeed. For a change, you're gonna say yes to *my* proposal. Ella Mae Tyson, for the last time, *will you marry me?*"

She smiled so wide I swear her dentures almost slipped out. "Yes! Yes! Yes! I'll marry you, James Butler. A thousand times, yes!"

41
Kevin

I woke up to my new bride peppering my face with kisses . . . as she'd done every morning since the ceremony. I was loving the whole husband-and-wife thing. Made all the difference in the world when you married the right person. I was particularly surprised by Charisse's enhanced sex drive. She'd practically chased me down all day, every day. Oh, we'd had a pretty healthy relationship before. But since we got hitched, she'd been way off the chain, throwing sex at me three, four times on weekdays and twice on Sunday. If I had known about this particular side effect of matrimonial bliss, I'd have married her sooner . . . much sooner.

"I love your cologne. Every time I smell you, I wanna rip your clothes off," Charisse said in her sultry voice as she ran her fingers across my chest.

"Is that right?" I brushed my fingers across the profile of her cheek, feeling the same warmth I had when she walked toward me down the aisle. "You're so beautiful."

"You know . . . you don't have to keep gassing up my head. I'm a sure thing now." She laughed.

"You were *always* a sure thing," I said, protecting my head from the pillow I predicted would be smacking me upside my head. "I'm kidding. I'm kidding. I just want to hold on to my sure thing, so I'm going to tell you how beautiful you are."

I rolled over on my back and glanced at the ceiling. Didn't realize my smile faded until Charisse shared her observation.

"What's wrong, baby? You worried about something?"

"I'm all right I guess. I'm just not sure how to deal with this Kristen situation. Both Greg and I want to confront her, but we can't exactly sever all ties because of the kids. We don't want any major dramatic scenes, but, man, we'd sure like to let her know she didn't get away with trying to play us . . . and in a way she'll never forget."

Charisse rolled over on her side, leaned on her elbow, and propped her head up on her hand. "You know this is my specialty, right? I've been in similar situations more times than I care to remember. I told you about Sean, right?"

"I think I remember you mentioning him. The married guy."

"Yep. He's the one. See, I've never been a fan of making big public scenes or burning bridges, but sometimes you've got to let folks understand they can't get over on you. And with the way Miss Thang treated me, showing up at my house with her little posse, I'd be more than happy to help you serve her some just desserts."

"So, you got any ideas?"

"Hmmm . . . Let's just say revenge is best served

over dinner while meeting up with old friends. Feel like going out tonight?"

Charisse decided on the M&S Grill, a semi-swanky restaurant in downtown DC. I had no idea why she insisted on this spot, but she said it'd be the perfect place for the night's festivities.

After calling Greg and telling him about Charisse's plan, we agreed we never wanted to be on her bad side. Talk about hell to pay. Once Greg was on board, I called Kristen, who had no idea Charisse and I had tied the knot. She'd assumed we'd broken up and that she still had a chance at a relationship. I'd called her from the airport, on my way to the Jamaican honeymoon, to let her know I had to fly away on emergency Bureau business to support a case. She made me promise to meet with her and provide the photographs to her as soon as I returned—a promise I would not keep. I let out a long breath now as I picked up the phone, dreading the sound of her conniving voice.

"Hey, Kris. How are you?" I'd never called her Kris before, so she'd definitely notice the informality.

"Kevin, I'm so glad to hear your voice. How'd your business trip go? Everything all right with the case?"

"Yeah, everything went off without a hitch," I said, laughing at my choice of terminology. Seemed almost too perfect as I'd just gotten hitched. I winked at my wife.

"So, listen. I was wondering if you and I might hook up tonight, you know, so I can give you the information you need."

"Wow, your timing couldn't be more perfect. I was planning to meet with my attorney about custody . . . and the divorce tomorrow."

"The divorce? It's like *that*?"

"Yeah . . . 'fraid so. Things seem to be getting worse. He's more distant these days. I can tell he's about to make a move."

"Is that right? Well, what do you think about dinner? We can talk about things. Maybe talk about . . . us."

"Us?" I could hear the smile in her voice. "Okay. What time and where?"

"Ummm . . . how about seven? The M and S Grill?"

"Sweet. One of my favorite restaurants. Meet you there . . . at seven."

"I look forward to it."

Charisse made reservations for five. She requested her favorite table, a semicircle with bench seating that would allow her and me a view of the door without our guests seeing us in time to make a premature departure.

Charisse and I arrived first. She took a seat at the bar shortly after me. I ordered one drink for myself and one for the beautiful woman sitting at the bar. She smiled and raised her glass to me in appreciation.

Kristen strolled in about ten minutes to seven, a little early. I figured she would be. That's why I told Charisse we needed to arrive extra-early. Kristen smiled as she rounded the partition near the table, wearing a body-hugging, navy-blue-and-white minidress that showed off her curves and all but a few inches of her legs. Certainly left little to the imagination. I knew I'd better keep my eyes glued to the table all night long or Kristen wouldn't be the only one in our group trying to get a divorce.

"Well, don't you look . . . *nice* this evening," I said, trying to be polite. But, for real, she looked good. Couldn't compare to my bride as far as I was concerned though, or at least that's what I'd tell Charisse.

She shot me a flirty smile. "I thought you might like this dress. I bought it earlier today."

"Yep. Very nice," I said, glad Charisse wasn't close enough to hear me. She'd have smacked me blind.

"So you got something for me?" she asked, getting right down to business, as I expected she would. Timing was everything, and Charisse and I had planned for the night to end quickly. I lifted a sealed manila envelope from the seat next to me and handed it to her.

"Here you go. I think I got everything you need," I said.

Kristen smiled smugly, as if she'd gotten away with stealing the Hope Diamond. I couldn't wait to bust her bubble. "I don't know how to thank you, Kevin . . . but I'm sure I'll think of *something*," she said with a wink.

I resisted the urge to roll my eyes.

Fortunately, the passing of the envelope was Charisse's signal to join us. My eyes smiled as she approached the table and Kristen's eyes followed mine . . . until she too laid eyes on her.

Charisse kissed me on the lips and Kristen's jaw went ker-thunk. "Evening, Kristen. Cat got your tongue?"

Kristen cut her eyes at Charisse. "What are you doing here?" She turned to me. "What is *she* doing here?"

"I'm sorry to intrude on your . . . *little date*. I'm just

here to enjoy dinner . . . with my husband," Charisse said, scooting in closer to Kristen to block her so she couldn't escape. Charisse hung her ringed finger in Kristen's face, which, on a scale of pleased to pissed, registered somewhere between *son of a bitch!* and *mothafucka!* "Nice dress, by the way. Ho's-R-Us having a clearance sale?"

I concealed my chuckle and glanced at my watch to check the time; we were expecting the next guest to arrive shortly. I gave Charisse a head nod on the sly, letting her know she needed to keep an eye on the door so we couldn't miss the visitor.

"You two are married!" Kristen said, unable to contain her disappointment.

"Yes, we are. And . . . according to the paternity test, we're expecting too . . . joint custody as it were."

"Paternity test?" Kristen faced me, looking wounded. "You tested Javon?"

"Yes, I did. I needed to make sure he was mine, so I could prove I'm his father and file the paperwork for joint custody and child support."

"Child support?"

"Yes. I want to make sure he's taken care of regardless of where he lives or who he lives with."

"Why are you doing this, Kevin?" Kristen said, careful not to express too much emotion in front of Charisse. "I thought we—"

Just as Kristen let the word *we* pass her lips, the second guest walked through the door. Charisse noticed her first, then I did. Kristen was still looking at me, shocked that her plan to hoodwink and hook me had failed miserably.

"Hey, Kristen. Isn't that your friend Sheila? Why

don't you invite her over to the table to sit with us? Sheila! Sheila! Over here!" Charisse said, waving to get her attention.

Sheila appeared somewhere between angry and confused until she noticed Kristen at the table with a crumpled face. She and Kristen stared at each other in horror. Kristen had no doubt realized that I, FBI agent that I am, recognized Sheila as the woman I'd photographed on her behalf—Greg's so-called mistress. Within seconds, she'd probably also caught on that Charisse knew Sheila was a friend of hers—and if Charisse knew, I knew. At that moment, the lightbulb came on and Kristen knew she'd been set up. She grabbed her purse and attempted to leave, but of course Charisse wouldn't stand for that. "Oh, no, honey. You can't leave now. Show's just getting started."

Greg, who'd been waiting outside until Sheila arrived for our "dinner date," walked in shortly after Sheila. He eased up behind Sheila before she could speak or bolt for the door and said, "Well, well, well. Looks like the gang's all here."

"Greg?!" Kristen nearly yelled, looking at him as if she'd seen the ghost of Christmas past. She shot a burning-hot glare at Charisse, who just smiled wide, and then cut her eyes at me.

With nary a single word spoken, Greg and I had delivered a message Kristen and Sheila heard loud and clear, but Greg felt it necessary to emphasize the lesson. He looked at them, his lips tight, eyes narrowed, and teeth gritted. In a voice barely above a whisper, he said, "Stop playing these *fucking* games. I've wasted nine years of my life with *you* and two months of my life with *you*." His eyes darted at Kristen and Sheila respectively. "And I'm not wasting another second of my time. I only want two things—a divorce and my kids."

He turned to Kristen. "You and I have two beautiful children together, so I've got to be civil to you because of them. Outside of that, I don't want anything to do with your lying, scheming ass ever again."

Then he turned to Sheila. "And you? Sleeping with me because your girl asked you to help set me up?" He pulled out a $50 bill from his pants pocket and tucked it in the front of her shirt. "Next time you need a *pimp*, come see me directly. I pay better."

He dropped an envelope on the table, which contained a summons for Kevin's joint-custody hearing, and Kristen picked it up. "Now . . . consider yourself served. I'm out. Later, Charisse and Kevin."

Greg spun around with the grace of a Temptation and rolled out, leaving everyone stunned silent. Kristen and Sheila looked at each other all embarrassed. They'd been had.

After a few moments of awkward silence, Charisse said, "Well, damn! Guess he got y'all told, huh?" She turned to me. "Baby, I've lost my appetite. Let's get outta here. You two enjoy your meal."

Just as she and I stood up to leave, I said, "Oh . . . one more thing." I dropped a second envelope on the table in front of her. "Greg will see you in court. You've been served . . . again."

As Charisse and I approached the exit, she said, "Man, I hope Kristen enjoys our honeymoon pictures."

Happily
Ever
After?

42

Six Months Later

"Honey?" I called out to Kevin, who was putting on his suit to go to work. I could tell because the smell of his cologne wreaked havoc on my sinuses. He always sprayed it on so thick he had his own ozone layer. For weeks, I'd been asking him to go to the doctor to see if he had some freak olfactory disorder. He didn't understand the key concept of wearing cologne well: less is more.

"Yes, dear!" he said, in a voice that told me I'd be repeating myself twenty times because he wasn't listening. Didn't matter to me. A sister had to do what a sister had to do, and this issue had been gettin' on my last nerve for too long now.

"You remember those steel bars sticking out of the walls in the bathroom?"

"Yes, dear."

"They're called *towel bars*. I think the builder, in his infinite wisdom, installed them so you, dear husband, wouldn't have to hang your sopping-wet towels on the bathroom floor."

"Yes, dear!" he said, adding a little more edge in

his voice. I didn't care. Apparently, he thought *wife* equaled *maid*. He'd married the wrong sister to try to carry me like that.

"And, honey?"

"Yes, dear!" he said, the edge in his voice even edgier.

"Remember the thirteen thousand rolls of toilet paper we got for like twelve bucks from Costco last week?"

"Yes, dear."

"Well, the builder also installed these little toilet paper holders too. When the rolls get down to that little cardboard thingy in the middle, you can actually take that off and put on a *new* roll."

The miracles of modern technology.

With the last smart-ass comment (which I probably should've kept to myself), I realized I had just instigated the next battle in our war for household supremacy. With all the progress I'd made in my journey to become a grown-up capable of having healthy relationships with good men, I still hadn't learned to keep my damn mouth shut. Always got something to say, always got to get in the last word.

Before Kevin and I got married, I never had the opportunity to discover how stuck in our ways we were. Usually when we started getting on each other's nerves, I could send him home to his condo, but that little piece of heaven had long been sold. So the farthest I could send him was to the basement . . . which wasn't nearly far enough when we were about ready to kill each other.

Nisey and Mom were always jumping on my ass,

saying I understood what I was getting into because I'd been married before, but they failed to realize my first marriage, to Jason, who was ten years my junior and still trainable, pretty much went straight from honeymoon to divorce. He'd been shipped off to Iraq within a few months of our wedding, and not a day after he returned, I discovered he'd been having an affair with a married officer in his army reserve unit (a woman). We'd been in constant crisis; we had no sense of normalcy, no routines. I'd never had to learn to actually live and share space permanently, to compromise, or to tolerate the annoying habits that made me want to back over him in the driveway.

More to the point, Kevin and I were both over forty years old. We weren't "a little stuck" in our annoying habits that drove each other completely mad, we were cemented up to our knees in them. No, we were more like those fossilized mosquitoes wedged into chunks of prehistoric rock for a gazillion years. Both stubborn and refusing to budge, determined to maintain our independence by any means necessary—usually my nagging and his complaining.

On the surface, our struggles might've seemed like meaningless disagreements that could be squashed by just picking up the damn towel or replacing the fucking toilet paper, but beneath that illusion, we were fighting for a way of life. We both wanted "my way," and in such struggles, only one of us could win, only one could reign supreme—me.

As I stood in the steamy bathroom mirror trying to put on my makeup, Kevin finally drifted in, in his own sweet, slow-ass time, to hang up his towel. I'd half hoped he'd compliment me on my new outfit, the way he did when we first got married. Used to tell me I was beautiful every day . . . for about the first month. Over time, *beautiful* evolved to *good*. Eventually *good* became *a'ight*. I'd started to wish he'd elevate the compliments back to *good* at least. I should've known better.

"Hey, baby," I said, holding my hands out to show off my pricey suit. "Notice anything special?"

He gave me the once-over. "Yeah. Looks like something's hanging out of your nose. You might want to wipe that." Then he handed me a tissue. I stood in front of him decked out in a black, booty-hugging DKNY suit, and all he acknowledged was a booger. Then he had the nerve to say, "Whatchu cookin' for breakfast? I'm starved."

As if.

His lackluster housecleaning and complimenting skills had hardly inspired the Julia Child in me. Oh, don't get me wrong, I'd been a culinary master for the beautiful hunk of man who showered me with love and attention a few months ago. I'd whipped up omelets, homemade biscuits, grits, home fries, hot coffee, and hot sex daily. Booger boy could jerk off and take his ass to McDonald's.

"I'm not. I've got an early meeting at the office this morning so you'll need to fend for yourself," I said, lying my ass off. I'm a real estate agent. We get in when we get in. I just didn't want to cook for him.

I grabbed my shoes from the closet and trotted downstairs with my ass on my shoulders. I had a long day ahead of me at the office. I'd just taken two listings the previous day so marketing mayhem had to begin. I had signs to post, flyers to create and distribute, lockboxes to install, and e-mails to send. Although my assistant, Nyla, kept my files well administered, control freak that I am, I kept my hand in everything.

As I poured the water in the coffeemaker, I thought about Mom and James. Hadn't spoken to them in a couple of weeks, so I thought I'd go ahead and check in. Right as I grabbed my cell phone from my purse, a call came through. Speak of the devil.

"Hey, baby!" Mommy said, sounding ultracheerful. "How's married life treating you?"

I wanted to say, *Like a slice of year-old cheese*, but I decided to put on my I-love-marriage game face to keep her from getting in my business.

"We're . . . *great!*" I somehow managed to choke out and sound halfway upbeat. Oh, but the words tasted bitter. "A better question is, how is married life treating you?"

She and James got married at the justice of the peace two weeks after our wedding. They'd have gone sooner but they wanted us to attend and we'd left for our honeymoon and come home to the Kristen drama. Four months later they were still in wedded bliss, and Kevin and I were sliding headfirst into marital mediocrity.

We hate her.

"We're fantastic," she said, as if she genuinely meant it. Fake ass. She was married. No way in hell she meant it. "James can't seem to get enough of me. Old frisky thing."

"Ewwwww, Mom. I keep telling you I don't need to hear all of your business. Too much information," I semi-snapped. Jealous like a mofo.

"Hmph. Sounds like a whole lot of hate to me. Maybe *you* need to get some. What's going on?"

"Nothing, Mom," I said, trying not to sound as if I was lying. "We're. . . *great!*"

"That's two *great*s. Now I know something's wrong. What is it?"

I drew in a deep breath and confessed, "I honestly . . . I don't know. Just seems like we'd been living this perfect dream for so long, now our relationship is getting extremely . . . *real*—and I want my fairy tale back."

"Baby, marriage ain't nothing if not real. And the longer a marriage lasts, the more *real* it gets. That's what you signed up for. You didn't sign up for a life-long fairy tale. You signed up for a lifetime of *real*. So, now you got *real*."

"So why aren't you and James gettin' *real* yet?"

"Because we ain't got nothing to do now except work on making each other happy . . . when we ain't pissing each other off. Trust me, we had our fair share of *real* when we were working and I was raising you. So busy living sometimes, we forgot to love. And that includes make love. You forget relationships take work . . . or you'll get an overdose of *real*. Y'all still having relations on the regular?"

"Moooom, jeez, you're gettin' awfully personal."

"You're my daughter; we don't get no more personal than that. And I'll take that as a no!"

"Well . . ." I said, squirming uncomfortably. "Not

as much as before. I find it's hard to get in the mood when we're drowning in so much *real.*"

"That's your first mistake. You can't let the sex get out of your marriage. If nothing else, it's thirty minutes when you ain't fightin'."

I laughed. Maybe Mom had a point. If I could focus more attention on extending the honeymoon than winning battles, Kevin and I would have more of what Mom and James had . . . and a little less *real.*

"Yeah, I guess you're right. How'd you get so smart about marriage?"

"*Dr. Phil,*" she said, laughing. "And *Oprah.* Anyway, so have you talked to your father lately?"

"Not in the last week or so, but I spoke to Trey. Nisey flew out to California to visit yesterday and she called me from his place. Dad's cancer treatments are still working and he's doing fine, thank God."

"What about my grandbaby? How's he doing?"

"He's wonderful, and Kristen's acting like she's got the sense God gave her now, so we're getting along for Javon's sake. We can't ask for much more until after the hearing. At least she's letting us keep him on weekends now. I have to admit, I love being a mother to him when he's here. He's got his father's good nature." *Too bad he's got a witch for a mother, but that's another story.*

"I know you do . . . which makes me wonder if you and Kevin are gonna make a baby before all your eggs dry up. You ain't exactly no spring chicken."

"I'd like to, Mom, but we probably need to start having sex again first."

"Don't wait too long. Your clock is tickin'!"

●   ●   ●

After thinking all day about what Mommy said, I realized that I wanted to make my marriage work. I wanted *real, honeymoon,* and *babies.* I wanted it all. I'd decided to stop focusing on the piddly, nit-nanny day-to-day irritations and concentrate more on remembering the reasons we got married in the first place. So, I called Kevin and asked him to get home on time because I had some things for us to do around the house—so to speak. I left the office early, hit the Safeway, and bought some T-bones, potatoes, and fresh veggies for dinner. Then I stopped at Victoria's Secret to get *his* dessert and went home to whip up a meal fit for a king. My king.

The whole house basked in candlelight. I'd probably overdone it, but the lighting looked beautiful. Like something out of a Dracula movie. I slipped into my hot, black Vickie number that sure enough wasn't keeping any secrets and would no doubt set his loins on fire. I positioned myself seductively on the couch, cranked up the Luther Vandross, and waited for my dear husband to walk in the door.

And waited.

And called.

And waited.

And texted.

And waited.

About eight thirty, a text came through on my cell:

Worked overtime. Going out for drinks with the fellas.
Will take care of stuff around the house tomorrow.
Be home later. Love you.

Tomorrow, huh?

Yeah, right.

It's jerking off and McDonald's for you. Inconsiderate bastard.

I schlepped around and blew out the candles, which set off three smoke detectors. As I walked up the stairs to change into my birth-control pajamas and go to bed, all I could think was . . .

This is soooo . . . real!

43

Ten Months Later

Charisse's icy foot nudged me when the alarm clock sounded, a far cry from the kisses she'd peppered my face with eight months ago. She'd put the clock on my side of the bed, claiming I had to wake up earlier so I should be in charge of turning the annoying thing off. I turned to look at her beautiful angelic face drifting back into a serene sleep . . . and she really pissed me off! I'd have slapped her if she wouldn't knock me out in return. All she did anymore was sleep and eat. What happened to the woman who only months ago woke me up with hot, butt-naked sex? I'd half thought about reaching out to a friend at the PG County Police Department and putting out an all-points bulletin that said, "Loving wife Charisse Douglass kidnapped and exchanged for a nagging, no-sex-having impostor. One-million-dollar reward for my beautiful wife's safe return."

I rolled out of bed and walked into the bathroom to take a shower but was stymied by the sea of delicates and unmentionables hanging from the shower walls. Pantyhose, drawers . . . they overwhelmed me, and I didn't want to touch them. Isn't that what the washer and dryer were for? So, you could actually wash and dry your clothes inside the machines and not dangle shit around the bathroom? After a few seconds of stewing, I seized the opportunity to ride Charisse as she'd ridden me on so many occasions.

"Ummm . . . honey?" I sang to Charisse, who was trying to sleep.

She stirred, then grunted and groaned for a few seconds. "Yeah?" Hated for anyone to interrupt her sleep.

"You know this large glass enclosure that goes around the shower?"

"Yeah. What about it?"

"Well, when the builder installed it, I think he intended it to keep the water from flooding the bathroom floor, not for you to hang your drawers and pantyhose on. Mind coming in here and moving your stuff so I can take a shower?"

"Baby, I'm still sleeping. Can't you move it . . . please?"

I stuck my head out the bathroom door "You know, I don't touch your stuff unless I'm taking it off your body, so can you come get it, please?" I said with sarcastic sweetness.

She snatched the comforter back and huffed as she stomped past me, pulled her things down. Then she rolled her eyes at me as she slammed her stuff in a clothes basket and got back in bed.

"Thank you, dear," I said with a devilish smirk.

"You're welcome, asshole."

I laughed to myself and shook my head. I didn't

often get opportunities to one-up Charisse but relished them when they came. I'd send her flowers later to make up for messing with her. Maybe.

Didn't take me long to figure out that Charisse and I had two different ideas of what marriage was supposed to be. I'd had an old-school upbringing, with old-school parents, who instilled old-school values in me. My mother did 99 percent of the cooking and cleaning, which meant picking up towels and replacing empty toilet paper holders. Dad brought home the bacon and Mom cooked it up, served it, and washed the dishes. There was no such thing as cooking when you felt like it . . . or not feeling like cooking. There was no such thing as being too tired to do anything.

What my father wanted, my father got when he wanted it. Of course I realized my mother didn't work outside the home like Charisse. While I supported Charisse's desire to have a career—and keeping it real, I liked living comfortably—I'd be lying if I said I didn't wish Charisse had more of my mother's old-school leanings.

My struggle to get a little more "traditional wife" collided with her struggle to make our marriage more of a modern "partnership" and led to a constant test of wills. I'd pretty much resisted doing virtually anything that sounded more like an order than a request, which meant I resisted doing just about everything Charisse asked me to do. Sometimes, it was just the way she said things that irked the hell out of me. She didn't always make it easy for me to do the right thing. Hell, lately, she'd made everything such a contest that, admittedly, I sometimes focused more on winning than on doing what it took to make the marriage work.

I got dressed and kissed my wife's plump cheek before I left the room. She didn't even bother trying to wake up and make me breakfast anymore. At least not over the several last months or so. My frustration was intensifying but I still loved her dearly. If I had to marry her again, I would. If I could do one thing differently, I'd force her to sign a contract agreeing to get with *my* program up front.

On my way to work, I decided to give Ma a call. Hadn't spoken with her in a couple of weeks, not since Mr. Tyson arrived in Winston-Salem. He said he was there taking care of some family business, a few properties he'd inherited from his parents when they passed. I had a sneaking suspicion he went there for more than some land. Everyone sensed the spark between him and Ma when she visited for the wedding, but she played off the attraction as harmless flirting. I knew better.

"Morning, Ma! How're you doing today?"

"Well, I'm just fine. Happy to hear your voice. What did I do to deserve this call today? Because you usually don't, not unless something's wrong. And from the sound of your voice, something's wrong. What is it?"

I got quiet for a few seconds, didn't really want to talk to Ma about my marital problems. Preferred to try to work them out myself . . . but maybe she could help talk some sense into Charisse.

"Kevin, don't make me reach through this phone!"

I chuckled. "I don't know. Seems like Charisse and I have totally different ideas about what marriage is supposed to be. Seems like . . . watching you and Dad all those years, I thought things would be different."

"Different like what? She's a wife; you're a husband. Just as God intended."

"You know what I mean, Ma."

"Listen, your father and I had the kind of relationship *he and I* agreed to have. You can't expect Charisse to live to a standard she didn't agree to."

"Yeah, I know. But I thought she'd cook and clean more. Thought she'd be a little easier to reason with. Seems like everything between us is a constant struggle. She wants to win. I want to win. But our marriage is losing."

"First of all, you've got to stop comparing what your father and I had with what you and she have. Your father and I got married in a very different time and we were very different people. He wanted me to be a stay-at-home mom and that's what *I wanted* to be. He agreed to pay all the bills and I agreed to take care of the home. You payin' all the bills?"

"No," I said, feeling a little sting.

"Hard as she works to help y'all live the life you're living, you can't expect her to be like me. I mean, did you marry her so she'd be your wife . . . or did you marry her so she'd be your mother?"

Ouch. She'd hit a sensitive spot right there. Truth was I wanted both. More wife than mother of course—but both.

"I'd like both to be honest."

"Well, then you shoulda married Superwoman, because Charisse can't be everything to you. Nor should you expect her to be. You knew *exactly* who you were marrying before you stepped to the altar. You knew the kind of hours she worked, and you knew she wouldn't stop because she married you. I sure enough wouldn't. Sounds to me like you need to get over yourself and find some middle ground."

"Wait a minute. Wasn't it *you* who said she didn't feed me enough?"

"Yeah, 'cause I'm your mother and that's what I'm s'posed to say. Now I suggest you stop wastin' my time on this phone and be thankful you found a wife willing to put up with a big mama's boy!"

Amazing how one conversation could change my entire perspective. Indeed, maybe I did need to stop expecting Charisse to be my mother . . . so much.

I turned my car around and headed straight home. I needed to apologize to my wife; maybe we could set our course straight.

When I walked in the house, Charisse was sitting at the kitchen table with a pile of used tissues, wiping her eyes and crying a river. I rushed to her side and put my arm around her shoulder.

"Baby, what's wrong? Why are you crying?"

"I don't know," she said, blowing her nose.

"What happened?"

"Nothing," she sniffed.

"Charisse, talk to me. What's going on?"

"I don't know, Kevin. One minute I was watching 'Wednesday's Child' on NBC. You know, the segment where they talk about the special needs kids and try to get them adopted? The next thing I knew I was crying like someone had stolen my BMW." She grabbed a new tissue, adding the old one to the pile. "Probably just stress . . . especially with the way things have been going between us."

"I know. That's why I came home to talk to you. Listen, baby, I know things have been tense between us, and I'm sorry for my part in it. But how about starting today, you and I recommit to doing what we need to do to make our marriage work?"

"Such as?"

"I've been unfair to you, expecting our marriage to be like my parents', and we're not them. That's not the way *we* should be. I'm sorry."

"And I'm sorry for giving you such a hard time. I promise I'm going to stop sweating the small stuff."

"Sounds like a good plan to me." I pressed my lips tenderly against hers. "What do you say tonight we have a little candlelight dinner. *I'll* cook . . . and you can bring dessert."

"Oh, my, Mr. Douglass. I think that sounds . . . Oh, crap. Kristen needs us to keep the baby tonight, remember? She asked us about a month ago."

"Oh, right! I completely forgot. Well, that's okay. I'll leave work a little early, take him to the park, and wear him out. After I knock him out, I'm gonna knock your boots."

When I walked into the bedroom, Charisse was waiting on me, wearing a sexy black nightie I hadn't seen before. I wanted her so bad I could taste her . . . and taste her is exactly what I'd planned to do.

"Baby sleeping?" Charisse asked, as I slipped out of my clothes and into the bed.

"Sound asleep."

She ran her fingers down my chest and gripped me in a way that made my body shiver.

"You want me, baby," I said in a sexy groan.

"Ooh, yes," she whispered, the sensation of her breath whispering in my ear sending shock waves through my every crevice.

She pulled me on top of her and kissed me hard and deep; I knew she wanted to bypass the foreplay and get straight to business.

I eased inside her; she was so wet I had to focus on the clock to keep from climaxing too soon. As I thrust inside, her screams got louder and louder. I couldn't hold it much longer. She felt too good.

When she finally screamed in the ultimate pleasure, I prepared to release everything I had inside with the force of a tidal wave . . . then I heard a piercing scream.

"Daddy, nooooo! Daddy, nooooo!"

The erection killer had entered the building. Thank God we were under the comforter.

"Uhhhh, Kevin?" Charisse said. "I think you forgot to lock the door."

"*Brilliant* observation."

"Umph," she said, as I wrapped myself in the sheet to put Javon back to bed. "Too bad for you, 'cause I got mine!"

44
One Year Later . . .

Lying in the dark, I stared at the ceiling for about an hour before I even thought about getting out of bed. So hard to believe it'd been a year since Kevin and I had said, "I do." We'd had one helluva crazy time, and Lord knew we'd been through some changes, but somehow we'd persevered and survived alive, relatively un-scathed . . . and together.

Since it was Saturday, I decided to let Kevin sleep until he woke on his own. I was dying to give him his gift though. Had Derek pick it up from the FBI gift store for me a couple of days prior to our anniversary when I got the news. The gift? A onesie that read MY DAD IS AN FBI AGENT.

Yep.

We were pregnant. With child. Knocked up. Baby mama and baby daddy.

I hadn't told anyone else yet. Not Nisey, not any-one. I needed some time to digest the idea myself. Because I was an over-forty, first-time mother-to-be, I'd be subjected to many tests, and so many risks were involved that having a baby was pretty scary. At the same time, the thought of a little Kevin or little me running around the house causing hate and discontent thrilled me like nothing else in my life ever had.

I'd gotten up to pee for the thirty-seventh time when Kevin started to stir. I could barely contain my excitement. As soon as he opened his mouth to say, "Happy anniversary," I'd break out his little gift bag and announce, "You're gonna be a daddy . . . again!" Couldn't wait. I was bubbling.

After I finished in the bathroom, I hurried and jumped back in the bed. Kevin rolled over and wrapped me up in his arms. I swear I loved feeling engulfed in him. The warmth of his body had become home to me.

"Morning, baby," he purred in his sexy, I-just-woke-up voice.

"Good morning to you too," I said, waiting for it . . . you know, the big "Happy anniversary!"

"I feel like staying in bed all day, but I promised the boys I'd play ball this morning. You got anything planned for today?"

Do I have anything planned?

How about I plan to kick your ass?

"I don't know. I thought we could go out to dinner or something. What do you think?"

"Ummm, nooo. I think we need to stay out of the restaurants for a while. You know I love you, but I noticed you've picked up a couple of pounds. I'll cook us something healthy at home."

"Did you just call me *fat?*"

"No, not *fat*, baby . . . just a little . . . *fluffy.*"

No, he did *not* just call me *fluffy*!? *And* he forgot our anniversary too?

"Fluffy?! You know what, Kevin? You can kiss my fluffy ass. I mean, just kiss it!"

"Did I say something?"

I looked at him as if he'd lost his natural mind.

"Nope! You didn't say *a thing*. I'm outta here. I'll see you later."

"Baby, wait!"

"Don't *baby* me."

You wanna talk about spitting mad? I was hot. I couldn't believe after everything he and I'd been through over the year, this fool didn't even remember the day we ordered ourselves into this life sentence.

Such a . . . man.

We hate men.

I stomped, banged, and crashed my way around the house until I mustered enough energy to get dressed and roll out. Kevin kept asking me what was wrong, but if he didn't know, I sure wasn't gonna tell him.

As I reached for the doorknob, he hollered, "What time are you coming home?" from upstairs.

"When you go to hell in a burning handbasket with gasoline drawers on!"

Okay, that was harsh, but I was beyond pissed.

I jumped in the Beemer and started in the direction of Nisey's house. I figured she wouldn't be busy doing anything because her man was in California.

"Hey, girl. What's going on?" I asked.

She didn't have the phone up to her ear, but I heard her giggling and some manly mumbling. Someone was with her. I'd just spoken with Trey not even a day and half ago; he'd made no mention of traveling to DC. I know this heifer would not even try to cheat on *my* brother. Not a Tyson.

"Nisey, I know you don't have somebody over there. Please tell me you ain't steppin' out on Trey."

"I'm not steppin' out on Trey. You know me better than that."

"Then who's there?"

"Who's here? Nobody. That's, uhhh . . . the TV. I was laughing at something on TV. Now I know you didn't call here to question me on who's in my house. What's going on? You sound a little upset."

"Can you believe Kevin forgot our wedding anniversary?"

"Girl, quit playin'. Are you for real?"

"Yeah. He didn't say a word this morning. Told me he was gonna play ball with the fellas, and then called me fluffy . . . said I picked up a few pounds. Can you believe that?"

Nisey laughed. "Well, I wasn't gonna say anything, but you have picked up a few pounds, girl. You need to cut back on the desserts."

"Not you too! You guys are right. I have picked up a few pounds . . . because I'm *fed up* with both of y'all!"

She giggled again. This time I heard wrestling in the background.

"Nisey, who's there?"

"Rissey . . . I swear . . . nobody's . . . here. Listen, lemme call you back later. Don't worry about Kevin. I'm sure he'll come through."

No, she didn't blow me off! I was half tempted to go to her house, but even if she was seeing someone else, it wasn't my place to be checking up on her.

I didn't know what the hell to do with myself, so I spent the day shopping with Kevin's credit card and eating for two. Then I went to the park for a little while to watch the planes fly in. While I was sitting there, I decided to call Lamar and see what he was up to. He and I didn't speak nearly as often as we used to. After Kevin and I got married, he found a girlfriend, one of the little Christian-lite women at his church. No, I didn't like her, but I'm not sure I would've liked anyone he dated. He'd always be a part of me, even if we weren't together.

He answered the phone and I said, "Guess who?"

He laughed. "Lemme guess. You're selling Amway products."

"I don't think so," I said with a light chuckle. "How are you? It's been a while."

"I'm good. We're good—me and Tina."

"Ohhh, Tina, huh? I think I'm jealous."

He laughed. "Don't be. There's only one you."

I blushed. "I was calling because I have a little bit of news to share."

"Oh, really. What's going on?"

"Well . . . I'm, uhhh . . . I'm gonna have a baby."

Silence. . . . More silence.

"Hello. You okay? "

"Yeah, I'm sorry. I'm just surprised. Congratulations," he said flatly.

"Why do you sound like I just killed your dog?"

He chuckled. "No, I'm excited for you. Really. I

guess this makes everything between us so final, like there's really no chance for us now."

My heart fluttered; he really did love me. "Well . . . don't be so sure about that. He forgot our anniversary and called me 'fluffy' today. We might be divorced sooner than you think."

"Wait. He called you fluffy knowing you're pregnant?"

"No, he doesn't know yet. You're actually the only person close to me that I've told. Nisey doesn't even know. She called me fluffy too. Heifer. I was planning to tell them today before they started calling me names."

"Everything will be okay. Go get yourself a Blizzard. You'll feel better. And if there's one thing you know about Kevin, he'd never hurt you intentionally, right? He loves you too much for that."

"Yeah. I guess you're right."

Against my better instincts, I went home after talking to Lamar. He may not be the most objective person in this scenario, but he was right about Kevin. Oh, I had every right to be pissed, but I knew Kevin hadn't forgotten on purpose. As a matter of fact, remembering our anniversary would've cost him far less in both money and grief than forgetting. So, I decided to go home and give him the tickets to his guilt trip.

I pulled up to the house and noticed Nisey's car parked in the driveway. *What the hell is she doing here?* I thought. Maybe she'd come to tell Kevin he'd forgotten our anniversary. When I opened the door, I almost gave birth. I heard a virtual choir sing, "Happy anniversary!"

I couldn't believe it! My heart pounded as I scanned the room to see the faces of everyone I loved. Nisey, Trey, James, Mama, Mother Douglass, and my father. Derek—who was standing underneath a handmade sign that read WE'RE HAVING A BABY!—had a sheepish grin. That sucker had told Kevin about the baby. I walked around to hug everyone and say hello . . . then I gunned for Derek, cutting my eyes at him. "You!"

He shrugged. "So, now you know I can't keep a secret. Sue me."

I punched him in the arm, then gave him a hug and shook my head. Gossiping-ass men.

Kevin weaved his way toward me, held his arms out, and said, "Happy anniversary, baby! Sorry, I had to trick you that way, but your nosy ass is impossible to surprise. I thought what better gift than celebrating our first year with the people we love."

I kissed him on the cheek. "I couldn't ask for a better gift, baby. I *so* thought you forgot. And you called me fat. You know you came within an inch of losing your life, don't you?"

He laughed. "You don't even know how hard it was for me to contain my excitement about the baby. I've been floating on air since I found out. You know I couldn't pass up the chance to mess with you."

While James and my father smoked a couple of stogies on the deck to commemorate the occasion, Mom and Mother Douglass recalled their labor horror stories. If they planned to scare the shit out of me, their plan worked like a friggin' charm.

Nisey, seeing me wince in pain, grabbed my hand and walked me out to the front of the house. She smiled at me, glowing with happiness, as we copped a squat on the front step. It warmed my heart to see her so incredibly happy.

"Congratulations, Rissey. You're gonna be a mommy!" she said, putting her arm around my shoulder.

"I know. Can you believe it?"

"Yes, I can. You were made to be a mother. You know that, don't you? Anyone who could put up with Marcus's bad-ass kids deserves a medal," she said, referring to my ex-boyfriend's devil children.

I looked at her eyes, which had grown a little misty. She was getting awfully sentimental over an anniversary and a baby announcement. She wiped her eye and I noticed some bling on her finger.

"Nisey! What's that on your finger? Are you and Trey *engaged*?"

"Yes . . . we are."

"Oh. My. God!" I yelled, wrapping her up in a bear hug. "I'm sooo happy for you!" When she turned to look at me, I noticed tears streaming down her face. "Nisey. This is great news. Why are you crying?"

"I'm moving . . . to California."

"What?" I said, my heart pounding in my ears.

"Yeah. You know he's in the military. He can't leave, so I'm moving to be with him."

I heard my heart break.

Nisey had been my rock. My ride-or-die friend for life. She'd been there with me though my best and my worst. My highs and lows. And God knows, I probably couldn't have survived half the shit I'd been through, at least not with any sanity, if she weren't by my side. I never imagined a time in my life when I couldn't drive ten minutes to get to her. I needed her here, with me. And now she'd be moving across the country. Whom could I run to? Who would be the Nisey to Rissey?

My eyes rained buckets. I'm not even sure where all the water came from, but I couldn't make it stop. All we could do was hug each other until we calmed down.

"Some friend you are," I said, sniffling and wiping my eyes. "You know I'm a hormonal mess, and you spring this on me."

"I know, Rissey. God knows, it wasn't an easy decision to make, especially with Jamal being so far from David. And me moving so far from you. But we're in love and we want to get married."

"Can't you get one of the video phones and commute on weekends?"

She laughed.

"Or . . . maybe Facebook and phone sex?"

"Rissey! You're a nut."

"I really am happy for you. Honestly. But . . . you can't leave me," I whined, smiling through the new round of tears. "Who's going to give me pregnancy advice? Where am I gonna run to when Kevin pisses me off?"

"We'll be fine. Listen. In three years, when Trey retires, we're moving back here. Until then, we'll call and we'll visit. You're making all the money, honey. You can afford it."

"I guess," I said, then a lightbulb came on. "Wait a minute. You know what this means, don't you? After all these years of being best friends, we're actually gonna be sisters."

She grabbed my hand and held it to her face. "Rissey . . . you *are* my sister. You always have been. And you always will be."

I lay in Kevin's arms, listening to the rumble of his snores, thinking about my life since he'd crashed back into it. Because of him, I'd persevered through the hard shit to find my for-better-or-worse kind of man; my father and my brothers had become integral parts of my life; Nisey had found her soul mate; and, miracle of all miracles, Mom had *finally* married hers. What could better measure Kevin's goodness than to watch him enhance my life and the lives of every important person connected to me?

No, Kevin *did not* turn out to be the man I thought he was.

Thank God I think small.